Relationships 201

Alix Bekins

Dreamspinner Press

Published by
Dreamspinner Press
4760 Preston Road
Suite 244-149
Frisco, TX 75034
http://www.dreamspinnerpress.com/

Relationships 201
Copyright © 2010 by Alix Bekins

Cover Art by Catt Ford

ISBN: 978-1-61581-660-6

Printed in the United States of America
First Edition
December, 2010

eBook edition available
eBook ISBN: 978-1-61581-661-3

Thank Yous

To Katie, whose idea sparked this whole story in the first place. Thank you for the brilliant concept, for all of your music help, and for being the most excited first-draft reader a writer could want, always eager for the next part.

To Stacey, for providing the gorgeous pictures that kept me going during the long dry spells and for the first-edit work.

To the inner circle for their support—Martha most especially for the daily hand-holding and poking and encouragement. To Jan, who made me step back and think about what I wanted this to be on a deeper level. To Connie, who edited and gave such encouraging feedback. And to her and Elin for the final read-through, smoothing out the rough spots.

Finally, thanks go to my husband, who put up with an abnormal amount of craziness, and to all my friends who listened to me whine about writing for the last year and feigned interest.

Chapter 1
Back on Campus

STEPHAN cracks open a beer as he flops down on the avocado-green couch, wincing at the creaking noise from the battered piece of furniture. It's probably a decade older than he is, bought by the university to furnish the "new" graduate student housing when it was first built in the late 1960s. Still, it's good to be back on campus.

"Lazy bastard," Jim groans, lumbering through the door with a box nearly larger than his torso.

"Fuck you; I'm finished," Stephan says with a grin, swinging his feet up onto the coffee table.

Jim makes a face at him. "It's going to be like this when you finish your homework and I'm still slogging through mine, isn't it?"

Stephan raises his bottle in a teasing salute. "Yup. Just like when we were undergrads. Half the joy in being done is rubbing it in the faces of all those who aren't."

"I'm going to remember this, you know."

"You remember everything; I can't even remember what the hell you're getting a degree in, man. Tree-hugging crap, that's all I know."

"Environmental Toxicology," Jim supplies in a long-suffering tone. "And if you drank less, maybe you'd remember more. You're killing brain cells as well as poisoning your liver, you know."

"Goody-two-shoes," Stephan says, flicking the bottle cap at his friend.

"Alcoholic." Jim catches the object midair and tosses it back at Stephan, plinking him in the forehead.

Stephan's mouth drops open. "Oh, it is *on*, Davis, you fucker."

"I'm shaking," Jim mocks, putting down his box and flexing his arms. Which are pretty impressive, actually, because Jim definitely puts in his hours at the gym, not to mention jogging more than can possibly be good for a person. In other words, he's *built*.

With a grumble, Stephan lurches off the sofa and over the coffee table, and tackles Jim to the ground. Jim might be bigger, but Steph's devious, and he's no stranger to the Soloflex, himself. Laughing, they roll across the mostly empty living room, coming to a stop up against a wall, legs entangled.

Stephan is pinned underneath, swearing and shrieking as Jim digs his fingers in between ticklish ribs, when someone speaks from the open doorway.

"God*damn*, Steph." The tone of voice can only be described as aggrieved. "First day back on campus and you're already rolling around with another guy."

Stephan reaches down and grabs Jim's ass, giving it a squeeze as he moans theatrically. "Come on, Eric, tell me you could keep your hands off this fine ass if you were alone with it."

"There's a person attached to that ass, you know," Jim huffs, managing to knee Stephan in the stomach as he gets disentangled. "And also? You suck." He makes for the door, giving Eric a grin as he brushes past on his way to get more of his stuff.

"If you were horny, you just had to text me," Stephan's boyfriend scolds, strolling in and making himself comfortable on the sofa. Well, trying to; the sofa is adamantly resisting all efforts at cushioning and doing its best to imitate stone, longevity having been more important to its design than comfort. Also, at four inches over six feet tall, Eric doesn't fit on most furniture very well. His lankiness, floppy hair, and pointy features combine to make him seem very boyish.

"Well, you're here now; let's go find out which box the lube is in," Stephan suggests with his naughtiest grin.

Eric laughs and sits down, kicking off his flip-flops. "Seriously, are you all moved in? I thought I'd drop by and see if you needed a hand."

As usual, Eric's completely oblivious to Stephan's disappointed sigh. "All moved in, not terribly unpacked. I'll get to it later. I was just kicking back, watching Jim lug boxes around, making fun of him, and *drinking that beer*," he growls, lunging to reclaim his bottle.

Eric holds it out of reach, using his unfairly long limbs to play keep-away as if Steph was some pathetic little kid reaching for his milk money. After a light punch to Eric's shoulder, Stephan gets up, grumbling, and retrieves another one from the fridge.

"So, do you wanna get dinner?"

Stephan gives Eric one of his *what the hell are you babbling about?* eyebrow quirks. "It's two p.m."

"Oh. Okay, um. We could play some PS2 or something, if you're not going to unpack.... Did you eat lunch? I bet the pizza place at the Student Union isn't totally swamped yet and might get it here in under an hour."

They play around for a while, getting the TV and game consoles set up with only one minor argument, and dividing a pizza and responsibilities for harassing Jim equally. Just like the majority of their evenings over the last nine months, they settle into companionable, mellow hanging out. Being with Eric is like being with one of his best friends, only with sex. Sometimes. Stupid Jim had foiled Stephan's plans and objected loudly to his suggestion that he and Eric play strip-SSX Tricky, and Eric hadn't taken him seriously about a strip-game anyway. There *is* some kissing and minor groping while Jim is in his room, cussing as he tries to install some shelves and stubbornly refusing any help. It's nice.

And Stephan's definitely getting laid tonight. Probably for sure. They've been together for nearly a year now, although separated for the last two months while Eric did a summer outreach program in his hometown, but now they're back together. It's easy and comfortable, reassuring, the way they just fit with each other. Physically and figuratively, both.

Finally Jim comes out, holding some ice to a reddish-purple finger. "Aww, look at you two, all cozy on the couch. So sweet and romantic."

And it is—it's almost sickening, the way they're leaning equally against the sofa and each other's shoulders. But it feels right, so Stephan isn't arguing. It's good to just *be* with his boyfriend again. Even if he is so horny he might explode. Literally.

Eric stretches his arms above his head, exposing a strip of tummy Stephan wants to lick in the worst way. "Are you sure you don't need to unpack?" he asks, clueless to the lustful look he's getting.

"Dude. It's good," Stephan sighs, rolling his eyes.

"Aw, come on, I'll help you at least make the bed and stuff."

"Does that mean I'm finally going to get you in it?" Stephan asks as he gets up, sensing the futility of arguing.

"Maaaaybe." Eric grins.

They're pretty much finished when Steph's cell phone buzzes, and the piercing voice of his friend Kristine greets him. It sounds like she's at a rock concert or something, with the volume of music and voices and her yelling into the phone, but after a few minutes he manages to glean that a bunch of people are going out to 99 Bottles to celebrate the start of the new year, and he should join them and bring everyone he sees along with him.

They meet up with the usual suspects, mostly friends still in school, and spend the evening alternately mourning the end of summer and anticipating the joy of the new semester. Surprisingly, it's mostly couples: Jim and his girlfriend Jamie, Eric and Stephan, and Kristine and her new girlfriend, Tina. It strikes Stephan as a bit odd that everyone paired off when he wasn't looking, but he guesses that it's just another sign that he's getting older. The coupling, not the unobservant thing. He's *always* been unobservant.

It's too loud to have any decent conversations other than idle chitchat about the upcoming year. A few of the others are first year grad students, too, and only one isn't in the Division of Humanities. They spend some time commiserating together about their nervousness regarding the differences in coursework from when they were undergrads and the orientation the next day, when they'll find out which classes they've been assigned to as teaching assistants. The wrong professor could make their lives utter hell.

The cheap beer and greasy appetizers are plentiful, and Stephan eats with the mental note to do an extra twenty minutes of cardio the next time he works out. Although maybe carrying all his boxes up to his new apartment counted? A few more beers and he decides that the exercise was definitely good enough, even with the pizza he'd eaten earlier. Eric, of course, at barely twenty-one, can eat whatever the fuck he wants, devouring grease and sugar like they're going out of style. It totally isn't fair, and Stephan would hate him except that he knows that one day the kid's metabolism will catch up, and on that day he is planning to laugh his ass off at Eric's soft little beer belly.

"Will you still love me when I'm a bear?" Eric asks, fluttering his eyelashes as Stephan dutifully passes him the last of the jalapeno poppers.

"Fuck no." Stephan shudders. "I've dated older guys, yeah, but not bears."

"Aw, Steph. Love is supposed to be unconditional."

Stephan wipes a bit of ranch dressing off the corner of Eric's mouth with his thumb, and then kisses him. "Sweetheart, I *do* love you unconditionally. Just so long as you never, ever get old. Or cut your hair. Or stop working out. Or change how you look in any way."

Eric sticks his tongue out in response and wiggles it suggestively. Stephan is pulling him close for another kiss, when they're interrupted by a tiny blonde throwing herself bodily at them.

Allison, a friend of Eric's, whom Stephan has always disliked. Not that there's anything wrong with her in particular, just that she keeps pawing at Stephan and never seems to pick up on the fact that he's really, truly, completely 100 percent gay, and will never be interested in her that way no matter what. Not to mention that she's also brought Chad with her—Chad, who's been Eric's best friend since they were freshman-year roommates. The guy seriously rubs Stephan the wrong way; he's constantly making comments, which Stephan thinks barely conceal Chad's inner homophobia, and which Eric always insists are just "manly teasing." And of course Chad has dragged along his flavor of the week, a perky little brunette, and Perky's friend for good measure. Stephan wonders if Chad is going to manage to get both girls into bed with him; women just seem to turn stupid around the guy.

Ignoring the newcomers and not wanting to cling too much to Jim and Jamie, Stephan finds himself with Tina and a guy she knows from the Philosophy Department, another first-year grad student, who has the most amazing blue eyes. Not a bad body, either, and Stephan has had enough beer to let his gaze wander appreciatively while Eric's busy talking to Allison and Chad and the rest of his crowd.

He's abruptly interrupted from his leering by a hard elbow to the ribs. "Hey, I was just looking," he pouts, rubbing his side.

Eric rolls his eyes. "Better be all you're doing, Burke."

Stephan puts his arm around Eric and grabs his ass, pulling him close for a quick little smooch. "Wanna go home and I'll show you how sorry I am, baby? You know you're the only one I want," he teases, nuzzling Eric's neck.

"Prove it." Eric grins, and Stephan's cock throbs a bit, reminding him that it's been forever since they've fucked.

It's technically true that they'd had reunion sex when Eric got back into town a few days ago, but Stephan had been couch-surfing at Billy and Scott's until he could move in on campus, so it was just blowjobs. Stephan would have done more, but he was trying to follow Billy's "No Spooge on the Couch" rule, and Eric is unbelievably shy about sex when someone might walk in on them. So Stephan is understandably looking forward to getting him alone.

They don't bother saying goodbye to anyone, just leave, and Stephan is relieved that Eric seems as eager as he is, for once. In fact, he surprises the hell out of Steph on the drive home, running his hands all over his own body in the passenger seat, teasing, telling Stephan what he's going to do once they're alone. Apparently two months without sex has loosened up a lot of Eric's inhibitions, and Stephan practically runs from the parking lot to his apartment, laughing as his boyfriend paws at him all the way.

They fall on the bed, kissing and laughing and shoving each other's clothes off as fast as they can once Eric has kicked the door shut with a bang.

"Good to have a bed," Stephan notes, rolling them so he's on top and can get his jeans off the rest of the way.

"Good to have a *door*," Eric groans as Steph bends over him to mouth at his chest and stomach, making his way down.

"Well, if you weren't so inhibited," he grumbles between licks and kisses. "Some people find the idea of getting caught exciting."

"Not by Billy and Scott."

"You just don't want anyone to see the silly faces you make when you come," Stephan teases, smirking as he runs the tip of his tongue along the length of Eric's cock.

Eric sucks in a surprised breath as his dick jerks and a few drops of pre-come trickle out. He finally retorts, "Shut up, asshole," with a stellar lack of wit.

Stephan grins a challenge at him. "Make me."

"With pleasure." Eric grabs Stephan's head and pushes it down toward his cock. Barely a few moments have passed before he's making little whimpering noises and pushing Stephan away again. "Wait, hold on. Don't you want to fuck?" he manages to ask.

Stephan raises an eyebrow, answering with his lips still touching Eric's erection, the vibrations making Eric moan. "Um, *yeah*? That was sort of my plan."

"Your turn, then," Eric says, sitting up and manhandling Stephan down onto his back instead.

Stephan thinks about protesting that he'd wanted to top, but then Eric's mouth is on his dick and those fucking magnificent hands are spreading him open, and he decides he doesn't care; it can wait. Eric is slow and gentle, like always, although Stephan doesn't mind so much tonight, since it's been a while. It takes him a few minutes to relax, far too long in his opinion, but Eric never listens when Steph wants to hurry up and says that he doesn't mind the burn.

Anyway, it's good. Great, even, especially when Eric's fingers are replaced by cock—wonderful, thick, glorious *cock*. Say what you want about the boy, but he has a great dick and he knows what to do with it. Every stroke hits Stephan's sweet spot, filling him up, making his eyes roll back in his head with bliss. They've been apart too long to make it last, but that's perfect—not quite fast, yet still urgent. Soon they're entirely twisted up in each other, arms and legs entangled as they both thrust furiously, eyes squeezed shut as they try to muffle their climaxes against each other's shoulder and neck.

Stephan's hands clench so hard on the bedframe when he comes that it takes a moment to unbend them, and he feels a sore spot on his shoulder where Eric bit him a little too hard. They pant for breath, covered in a sheen of sweat, then gradually untangle. Stephan peeks into the hallway to discover Jim's door is shut, and quickly retrieves a glass of water and a washcloth from the bathroom to clean up.

Even the wet cloth doesn't wake Eric from his doze, and Stephan climbs back in bed, content to just crash out too. Their legs tangle together under the covers, his boyfriend's quiet breath ruffling his hair. Stephan lies there listening to Eric's heartbeat, the chirp of crickets, and the distant sounds of the undergrads' all-night partying which drift inside with the cool autumn night air.

He's back at school, back with Eric. All is right in his world again.

Chapter 2
Pedagogical Bonds

THE Humanities Division's graduate student orientation is the next day at eight thirty in the morning, a time clearly designed by someone with a personal vendetta against Stephan. It's just too damn early; the museum he'd worked at for the last year hadn't opened until ten thirty, and the idea of being alert at this hour is just offensive. All the coffee beans in Brazil aren't going to make it acceptable, but damned if Stephan isn't going to try.

The orientation is held in one of the big auditoriums, and he actually gets there early, nursing his fourth cup of coffee and making a note to himself to kiss Jim's feet for setting up *and* turning on the automatic coffeemaker the night before.

He meets up outside with some people he knows and feels the conflicted sort of familiarity—been there, done that—of someone who's been on the campus for four years already, mixed with the uncertain anticipation of beginning something brand new. He *has* been here, but he hasn't done *that*, and in some ways it's like being a freshman all over again. Only without the pimples. And with more sex and booze.

The orientation starts, and it's mostly just a lot of garbage about the different departments and what the faculty in each of them is focusing on. The division is trying to emphasize interdisciplinary relations this year, get people to work with the experts no matter what department they're in. On one hand it seems like a great idea, but on the other hand it sounds like a massive pain in the ass, a great idea strangled by the usual university red tape. The graduate classes are fairly small, though, and evidently the budget cuts mean a general pooling of resources. Including teaching assistants.

When Stephan realizes this could mean that he might end up TAing for one of Eric's literature classes he has to clench his jaw to keep from laughing out loud—that would be so fucking awesome! He can't keep the malicious little grin off his face and ends up having to pass a note to Kristine to explain after she jabs him in the ribs with her sharp elbow.

Unfortunately before Kristine even passes the note back, his evil glee is ruined by the Dean's overview of the Academic Code of Conduct and his sharp emphasis about inappropriate relations with students and abuse of positions of authority. It's such a load of bullshit; no one really cares what the grad students do, whether they fuck undergrads or faculty or *sheep*, but the university has to cover its ass, he supposes. It's improbable he'd be assigned to one of Eric's classes anyway, and it's made clear that all he'd have to do is make sure Eric's not in his section.

Finally they get to the part that they've all been waiting for, where the Assistant Dean talks about the TAships. *Unfortunately*, the Assistant Dean this year is one of the Theater Arts faculty, an energetic and unbelievably sincere man who gives new meaning to the word "flamboyant" and makes Stephan cringe just on general principle.

The Assistant Dean talks a little bit about the need to be at each lecture for the classes they are assigned to, and if there are sections they are assigned to teach, that they're not allowed to cancel more than one meeting without getting in trouble. He makes a very stern frowny face and emphasizes the need to get assignments graded on time. Then, in conclusion, the guy stands up in front of the lecture hall and says to the hundred or so new graduate students seated there, "The pedagogical bond between Student and Teacher is a sacred one. I could never presume to *tell* you how to teach your classes. Just go out there and *do your thing*!"

After a very long moment of shocked silence, the Dean clears his throat and moves on to talk about how and when they will be paid for their TA work, while the students blink at each other, dumbfounded.

That, it seems, was the sum total of their training on how to be teachers: "Just go out there and *do your thing!*"

Un-fucking-believable.

Stephan zones out on all the financial stuff about grants and loans and fees and payment schedules, and doesn't really tune back in until he receives another jab in the ribs from Kristine. The girl really should wear elbow pads; he makes a mental note to sit next to Tina after the break.

Kristine has helpfully awoken him from his *That's honest-to-God all they're going to say about teaching?* stupor in order to check out the lists being projected onto the screen above them of which classes have had which grad students assigned to them. Stephan's thrilled and relieved to hear that he's TAing for the big Intro to American History class, as are two other students. It has the temporary downside that no faculty ever wants to teach the Intro classes, so it's unassigned at the moment and will go to whomever is lowest on the faculty totem pole, but it doesn't really matter.

Looks like he won't be grading his boyfriend on his sexual skills after all. Unless he can get Eric into some role playing or something, and he decides to follow up on that subject later. His sudden awareness of his dick makes him also realize those four cups of coffee need an outlet. He's almost squirming by the time the Dean finally announces a short break and he can run to the restroom.

He looks over the guy already in the can: older, a little rough around the edges, rugged, maybe. Facial hair somewhere between stubble and beard, but it's his eyes that really make Stephan do a double take. There's nothing really special about their color, but they're just... *warm.* Welcoming.

Their gazes catch and hold for a moment in the mirror above the sinks, but then the door bangs open and Mark, a guy Stephan sort of knows through Jim, comes in followed by two others, and no one stands around a men's room staring at another guy without getting his ass kicked, so Stephan heads out and makes his way back to his seat.

Armed with a fresh cup of coffee, of course; if the university's going to welcome them with free coffee and bagels, who is Stephan to say no? Although honestly, those bagels? Probably older than he is. He tried one once, as a sophomore, and nearly lost a tooth. He's not surprised that no one seems to have touched the artistic display the catering staff has made.

He wonders idly if they're the same bagels, every time, at every function. Maybe they've been shellacked or something, glued together to stay in formation.

Okay, maybe he might have had a little too much caffeine on an empty stomach.

Once they've all reassembled, the Dean introduces the faculty: their names, classes they're teaching this year, and what sort of research they're doing. Stephan dutifully notes down all of the History faculty, along with anyone else who sounds like they're doing work in his area of interest, namely the history of religions in America.

The only History faculty member who's new since Stephan graduated is introduced as Professor Jeffery Tegan, and it's the guy from the bathroom, with the warm eyes. He waves at the auditorium and corrects the Humanities Dean, saying, "Just Jeff," in a gravelly but friendly voice, before he sits down again. His focus is American history, and Stephan makes a mental note to see what he's about and if he'd maybe make a good advisor for his thesis. Or something.

After an interminable speech about how hard they can expect their classes to be now that they're grad students, and how there won't be any slacking off, that they're "adults now," they're released. It's such bullshit; everyone Stephan's talked to (including his undergrad faculty advisor) has told him over and over that the coursework is about the same; he's just expected to take it a lot more seriously than most undergraduates do. Since being serious enough was never a problem for him, Stephan figures he's pretty much set. He's used to working hard, putting in long hours, missing parties in favor of working on research papers.

Well, *some* parties. Not all of them, because that would suck, and you're only young once, right?

Still, he loves what he's studying, is fascinated and turned on by it in an amazingly geeky way. It's kind of weird, because he doesn't talk to his parents more than every couple of months and only sees his family over the Christmas holidays, but it's largely his upbringing that spurred his interest in religion. They're all very good Christians, churchgoing, involved with the community, and have been his whole life. They're less than thrilled about his "sinful lifestyle choices," so it's not a topic they talk about, and therefore, they don't have much to say to each other beyond the pleasantries.

The whole religious *you're-going-to-hell* thing has always mystified Stephan, and especially since he figured out that he was gay and discovered that some churches didn't have a big problem with that. It's funny to him, and a little bit sad, that so many churches teach that everyone but the individuals in their congregation is going to hell. That's just illogical, not to mention kind of meanspirited.

And hey, if he's going to hell for liking cock? Then heaven would probably suck anyway.

Just as Stephan's about to leave the auditorium, he notices the other two students assigned to TA the American History intro class waving him over. They exchange names and e-mail addresses, and plan to hook up again right after the first session next Monday. The guy, Will, says that he talked to the Chair of the History department, who said that someone would be e-mailing them sometime within in the next two days about which faculty has been assigned to teach. They laugh when Lauren, the other TA, points out that if the university follows its usual communication patterns, they'll probably find out when they set foot in the door of the classroom. They both seem pretty cool, easygoing but organized, and Stephan's glad they're all in the same boat.

Lunchtime seems like a blessing, and Stephan's not surprised when he checks his cell phone and has a message from Eric, suggesting they meet up somewhere. It's sweet, makes a little fluttery thing happen in Stephan's chest area, but it's also a little weird. They've been together since around New Year's Eve—their first kiss, Steph's embarrassed to admit, it's so nauseatingly romantic—but since Eric was at school and Stephan was working at the local history museum all year, it's going to be weird now to be seeing so much more of each other. Every day, even. Of course, Eric's living off campus while Stephan's on, but still.

It's not bad, just different.

"So, how was it?" Eric asks, joining Stephan at one of the cafés scattered around the sprawling campus. One of the upsides of having the campus be its own little island apart from the town is that it's fairly insular. There are coffee shops or small cafés near almost every large cluster of buildings, and the buildings are grouped more or less by academic division. Stephan can't even remember the last time he was at Science Hill for anything other than the taqueria located there.

"Not bad. Long. Boring as shit. And they had those bagels," Stephan says, eagerly starting on his sandwich.

"The ones from catering?" Eric grins. "Wow. They must really have it in for you guys."

Stephan nods. "And there was a possibility that I'd end up TAing one of your classes, but no, I got assigned to Intro Am Hist."

"You're lucky I speak your code language," Eric says, shaking his head with a smile. "So who's teaching it?"

"Dunno yet; it's unassigned. But I met the other two TAs, and they seem cool. We're all new, so we're all equally lost."

Stephan goes on to tell Eric about the great one-line "teacher training" they got from the Assistant Dean, and Eric almost chokes to death on his Coke, laughing so hard.

"Wow. Sink or swim, huh?"

"No kidding. And now you know exactly how much they care about the undergrads, letting us try and teach you guys with no guidance whatsoever. No wonder most of my TAs sucked so much, and those study sections were such a waste of time," Stephan says, shaking his head with disgust.

"Well, *some* of them know what they're doing," Eric offers. "I had a great TA last year who really helped me with my writing. Of course, she was PhD track, so she'd been doing it for a while...."

"Yeah." Stephan wads up the paper wrapping from his sandwich and twists it into a ball. "Bet I can make it into that trash can?" he asks, indicating the one in the corner.

"Maybe? That's not a good bet. How about if you make it, you get a reward?"

"What kind of reward?"

"PDA? Maybe we can gross out those freshmen dudes at the other table."

"You're on," Stephan says. He aims carefully and the trash lands in the exact center of the bin. Eric wads his trash up and follows suit, then hooks his foot around the rung of Stephan's chair, drags it over with a loud screech, and bends him backward in a kiss straight out of some old black and white movie.

The idiots at the other table are making grossed-out noises and muttering under their breath, but Stephan doesn't care. He doesn't even mind being bent over backward like this, obviously the "girl," because the thrill of being manhandled by Eric cancels out just about anything else. Eric rarely takes control or uses his size to his advantage, and Stephan doesn't care if it makes people think he's submissive or whatever—it's fucking *hot*.

Plus, the campus is pretty safe. It's super-liberal and full of leftover hippie types, and has a pretty big GLBT community. The town is like that, too, and it's really one of the best places to be gay, probably in the whole country, as far as Stephan knows. The freshmen guys are going to learn pretty goddamned fast that if they want to be homophobic, they'd better keep their thoughts to themselves or they're going to be subjected to some seriously uncomfortable "interventions" by the residential staff in the dorms.

When he starts giggling, remembering some of the "outreach" he participated in as an undergrad, Eric lets him up, looking puzzled.

"It's that funny?" he asks, pouting a little.

"Nah. Just thinking about some of the things we did to the homophobes when I lived in the dorms. Remember when I told you about how Mike and Jim made those two losers wear feather boas and tiaras and high heels for two days after they made fun of drag queens?"

Eric snorts. He wasn't there, of course, being three years younger, but he's heard a lot of the stories. "Where is Mike, anyway? Haven't seen him in ages."

"Took a few months off or something. He turned twenty-seven in July, if you can believe it, and decided to do some traveling, 'find himself' or some bullshit. He's been sending me random-assed e-mails from God knows where." Stephan grins.

"Is he back in town? On campus? Or did he finally finish his doctorate?"

"Man, I don't think that guy's ever going to finish. I think he likes school and doesn't want to be faculty. Just likes working in the labs, doing 'research'," Stephan says, making little air quotes with his fingers.

"Inventing new drugs," Eric clarifies, shaking his head with amused disapproval.

"Hey, he's in Biochem—that's what they do. And he's cooked up some seriously good shit."

Eric snorts and Stephan rolls his eyes. His boyfriend can be so uptight sometimes. It's not like Stephan does a lot of drugs, and nothing aside from Ecstasy and smoking pot in the last couple of years. Well, and mushrooms that one time over the summer, but still. It's not like he's an addict or shooting up heroin or dropping acid every weekend or whatever.

"Anyway, yeah, I think he's back. I should call him or something," Stephan says, changing the subject.

"Yeah, I'm sure there'll be a few parties this weekend." Eric nods. "I'll check around, let you know. We can decide what we want to do."

"Sounds like a plan."

Eric kisses Stephan again, and they walk across campus, headed toward Stephan's apartment. They've got all day to hang out, play games, and eat junk food, and he's not going to waste it. Classes start soon, and these last few days to goof around, before he's buried in coursework, are precious. He doesn't know what's ahead of him, exactly, but it feels big, like it's important to store up these moments, these last dregs of frivolous playtime with Eric.

Just in case.

Chapter 3
History Geek

CLASSES start on Thursday, which is baffling and always has been. Who the hell thought that up, and what the fuck were they smoking? *Thursday?* Honestly.

The day before was spent unpacking, getting the apartment organized, and thanking God that although Jim's taste in music sucks, he's as much of a neat freak as Stephan is about the kitchen and bathroom. Living together looks like it's probably going to work out pretty well, which is actually a little bit of a surprise. He and Jim have known each other for years, but they've never been super close, hang-out-all-the-time, best buddies or anything. But Jim's mellow and his girlfriend is pretty low maintenance, and their relationship seems relatively drama-free. Jim and Jamie have been together forever, and she's got some job at the County Planner's office or something. They both seem to like Eric well enough; sometimes Stephan thinks Jim likes his boyfriend more than he likes Stephan; they're both so conservative about some things. Anyway, it looks like they'll all get along fine.

All the History grad students get together at a local bar for an afternoon meet-and-greet and for the more experienced ones to offer some tips to the newbies: figure out who you want your advisor to be right away and ask them before the end of your first year, because no faculty wants more than two or three advisees and the good ones get taken up fast. Don't ask Garcia to be your advisor because he's got some weird deep-seated hatred of grad students and will make you rewrite your thesis over and over until you quit school. Always have at least five discussion topics for your TA sections, and if it's going miserably and none of the students will talk, see another TA or the professor teaching the class before it gets too bad.

Finally, they say, whatever you do, make nice with the department secretary and bring her chocolate. If you cross her, you will Rue the Day. They all nod somberly, and Stephan can see the capital letters. It's all good advice so far, so he decides to take them seriously on this, too, and pick up a box of Godiva's next time he happens to be at the bookstore—he knows the secretary already from when he was an undergrad, but he's not above a little bribery.

Eric decides to hang out with Chad and the rest of his housemates that evening, so Stephan gets to be alone all night to obsess about his first day as a grad student and generally let his neuroses have free rein. He's not *actually* a total spaz, just, well, sometimes. He likes to relax and have fun, sure, but he's also a control freak about most things, and not knowing what to expect in situations makes him tense. Nervous.

Fine, a total spaz.

Around midnight, after he's tried on four different shirts and asked Jamie if she has an iron because maybe the last one was too wrinkled, he gives up and decides to watch whatever crap on TV will calm him down while he has a couple of beers before trying to go to sleep. While Jim's in the bathroom, Jamie's puttering around getting ready for bed and work the next day. Once she seems to have everything done, she comes over to Stephan, and he turns down the volume, assuming that's what she's going to ask him to do. She laughs and sits down on his lap, messing up his hair with her hand, and giving him a kiss on the cheek. "You're going to be fine," she says, smiling. "You're good at school; you love this shit. Stop worrying."

Stephan grins at her, feeling more relaxed by her offer of girly mothering comfort than he really has any right to be. "Yeah. Thanks, Jamie," he says, arms wrapping around her waist to give her a hug.

"Stop trying to steal my girl," Jim calls from the hallway.

"It ain't stealin' if she's givin' it away," Stephan drawls, then laughs as Jamie gets up in a dramatic huff. He pinches her butt, and she squeals and runs off to Jim's room giggling.

"Steph get you all warmed up for me, baby?" he hears Jim tease, and then the door shuts, and Stephan turns up the volume a little so he doesn't have to hear anything else.

Thank goodness they're both fairly quiet. He offers them a silent toast with his beer. It's fun to tease your housemates about overhearing them having sex, but it gets annoying pretty damn fast. He should know; he shared a wall with Danielle when they were housemates their third year. She might be his best friend, but he did not need to know that much about her sex life. Moaning and bedsprings squeaking are bad enough—hearing her yell "Ride me, Daddy!" was seriously TMI.

Steph's schedule ends up being fairly light, at least at first glance. He's got his required introductory seminar, Historical Method and Theory, for two hours on Tuesdays and Thursdays, with an hour each of Introduction to the Literature of American History up to the Civil War and French language on Mondays, Wednesdays, and Fridays.

He can't get over how unbelievably stupid it is that he has to waste two whole semesters on taking a foreign language when his focus is on *American* history. The requirement makes sense for the other tracks; of course they'd need to occasionally read something in French or German or ancient Greek. But him? All of his source material's in English, thanks, and he already speaks that language pretty fucking fluently.

Oh well. The most annoying thing about school is always all the stupid hoops they make you jump through for no apparent reason. And maybe he can go to France or something, someday, and it won't be a total loss.

Or maybe there will be some hidden stash of papers from French explorers that he'll need to read for something he's working on someday.

Or maybe he'll meet some hot French dude he'd like to fuck. After all, knowledge is never a waste, right?

Stephan will have to wait until Monday for the first session of the class he's TAing and there's still been no word on which professor's been assigned to the class. Annoying, but typical.

He gets to his seminar Thursday morning nice and early and isn't that surprised to find Tina there. They sit next to each other, both a little nervous and glad to have found a friendly face. Two hours later, they stagger out of the classroom with identical looks of panic on their faces, overwhelmed by the sheer number of texts they're expected to read for just this one class. Sixteen weeks is not going to be nearly long enough.

They grab lunch together and then go to the bookstore, which is packed. It takes over an hour to find all of their books, lug them to the massive lines at the cashier counters, and pay. Poorer by more than $500, arms aching from the weight of so many hardcovers, grouchy and tired, he heads back to the grad student housing complex, thanking God that he doesn't have to carry all his books to the bus stop and then to his apartment off campus, the way Tina does. Sure, he has a pang of guilt, a chivalrous urge to help her out somehow, but the *I'm-a-self-sufficient-woman* glare she shot him when he started to offer shut him up fast.

The next day isn't so bad; he's starting to get a feel for the rhythm of how his days are going to go, settling back into the student groove. Being able to find and make a cup of coffee first thing in the morning before his eyes are all the way open, without running into any walls, is also a big plus.

His Friday starts with French, which is taught by a petite woman, very no-nonsense, but with a wicked sense of humor that slips out occasionally. It's a mixed class, mostly undergraduates, but that's actually a relief since it means the pace will be a little more manageable, Stephan thinks. Madame Georges seems strict about the rules, that homework will be due every day, no late work accepted at all, and there will be a quiz every week. But the chapters in the book are short, and she seems more focused on them actually retaining the information than just flying through as much as possible at breakneck speed. Stephan took French in high school, so hopefully this won't be too hard, even if that was six years ago. If he does well, maybe he'll try to pass the GSFLE reading test in December and not have to take the second semester after all.

His Intro to the Literature of American History class that afternoon brings a pleasant surprise: Danielle. He's a little shocked to see her there, actually, not because it's illogical—which it's not, since she's a second-year Am Lit grad student—but because she's supposed to be one of his best friends and he hasn't talked to her in almost a month. She hasn't returned his texts or voicemails or e-mails, and he's had no idea if she'd been swallowed by a whale or what.

She sits down next to him and leans her head on his shoulder. "Can you ever forgive me, baby?" she asks in a pathetic voice.

"I'll have to think about it," he answers, wiggling to get her to sit up. What he sees when he finally gets a close look at her makes his forehead wrinkle, all banter aside. "What's happened?" he asks, reaching up to run his thumb lightly across the dark circles under her eyes.

She shrugs. "Short version? Broke up with Bryan. I ended it, but it still sucks." She sighs, pulling him into a hug and burrowing into his chest.

He wants to say something comforting, but the best he can come up with is, "He was kind of a dick. I'm sorry," as he wraps his arms around her.

"He was," she says, and he can feel the half-laugh even though it's silent. "From now on, you pick out all my boyfriends, okay?"

"Yeah, good plan," he agrees, giving her a squeeze as they disentangle when the professor comes in.

The class looks amazing. They're working closely with the primary sources, using literature to construct a picture of the society at the time. It's the kind of thing Stephan gets the mental equivalent of a hard-on for, taking a text or an object from history and coming to his own conclusions about the people who created it, rather than working from what all the other scholars have said. Seriously, he gets *really* excited about this stuff.

Yeah, he's kind of a history geek that way. So what? At least he's got the "good-looking" thing going for him.

Anyway, the class looks great. A shitload of work, but work he's excited to do, and he's grinning like a total dork by the time the professor wraps it up and everyone heads outside. He's not the only one who's excited; it's a smallish seminar, less than twenty students, and everyone seems pretty happy.

Well, except Danielle. Who looks happier, but not *happy*. Then again, he knows her pretty well, and how upset she must be if she's gone incommunicado for a whole month. Wrapping an arm around her shoulders, he guides her outside into the afternoon sunlight.

He nods his head at a bench, then goes to get two drinks from the coffee cart across the way. He remembers to get hers with two shots of espresso and with soy milk and fake sugar, even though usually he'd argue about it since he thinks she's already skinny enough and she looks even thinner now than the last time he saw her. She doesn't need to hear that today, but he does buy an enormous brownie, hoping maybe it will tempt her into consuming some actual calories.

"Want to talk about it?" he asks, sitting down next to where she's sprawled out, sunglasses on, eyes closed, face turned up to catch the last rays of the afternoon.

She's quiet for a few minutes, thinking. "Not really."

He's always liked that about Danni; even a simple question, she takes a second to consider and answers honestly. And he's relieved she doesn't want to have a big breakdown and start bawling, at least not right now. She's cried on him a few times over various assholes, and he doesn't mind, but he'd rather not do it outside, in public, without a huge box of tissues nearby.

"I don't have any Kleenex," she says, the corner of her mouth twitching upward a little.

"Me and my shirt appreciate that," he says, laughing. "So, we're not going to talk about the asshole, then, or why you didn't tell me what was going on. Fine. What classes are you taking, are you still sharing that hideous condo with Melissa, and did you get all your books already or do you need help? Also, I hope you don't have plans for tonight because I'm taking you to dinner and a movie. I gotta warn you, though, I'm not going to put out."

As he hoped, she laughs and nudges him with her knee. "They say a mouth's a mouth, Steph."

"I doubt Eric would see it that way," he snorts.

"You two are still together, then?"

He nods, not wanting to talk about his relationship and rub his happiness in her face. "So, books? Dinner?"

"I've got my books. Dinner… would be really nice, actually. I haven't been getting out much," she admits, reaching for the brownie.

He pushes it toward her without looking. "Just you and me, or should I ask Eric if he wants to come along and annoy us?"

"Whichever," she shrugs. He gives her a look, and she shrugs again. "Seriously, whichever. Not like seeing you happy is going to make me start sobbing. Eric's a good guy; I don't mind if he comes along." She pauses a moment, then reaches over and wraps his hand around hers. "Just so long as *he's* the third wheel. And no making out with him in front of me," she adds, a mischievous look in her eye. "It's my date with you, so I get to make the rules."

"What have I gotten myself into?" Stephan sighs, the weight of the world in his voice, but a smile playing around his eyes as he digs out his cell phone to call Eric.

Chapter 4
Go Baby, Go

FRIDAY night had actually turned out pretty well, all things considered. Eric was slightly pissy about not having Stephan to himself, for about thirty seconds, until he got a good look at Danielle and how miserable she was. She suggested an action movie, and that pretty much won Eric over completely. They'd gone out for Chinese after, and he managed to talk her into ice cream too. Stephan was pleased to see that she ate a decent amount and considered it a job well done when they dropped her off at her place and headed back to Eric's.

To sleep. Mostly.

Chad gives Stephan a squinty look over the coffeemaker, but Eric smacks Chad upside the head before he can make any smart-assed remarks about how disgusting gay sex is. Stephan downs a bowl of wretched sugary cereal and two cups of coffee, and then kisses Eric goodbye until later so that he can go study.

Yes, already. He has homework again, and is starting to remember, with a creeping sense of doom, that feeling students have that there is always *something* they should be doing instead of relaxing and having fun. Or fucking. Or sleeping. Or eating. So he spends the day stretched out on his bed, reading brain-meltingly dull books about historiography and coloring his fingernails with different hued highlighter pens until evening.

Eric's other housemate's girlfriend is having a birthday party, turning twenty-one, so that's where they start out on Saturday night. Stephan wants to get there early, since it's all newly legal kids and that means there's going to be vomit on the carpet, probably before midnight. In all fairness, he readily admits that someone usually pukes at his friends' parties, the big ones, anyway, even though everyone is well above drinking age. Usually they make it to the bathroom or some bushes outside, and that's an important distinction between what Stephan thinks of as a "post-college" party and a party where the only point is to get drunk because it's so awesome that you can do it legally now.

They show up while the crowd is small and the hostess is still capable of standing upright. They've brought the required bottle of hard liquor, and they add it to the collection in the kitchen, which is covered with bottles and cups and sticky sheets of paper with recipes for every sex drink possible. Eric happily makes himself a Sex on the Beach and grins when Stephan plays along and makes a Cock-sucking Cowboy.

Drinks in hand, they weave through a mostly talking, semi-dancing crowd to pay their respects to the hostess, Melanie. She insists that the party has four rules and manages (with some difficulty) to list each one on a separate finger: one, no puking on the carpet; two, you have to bring a bottle of booze; three, everyone has to wear a hat; and four, everyone has to kiss the birthday girl. The best kisser gets to give her a birthday spanking, she adds, wiggling her eyebrows comically.

Rule number one looks like it's probably going to be broken fairly soon by the giggly blonde in the corner; she and her friends are a little green around the gills already. Stephan and Eric are good for number two, and after a quick mind-reading glance at each other, they both grin and lean in at the same time to plant sloppy wet kisses on Melanie's cheeks.

She laughs, stretching up to hook an arm around each of their necks. "Why do gay boys think they can get away without real kisses?" She tsks. "I demand do-overs!"

"No way," Eric laughs. "Stephan's a pretty good kisser, and you're not allowed to have him spank you."

"Ha! I knew you were a big subby bottom, Eric," Mel says, grinning. "Fine, you can keep your Dom. Come here and give me a kiss anyway."

Eric's kiss is chaste, mouth closed, and even Stephan can see it's about as soft and innocent as Eric kissing his nephew goodnight. Trying not to cackle evilly, Stephan downs the rest of his sticky sweet drink, pulls Melanie to him, bends her over backward, and lays the most flamboyantly passionate kiss on her that he's capable of. Her lips are soft, and her body feels wrong, small hands gripping his shoulders in surprise, but it's actually an all-right kiss—to be honest, it's the best kiss he's ever had with a girl.

Possibly this is because Eric is watching them, and even though he's laughing, Stephan can tell by the way Eric's hands have tightened into almost fists that he's a little pissed off—jealous, maybe. Stephan finds this satisfying. He lets Melanie up, and she stumbles a little bit, and he's not too modest to hope that it's from the kiss and not the fact that she's drunk.

She raises a hand to her lips slowly, eyes still locked on Stephan. "You... you...." She glances across the room at her boyfriend, who's been mostly ignoring the whole process. "You suck. You look like that," she says, waving her hands around in a gesture that seems aimed mostly at his chest, "and then you kiss like *that*, and then you have to go and be gay. So not fair," she pouts. "I hate you. Go get me another drink. Something blue!" she shouts as he turns and starts back to the kitchen.

He finds a guy who's decided to play bartender and comes up with "something blue for the birthday girl" impressively fast. When he returns to trade the drink for his boyfriend, he finds Eric pawing through a huge box of hats, intent on fulfilling rule number three.

As he suspected, the hat rule is designed to make him look like a dork. He contemplates going out to his car and grabbing a baseball cap so he can claim he's following the letter of the law, even while violating the spirit. Eric, though—he's into it. He drags out a huge black witch's hat, then a tattered Indian chief headdress, then a tiara, and finally a plastic Viking helmet, complete with horns.

"No," Stephan says as firmly as he can.

"Oh yes," Eric grins. "It's a rule."

"But my hair looks good tonight. And we're going to Billy's after this," he whines.

"Billy has seen you look like shit before. He won't mind now."

"You suck," Stephan says, grabbing the Viking helm and plopping it on his head grimly.

It takes Eric a few minutes to stop laughing, and by then the moment for any witty comeback has passed. Instead, Eric grabs the tiara, which looks like a leftover from a beauty pageant or something, and delicately perches it on his head.

"Princess Erica," Steph grins.

"You're not going to ravish me, are you, you barbarian?" Eric asks, eyelashes fluttering.

Stephan nods. "I'm pretty sure I have to."

"But I'm a pretty princess. I'm more powerful than you are."

"Dude. *Viking.* I think I can take you."

Eric looks him up and down, smirking. "I dunno. You're a little short for a Viking."

"Fuck you. You're a freaky giant of a princess. You're lucky anyone wants to ravish your ass at all," Steph scowls.

"Now, now—no fighting, boys," Melanie interrupts, wrapping an arm around Eric. Her boyfriend's got her on the other side, and while she's still smiling, she's also clearly about to fall over if he stops holding her up. "I'm sure everyone wants to watch a horny Stephan ravish Princess Erica, but not until after the cake."

"Cake!" a guy's voice shouts across the room, and then a chant begins, ending thankfully quickly when two girls bring over a huge sheet cake with what appears to be twenty-one candles but is actually a fire hazard of nearly epic proportions. Everyone not completely inebriated takes a hurried step back, and the requisite song is sung at breakneck speed. A sober friend, who Stephan thinks Melanie should probably buy dinner for tomorrow in gratitude, grabs the birthday girl's long hair and pulls it back from the flames before it's singed off as she blows out the candles.

Disaster averted, wishes made, and hair still intact, everyone cheers or breathes a sigh of relief—depending on how drunk they are.

Eric, of course, insists on sticking around for a piece of the cake, but once he's had his sugar, he's willing to take off and head over to Billy's. Well, Billy and Scott's, but Stephan always thinks of it as Billy's house because Billy is the one who bought it when his grandparents died and left him the money. Stephan lived there for a while, too, but it turned out that being friends with Billy was pretty much contingent upon not living with him, and since he and Stephan wanted to stay friends, Steph moved out as soon as he could.

Just as they leave, the blonde girl Stephan noticed earlier bends over and pukes, right on the carpet. He laughs all the way out to the car and for a good part of the drive across town.

BILLY'S (and Scott's) house is smallish and seems even smaller packed with people. In reality, it doesn't take more than a dozen warm bodies to make it seem like there's not enough space to breathe, but it's a nice contrast to the group that they just left of at least fifty people Stephan didn't know.

As usual, it's not so much a party as a bunch of friends hanging out. Stephan's one of the last few still in school, but Santa Cruz is a college town and everything turns on the university's calendar, so it's not that weird to be having a back-to-school party. People graduate and stick around, at least until they "grow up" and the cost of living and limited job opportunities force them to leave the area. Most of Stephan's friends are older but not at that stage yet, still figuring out what they want to do. Billy might have four years on him, but Stephan's always felt like he was the one with more of his life figured out.

They met when he was a freshman, just a few weeks into college. Billy was sitting on the lawn in the undergrad housing quad, playing his guitar and singing during an impromptu dorm party. He was drunk off his ass and the instrument was badly out of tune, and Stephan just went up to him, took the guitar away, turned a few pegs to tune it, and handed it back without a word. When he started to leave, Billy grabbed him by the ankle.

"Got yours with you or did you leave it at home?" Billy asked with a grin.

Stephan returned it, if a little tentatively. "It's at home. But my roommate's got one he'll probably let me borrow." A few minutes later Billy was teaching him the melody of the song he'd been singing, and they'd been friends ever since.

Now Billy has an office job he hates, which he quits every few months for a new one, and Stephan can never keep track of what he's doing. He works enough to pay the bills, but his heart's pretty set on making it big as a musician. He's good, plays a lot of local gigs and even a few in the city, and Steph hopes he gets his big break soon; he's talented enough and he deserves a chance to show the world.

Scott's the more practical part of the couple. They've been together for a few years now, and living together for the last two. They started off playing in the band, then started fucking, then split up musically, then split up romantically, and got back together with the band. Basically, they tried every combination possible, and it was a big mess for a while until they figured out that they could play together or have a relationship, but not both.

Stephan thinks they made the right decision, choosing love. After all, you can always find other guys to make music with. They still mess around at home, write music together, occasionally play at parties, but they have their own bands and don't have to "compromise their artistic visions" or some such shit, and it seems to work for them. Together, but separate. Stephan's always kind of envied that.

Well, not always. Just in the last few years, since they found out what works most of the time. Billy can still be a raging asshole, and Scott can be a bit of a pushover. Together, though, they're a pretty awesome set of friends.

Scott apparently barbecued enough chicken earlier in the day to feed a small army, so even though it's nearly midnight, everyone's eating and drinking beer, talking at a normal volume over the quiet music in the background. Eric brings a plate stacked precariously high with drumsticks in from the kitchen and shares with Stephan after a moment of fake pouting.

"Your barbecue sauce is awesome," Eric tells Scott, licking his fingers, totally oblivious to the fact that *some* people might find the gesture suggestive. *Some* people sitting right next to him, remembering how nice that tongue felt just a few weeks ago, right here on this very couch.

Some *person*, who hopes his semi-erection isn't noticeable. Apparently Stephan's body needs a few more weeks of regular sex to stop responding like a boy a decade younger than he actually is.

While Scott tries to explain the recipe to Eric, who is actually scrawling it down on a Post-it note despite the fact that he's never cooked anything that didn't come directly out of a box or a can, Stephan steps out to the patio for some fresh air and to see who's hanging out outside. Smoking out there, to be more specific.

"Steph! Baby!"

Octopus-like arms wrap around Stephan from behind and squeeze the breath out of him. When he can inhale again, he notices that the air out here smells less like tobacco and more like pot, which makes sense because it's Mike who's got him in a bear hug.

Stephan grins and settles back into Mike's embrace. "Gonna have to get me high *before* you try to take advantage of me, man."

"Can do." There is a chuckle of warm breath next to his ear, and a pipe is passed over to Mike's waiting hand. One arm still wrapped around Stephan's waist, Mike brings it to Steph's lips while a guy Stephan doesn't know helpfully flicks a lighter.

Eric doesn't smoke pot, ever, so Stephan doesn't have any qualms about taking a huge hit—Eric can drive them home. Besides, he needs to calm his hormones down somehow, and beer's just not cutting it tonight.

The smoke fills his lungs, *smooth and warm and kind of velvety*, Stephan thinks on his second hit. Which is when part of him notes that *holy shit*, that's seriously strong stuff if he's having "velvety" thoughts already.

He giggles a little. "Wow. Where'd you get this?"

Mike's still holding him, maybe pressing their bodies a little closer together than is strictly platonic, but whatever. "My own backyard, man. Like Dorothy, I went to Oz only to discover that the best grass is right here at home."

Stephan's laughing at Mike's mixed metaphors so hard that his face hurts, limbs gone all loose and lazy. His head's resting on his friend's shoulder, and he suddenly realizes, "Dude, you snuck up on me. I haven't even actually seen you yet."

"Feeling's not enough?" Mike purrs, pressing his hips into Stephan's ass and rubbing them slowly together.

This just makes Stephan giggle even harder. "Eric will so totally kick your ass."

Mike tries to sound serious, concerned, for a moment. "You dating some big, jealous tough guy?"

Music from inside drifts out through the window, and Stephan glances in to see Eric standing next to the stereo, holding the latest Garbage CD. He pulls free of Mike's embrace, grabbing him by the hand and dragging him inside.

"Hey, babe," he says with a smile, bumping his hip against his boyfriend. "Mike forgot how big and burly you are and tried to hit on me. Beat him up."

"I *did* hit on you, idiot. I'll never stop. One day you will be mine!" Mike cackles, and he and Stephan almost fall over laughing.

"You are so high," Eric smiles, shaking his head.

His disapproval is mostly a joke, but not completely. Despite Mike's many long lectures about how alcohol is harder on your body than THC, Eric still goes by the laws of what's legal and what isn't, most of the time. Stephan only smokes or does drugs at parties these days, anyhow, so it's not really a big deal for them, but it does keep Eric from liking Mike as much as he might otherwise.

Which is kind of too bad, but it's not something Stephan can fix, so whatever.

"You put on this music for me?" Stephan asks, changing the topic and fluttering his eyelashes at Eric.

Who nods. "Gonna dance for us?" he suggests with all innocence.

"Only if you dance with me," Stephan challenges, although his hips are already kind of wiggling a little bit to the beat. He can't help it; he likes to dance, likes to feel rhythm and music in his body, whether playing his guitar or as one of a big crowd at a dance club.

"I'm not really the rainbows type," Eric says, as that part of the song comes on.

"No, you're not very feminine-looking at all," Mike says in a disappointed tone of voice, shaking his head sadly as he reaches up to comb his fingers through Eric's hair, which is so long it's curling a little at the ends. "You might be young, but I doubt you could pull off drag."

"Not everyone can be as versatile as you are." Stephan snickers, remembering the week Mike spent in a dress for reasons no one can ever remember. Even Mike doesn't seem to know, although he tries to hide it by pretending that he's being mysterious.

"I like my boys to look like boys and my girls to look like girls," Eric puts in.

"How very 1950s of you," Mike snorts, and Eric makes a face in response.

"Hey, lay off him," Scott says, coming over to smooth things out the way he always does, before they go from teasing to actual grouchiness. He takes the CD out of Eric's hands, saying, "Let's turn that off, anyway; Billy wants to play you the new song he's been working on, Steph."

"That'll get the taste of that technopop out of your head." Billy smirks, coming over to push a guitar at Steph. "I know how much you hate it."

Stephan's cheeks flush a little; he actually kind of *loves* it—it's one thing he and Eric bonded over in the beginning. All the rest of his friends tease him mercilessly about his taste in music, Billy in particular. It's not that he doesn't like the kind of country-rock that

Billy and Scott sing, not at all—he just likes almost everything. He's a musical omnivore, as Eric says.

Musical *slut*, Stephan usually corrects him with a leer.

Anyway, Billy sits him down and teaches him the chords for the harmony, and then in no time at all Billy is playing the melody and singing. The song isn't quite polished yet, but it's got a good feeling to it, makes something sort of pull in Stephan's chest. The lyrics are about love sought and finally found, and how what's easy isn't always what's right. When Billy finishes, a muscle in Scott's jaw is twitching with the effort of keeping his emotions bottled up. He breaks once the smattering of applause fades out and grabs Billy and shoves him into the bedroom, the door closing with a very final-sounding slam. Eric's got a soft smile on his face, eyes only on Steph, and Stephan's glad he's got such an awesome boyfriend.

"Late birthday present for Scott?" Mike asks.

"Sounds like it."

Someone turns up the stereo to block out the muffled sounds coming from the bedroom, but the crowd takes the hint and starts drifting out. It's late, anyway, and with the hosts busy fucking their brains out, it's clearly time to go.

Kristine and Tina are the last two to leave, and they help Stephan and Eric clean up anything that's going to be seriously gross in the morning. Mostly it's just a matter of getting the food trash bagged up before the ants get to it, and they're done in a matter of minutes. Stephan turns off lights and locks up, and he's pretty well dragging by the time Eric's wrapping an arm around his waist and guiding him to the car.

It's been a long night, and a long week. And although he'd like to take Eric home and do a little bit of what Scott and Billy are doing, he knows it's just not in the cards.

"Morning sex?" he mumbles as Eric tucks him into bed and then climbs in with him.

A heavy arm wraps around his waist, but he doesn't hear an answer before he falls asleep.

Chapter 5
Warm

STEPHAN probably shouldn't feel as surprised as he does when he arrives at the big lecture hall on Monday to see that Professor Tegan is teaching Intro to Am Hist. He was, after all, the only new faculty member in the History Department. And it wasn't like Stephan had forgotten about him, exactly, or about that moment their eyes met in the mirror of the men's room, it was just that he hadn't let himself focus on it.

Which is why he feels a little off-balance, walking down to the tables and podium at the front of the classroom fifteen minutes before class starts, and meeting those warm eyes again. This time, though, they're joined by a smile that makes Stephan's breath sort of catch in his throat for a moment. He smiles back, positive he looks like a total idiot, and takes a couple of deep breaths as he makes it down the last few steps.

"Hi, I'm Jeff," the guy says, sticking out his hand.

Warm, Stephan thinks, and mentally kicks himself in the hopes of getting his brain back in gear, or at least coming up with a new adjective. "Stephan," he says. "One of your TAs."

"Yeah, I figured. I recognized you from the orientation last week."

Stephan tries really, really hard not to blush like a schoolgirl. Luckily, they're joined by Lauren a moment later, and then by Will. Since it's the first day of class, some students are actually early (*freshmen*) and want to talk to the professor. Jeff says that he'll introduce them during class and they can talk about TA duties after, if that's all right.

Class is kind of slow at first, mostly just going over the syllabus and course information. Then Jeff gives a short lecture about why anyone would even bother to study American history at the university level, after being bombarded with it all through elementary and high school. He talks about the differences between learning facts to regurgitate for tests and thinking about *why* things happened they way they did.

He's actually a pretty fucking amazing lecturer. Stephan had thought this class would be a total snooze since he knows the information backward and forward, but just watching Jeff lecture has him interested, even eager, for the next session when they really start to get into the meat of things.

The students seem pretty engaged as well. There are a lot of stragglers afterward, asking for permission codes for changing their section schedules and what to do about books being sold out at the bookstore and all the other crap that goes with the first day in a huge class. When the professor for the next course comes in, Jeff suggests the remaining students e-mail him and finally turns to the TAs, who have been waiting patiently off to the side.

"I could sure use a cup of coffee right now; how about we do this over at the café in the Student Center?" Jeff asks.

The three-minute walk seems a lot longer as Stephan tries not to stare at the man leading the way. Lauren's next to Jeff, chatting about her classes. Stephan thinks she's flirting, but he's not sure. Jeff doesn't seem to be responding, at any rate, and that shouldn't make him glad, but it does.

After all, only a total skeeze would flirt with one of his TAs on the first day of class, right? Even if he's into her, Jeff's probably not stupid enough to do something like that on day one. He's a smart guy. Interesting. Engaging.

And has a really nice smile.

And if he can't stop thinking thoughts like that, Stephan is going to be so screwed. There's nothing wrong with a little crush, with random attraction here and there, but dude! He seriously needs to get it together.

Once they've all got a drink and snagged a table, Jeff pulls out the class roster. There are about a hundred students in the class, but since it's a freshman-level intro class, they have six small sections of about fifteen to twenty students each. It breaks down to two sections per week, which suddenly sounds like more work than Stephan had anticipated.

"Now, don't freak out," Jeff says with a small smile. "I know you're all new TAs, and I don't expect you to know the answers to everything. You have trouble with the kids, with grading assignments, with your discussions not going well, you just let me know. I'll do what I can to help. Also, I'd suggest you three brainstorm discussion topics for each week together, make sure you're all more or less on the same page."

"How will we know what kind of grading criteria to use on their papers?" Will asks.

Jeff grins. "When I was a grad student, the first guy I TAed for had us all get together for a pizza-and-grading party when the first papers were due. Kind of sucked as far as parties go, but I think it's a good idea in general. We can talk about what we're looking for in the papers, and how to give constructive criticism. And make sure that you, Stephan, aren't giving C's for work that Lauren is giving A's."

"What, you can already tell that I'm a hard-ass?" Stephan protests with a laugh.

He's pretty sure he imagines the sparkle in Jeff's eye. "It was just an example."

"Well, you're probably not wrong," Steph accedes. "I've kind of been known as an overly studious geek most of my life."

"You?" Jeff grins, one eyebrow lifted.

Stephan shrugs. It's true; he *is* aware that he's pretty damn good-looking, because he has a mirror, right? That doesn't make him conceited, just not stupid. So maybe he doesn't look like your typical nerd—fair skin with a scattering of freckles, reddish-blond hair, striking hazel-green eyes, and a body he takes care of—but he kind of is. He worked hard in high school so he could get a scholarship to a good college, a better one than his parents would have been able to afford otherwise. And he worked hard to stay here, to keep his financial aid all four years. And he *likes* school; he kind of even loves it, to be honest. Sure, it stresses him out, and he hates the administrative crap, and some classes truly do blow, but mostly he loves it.

He loves hanging out with his friends, too, going out dancing, hiking, whatever. But he's equally happy studying all day at the library, researching something interesting. So while he might not look like a geek, he is one, and he's reached the point of being amused rather than irritated when people are surprised that a guy who looks the way he does can also be totally fascinated and even excited by a treatise on immigration written in the 1820s.

"What was your undergrad thesis on?" Jeff asks, and his tone is a mixture of challenge and simple curiosity.

Stephan grins. "*Pentecostalism in America and the Increased Leadership Roles of Women.*"

Lauren laughs. "Wow. Not only a history geek, but a guy unafraid of dabbling with the women's studies crowd. Impressive."

She's totally flirting with Stephan. He shrugs it off. "They're not as scary as they look. Mostly."

"Mine was on the *Supreme Court as a Force for Social Change,*" she offers. "How about you?" she prompts Will, who's been quiet so far.

"*European Views of Post-Colonial America.* Pretty boring, actually. I kind of hated it and decided I wanted to focus more on modern political relations as a grad student. I think," Will answers, fiddling with his empty coffee cup nervously.

Jeff nods and they chat for a bit about how sometimes you find the right subject that just excites you, grabs your interest, and how *sometimes* you get twenty pages and several months into a project and then realize that it bores the shit out of you.

"I have a ton of articles and two entire books published that I can't bear to even look at," Jeff admits with a self-deprecating grin. "Plus, sometimes your interests just change. It sucks when that happens halfway through a project you've committed to, but it's human nature. We're fickle creatures."

He's got an odd tone of voice there, and Stephan wonders if maybe he's talking about personal things more than academic, but it's really not his place to ask. He is intrigued, though.

"So you just moved here," he prompts. "Where were you before and why'd you move?"

Jeff takes a drink of his coffee before he answers. "I was at U-Dub. University of California offered me a move from Assistant faculty to Associate faculty, which puts me on a path for tenure. And my marriage ended, so it's a fresh start on a lot of levels." His voice is even, face placid, but the way he holds eye contact with Stephan is a little unnerving.

Lauren offers her condolences, and Jeff nods politely before he changes the topic. "So, since I'm new in town, maybe you guys could tell me which places have the best food?"

It turns out Will just transferred from Chapel Hill, so Lauren and Stephan do their best to brainstorm fast, cheap, good food and other useful resources about both the town and campus. Lauren's a native to the area, and Stephan's been here for almost six years, and between them they come up with a pretty good list of places to eat, the closest Laundromat to Will's apartment off campus, the secret best-places-to-park on campus list, and realistically how long Jeff can expect it will be before Housing Services gets his DSL working. They told him it would be two days, and Stephan almost snorts coffee out of his nose, laughing.

"Man, I'll buy you a drink if they get it done within two *weeks*," he offers.

"Great," Jeff says shaking his head. "I'll take that bet and just hope that maybe they're more responsive to faculty than they are to students. You're living on campus too, then?"

"Yeah, Grad Student Housing is just over the hill from Professorland." He makes a face, embarrassed by his slip. "Um. Faculty Housing, I mean."

Jeff laughs, shaking his head. "College campuses always have a ton of nicknames. Just one more thing for me to have to figure out."

"God, no kidding," Will agrees. "I was told to go to 'Apple's Eye' because that's where the post office is. I finally had to ask someone, who helpfully informed me that I was looking for 'Apl Sci', the Applied Sciences building."

They all laugh, and Lauren and Steph offer their condolences.

Stephan thinks for a moment, and then goes back to the original topic. "The Wi-Fi signal from the Student Union might actually reach your place, Professor Tegan. Give that a try. Otherwise the main library has the best tables, and the coffee cart there is open longer than the ones in any of the other study centers."

"Thanks." Jeff grins. "I'll remember that. But don't call me 'Professor Tegan,' kid. You'll make me feel old."

Stephan gives him a considering look. The guy can't be much older than forty, if he's even that. He's got a little bit of gray in his facial scruff, but none on his head, and Stephan seriously doubts he's the kind of man who colors his hair. There are some fine lines around his eyes, but in general? He's totally hot.

Jeff is absolutely the kind of guy Stephan usually goes for, except for the part where Jeff's even interested in the same stuff he's studying, whereas most of Stephan's past boyfriends have thought he was a total geek. Eric's the only guy Steph's ever been with who was younger than him. Ever.

While Stephan is pondering those facts and trying to rein in his stupidly growing crush, the others wrap up the conversation. Jeff says his goodbyes and leaves to go do some things for his other class.

"He's positively tasty," Lauren sighs as soon as he's out of earshot.

Stephan nods.

"Also single. And straight," she grins, with an expression that's both teasing and a little too victorious.

Stephan shrugs. "He's all yours."

"Damn, woman, the poor man just ended a marriage," Will chides. "He might not even be interested. And you're his TA! That's so inappropriate."

"Oh please. It's not like it would make any real difference. And I can wait if I have to," she shrugs. "Nothing wrong with flirting until then, though."

"God, you're like a shark," Will says.

"You might not be his type," Stephan adds, wondering why he feels like challenging her. He can tell she's mostly teasing with the man-eater act, but there's an element of possessiveness there that he doesn't like.

Lauren rolls her eyes. "Well, Pretty Boy here is off the menu, and a girl has to find something to eat." She gets her things together and pulls on a cardigan. "Seriously, I'll make sure it won't impact you two at all. Equal work for equal pay," she says with a grin as she leaves.

Will twists around in his chair, watching her go. "I think for the first time in my life I'm actually *relieved* a beautiful woman isn't at all interested in me," he says thoughtfully.

Stephan chuckles. Inside, he's tense and edgy, almost irritated, and wondering why on earth he's so upset about it. Lauren seems all right, if a bit blunt about her sexual interests, and Stephan can't really fault her for going after what she wants. And Jeff *is* straight, right? So what's his problem?

And he has a boyfriend anyway. It's just a stupid little crush, and he mentally snorts at himself, thinking that he is feeling both stupid *and* crushed.

"Well, best of luck to her," he says out loud, grabbing the trash from the table and tossing it into the garbage as he and Will both get up to go. "See you at the planning session."

Chapter 6
Study Break

CLASSES are going all right for the most part, and by the second week, Stephan's settling into the groove fairly well. Get up, drink the coffee Jim's made because he's a god, study, go to classes, study, answer student e-mails, study, maybe hit the gym, study, and sleep. Rinse, repeat. He's staked out his old favorite table in the library, had his first TA sessions, and has decided that he likes Lauren after all.

She's a little abrasive, but she's funny as hell, too, and so long as she's not angling for him, he doesn't really mind her constant objectifying comments about every man she sees. It's funny how uptight it makes Will. Plus Stephan usually agrees with her; she's got pretty good taste.

What's weird is that he hasn't seen as much of Eric in the last couple weeks as he thought he would. They're both on campus all day, every day, but they haven't been meeting up for more than the occasional lunch or dinner, and had only spent the night together once so far this week. Then again, Steph's pretty damn busy trying to get organized for his TAing and keeping from falling behind in his Method and Theory class. Eric's usually a pretty laid-back student, but he's suddenly realized that this is his final year, and he's throwing himself into his class work too.

They should study together, Stephan thinks idly one afternoon. No, like *really* study together, not just open their books and then fuck. They're both serious students—they could get actual work done, right? They've been together for a long time. They're adults. And Stephan is fully capable of reining in his horniness until it's time for a study break. Absolutely.

Come study with me? he texts Eric. Their schedules have been so chaotic, he doesn't even know if his boyfriend is in class at the moment or not.

OK. Need anything from the store? I'm getting supplies.

Snacks. Condoms. Your ass.

My ass is not a snack. Be there in 20.

About an hour later Eric's lying on Steph's bed, taking notes as he reads his book and getting cookie crumbs all over the place. His shoes are on the floor. He appears to be doing pretty well with this studying-together experiment.

Stephan is not. He's at his desk, trying to brainstorm discussion topics for his TA sections in one window and hunting through academic article databases in another. Both tasks are going a lot more slowly than he'd thought they would. Also, Eric stretched out on his bed, licking his fingers and making little noises whenever he reads something particularly interesting? Distracting.

Like, a lot.

He types a few more possible questions for his students into the outline for tomorrow and saves the file. Watches the way Eric's huge hands curve around his book. The way his shirt stretches across his shoulders....

"I can't read with you ogling me, asshole," Eric grumbles.

"Excellent; my evil plan is working. Time for a break."

"Or you could stop staring at me."

That wouldn't be fun at all. Plus, Stephan's bored. And maybe if they had sex first, *then* he would be able to focus and get some work done. That sounds totally plausible.

Eric laughs in the face of this very logical and reasonable idea. "Let me finish this chapter." Pouting isn't one of Stephan's strong points, apparently, as it just makes Eric smirk. "Watch porn for a few minutes or something," he suggests, turning a page.

He's teasing, of course. But Stephan's sitting in front of the computer, and goodness knows he's got a lot of porn on the thing....

It takes a few minutes before Eric glances up, and then he does a double take when he gets a look at what's on the computer screen. "Dude! I was kidding!"

Stephan shrugs. "I'm trying to be patient. I even turned the sound off so it wouldn't bother you," he smirks, one hand resting on his crotch. Now that Eric's watching, he curves his hand around his hardening cock and gives it a slow rub.

The way Eric's eyes kind of glaze over is very gratifying, even if he does huff out a breath, sounding thoroughly put-upon. "Fine, c'mere," he sighs, shoving his books off to the side, and Stephan's over there, on top of him before the pages have settled.

Their lips meet, Stephan's admittedly more hungrily than Eric's, but he's into it, licking into Steph's mouth soon enough. His hands come to rest on the curve of Steph's ass, then slip down, long fingers reaching underneath loose denim, making Stephan moan and press forward. Eric moves his leg so Steph can ride his thigh. He bites on the hard tendon of Stephan's neck as they grind together, kissing sloppily as they get carried away.

"Want to fuck you," Stephan growls, leaning his full weight on Eric's arms, pinning them by his sides.

"Jim's in the living room," Eric objects. "And we don't have time. I have to go to my study group in less than an hour."

Stephan gives him an incredulous look. "It won't take *that* long," he says, pressing his erection into Eric's hip meaningfully.

Eric takes a deep breath, closing his eyes. He opens them and pulls his hands away from Stephan's ass, moving to cup the back of Stephan's head as he gives him a gentle kiss, which frankly baffles Steph.

"I'm just not in the mood for that; sorry. How about hands? Or I could suck you off," he offers.

Something feels very weird and wrong, but Stephan has no idea what is going on, and honestly? Most of his blood flow is in his throbbing cock at the moment. He'd really much rather get off and *then* talk, if that's going to be possible.

"Um, yeah, hands are fine," he says, trying not to lose the mood entirely. He starts to say something about not wanting Eric to suck him off if he's not into it, but can't think of a way that doesn't make him sound like an asshole trying to guilt trip his partner into a blowjob.

And Eric's good at this, so really, he shouldn't be complaining. In very little time at all, Steph's pants are on the floor, his shirt is, well, somewhere—he sort of lost track of it—and Eric's shirt is off too. There's a lot of delicious skin everywhere, and while Stephan would rather sex be a little bit more mutual, he doesn't care all that much once Eric licks the palm of his hand and wraps his fist around Stephan's cock. He's good with his hands; in fact, Eric's good in bed, in general. If only he was a little bit more into it....

Stephan sucks a perky nipple into his mouth, enjoying the flavor of his boyfriend's warm skin and thrusting his dick into Eric's grip. He moans a little at the whispered, "That's it, come on, Steph," and he closes his eyes. It feels good, tons better than jerking off by himself. Squeezing his eyes shut, he imagines it's Eric's ass he's plunging into, hot and tight and so good. He gets into the fantasy a little too much and bites down, making Eric gasp. In his mind, though, it's a better kind of noise, helpless and surprised pleasure, and he comes, hips jerking as he empties himself into Eric's hands.

He's still breathing hard, eyes shut, when Eric moves away, leaving sweat cooling on Stephan's body. There's the sound of tissues being pulled from the box, Eric cleaning up. Warm lips press against his, and Stephan has no idea if he's imagining the hint of apology in his boyfriend's kiss or not.

"Thanks," he says, finally opening his eyes.

Eric smiles. "No problem. Think you can study now?"

Right, studying. That's what they're supposed to be doing, why Eric's here. Dammit. "I dunno." Steph yawns. "Might need a little nap." He stretches, arms and chest flexing, and catches Eric watching him. "Unless you think maybe you'd be interested in round two?"

Shaking his head, Eric smiles. "Can't. Have to go in… about twenty minutes, now."

"How are your classes going?" Stephan asks, feeling like he probably should have asked earlier. Or should have just *known*, to be honest. But it's not like it's entirely his fault they haven't been talking all that much.

"Good, really good." Eric shrugs, pulling his T-shirt back on. "For once, I like all my classes; no duds at all. And I think I might already have a topic for my thesis next semester, which is a good feeling. Usually I can't decide and end up hating whatever I get stuck with at the last minute."

They talk for a while about thesis topics, bouncing around ideas, Stephan doing more to tease inspiration out of Eric than actually contributing anything of his own. But Romanticism's not his subject; all he can do is push his boyfriend toward topics that sound interesting, things that Eric gets fired up about. It's always easier to write about something you can argue about, and if Stephan manages to get Eric to start waving his hands around as he explains the importance of William Blake's madness, then it's a pretty good bet that he'll be interested enough to maintain his focus for an entire semester and a fifty-page research paper. Probably.

He makes a mental note to share that suggestion with the kids he's TAing, and then wonders if it's even relevant to freshmen at all. Ah well. He'll tell them and hope they remember it when it becomes important.

Eric leaves to go to his study group, and Stephan finally manages to get a list of discussion topics jotted down for next week. He gives up on the article databases in favor of his French homework; Madame Georges has turned out to be as anal retentive as Stephan feared, but at least the work is more memorization than anything truly difficult.

Stephan is sick to death of his flashcards by the time he throws them across the room and grabs his phone. "Voulez-vous coucher avec moi ce soir?" he sings when Danielle picks up.

"Only if you take me out to dinner first," she replies. "I'm actually hungry, for once. Also, you know that technically only means go to bed, right? Not fuck."

"I know," he says, rolling his eyes. "Like I'd fuck *you*; you've got the wrong parts."

"Why so cruel, Steph? What'd I ever do to you?" she says, laughing.

"Other than make me listen to you moan and whimper through the wall for a year? I never wanted to hear your orgasm noises; I'm scarred for life."

"Suck it up," Danielle demands. "Come get me and take me to get food. My car's broken again."

They make plans, and she and Stephan are at one of the many Thai restaurants in less than an hour. The town has something like a dozen really excellent Thai places and *zero* Indian restaurants, a fact which mystifies all of the locals. Still, the Thai is pretty good.

Stephan talks her into splitting a dish of coconut ice cream with him; she needs the calories, and he needs to not eat the whole thing by himself. They're clashing spoons, fighting for the last bite, when she asks about Eric. He shrugs. "He's good. Busy with classes. Came over to study this afternoon."

She raises an eyebrow. "And did you actually get any work done at all?"

"Sadly, yes." He sighs with mock disappointment. "Though I did manage to score a hand job as a study break."

"Please, spare me the details. I love you, but I don't want to hear about your spooge. Plus, I'm *so* jealous; I haven't gotten laid in months and think my vibrator's wearing out. Do you know how expensive those things are?"

"Yes, actually," he commiserates.

"Well, at least you've got a boyfriend," she sighs. "I really envy your relationship with Eric, you know; it looks so easy and comfortable."

Stephan nods, a strangely uncomfortable feeling growing in his chest that he washes down with the last of his iced coffee. "It's pretty drama free. That's been a nice change."

"No kidding," Danielle snorts. "You tend to go out with jerks almost as often as I do. But I like this one." She fiddles with her spoon for a minute, then puts it down. "So how is the sex?"

"Thought you didn't want to hear about it," he says, trying to tease, and gets a kick in the shin for his trouble. "Ouch, woman! It's fine. We're good," he answers, making a face as he rubs the bruise out of his leg. She gives him a look that says she knows he's not telling her everything. As usual, he caves pretty quickly. "It's... good," he repeats. "Comfortable. He's practically like my best friend, only with sex. That's how it's supposed to be, right?"

"Supposed to be?"

Stephan shrugs. "You know. Like, real. Not that breathless, all-consuming passion stuff, like in the movies and books."

"I don't know," Danielle sighs. "I know the passion stuff doesn't really last. But... there should be *some* passion, don't you think?"

He nods, thinking about how he always seems to want Eric more than Eric wants him, and how rotten that makes him feel inside when he thinks about it. He knows Eric loves him; he's said so, and that's not something most guys say lightly. And he knows Eric likes sex, likes sex with Stephan, thinks he's hot. But there's something off, still, and it bothers Stephan.

Not like he can say any of that to Danielle. Even if she is his best friend and a girl. She's single and lonely, and he's not going to rub his minor little romantic problems in her face. That's just mean. Besides, it's probably all in his head. Eric's just been busy and stressed out about starting his senior year, and Stephan's probably being hypersensitive, as always. It'll work out.

It always does. One way or the other.

Chapter 7
Smash

STEPHAN runs into Jeff at the library a few days later—literally—almost knocking them both over in his haste to get to the coffee cart before it locks up. They've already got the awning pulled down and are cleaning up as Stephan dashes across the atrium, hands digging into his pockets for enough loose change to get one more cup of God's Own Elixir into him before the library shuts down for the night.

Jeff, it seems, was on a similar trajectory with the same goal, and barely manages to catch Stephan by the arms and steady them both before they fall over. They wobble, holding each other up on their feet, Stephan apologizing and Jeff reassuring him that he's uninjured, if startled. The girl working at the cart is outright laughing at their collision and slips them the last two scones in thanks for their improv slapstick routine. Stephan could care less who's laughing at him; he has his coffee, and it's not even that stale.

"Way to destroy my professional dignity, kid." Jeff laughs, nudging Stephan's shoulder as they head back toward the library.

"Sorry," Stephan apologizes for probably the twentieth time. "I need caffeine if I'm going to finish up the stupid research I'm doing before the library closes in…." He looks at his watch. "Twenty minutes."

"Stupid, huh? What class?"

"Method and Theory. God, is anything more boring than the history of history?" he laments.

Jeff snorts. "Well, it's valuable to know where your so-called 'facts' came from. But yeah, I'm with you; too theoretical for my tastes."

Stephan nods and drinks his coffee. "So, what are you doing here so late?"

"Still no DSL in my apartment, and the Wi-Fi signal you mentioned from the Student Center seems to be blocked by a tree. It's intermittent at best, so I've been coming here."

"Ha! You owe me a drink," Stephan crows, delighted that he's been proven right about the suckitude of Housing Services, and not at all because he'll have to spend extra time with Jeff. That would be silly. Didn't even enter into the equation.

Jeff smiles an easy grin. "You want that at a cafe or a bar?" he asks, then he smirks a little as he adds, "How old are you, anyway? Can you get into bars yet?"

Stephan makes a face at him. "I'm twenty-four. And yeah, a beer would be good, although not tonight. It's already late and I've got an early class in the morning. How about tomorrow?"

With a nod, Jeff agrees, and they decide on a local wannabe-British-style pub, so they can grab some food, too, if they want. Stephan realizes that Jeff probably doesn't know many people in town yet and might be a little lonely. He needs friends.

"How old are you?" he asks before engaging his brain.

He gets a raised eyebrow in response, then a grin full of teeth that look more sharklike than amused. "Thirty-eight."

"Huh, you're only fourteen years older than I am. I think the beard makes you look older," Stephan says, and then wants to crawl into a hole and *die* because, wow, how rude can he get?

Luckily, Jeff seems more amused than pissed off by his lack of tact. "I'm not very fond of sunscreen, either," he admits, "and I used to do as much kayaking as I could in Seattle." He shrugs. "I feel like an old fogy, though. I'm a pretty boring guy, in case you couldn't tell by the fact that I'm hanging out at the library at almost eleven p.m."

"Well, hey, I'm here too," Stephan points out with a relieved smile. "Although actually…." He glances at his watch and sighs. "I doubt I'm going to get anything else done before they kick us out." As if on cue, the fifteen-minute warning bells ring.

"You'll get better work done tomorrow, anyway, if you're anything like me," Jeff suggests in a consoling tone. "You're frustrated with the subject and could probably use a break. Long day?"

Stephan nods and puts his backpack on again; Jeff slings his laptop case over his shoulder. They both turn and head out of the building toward the bus-and-shuttle stop. The evening shuttles only come every fifteen minutes or so, and they're the only ones waiting out there; it's too early in the semester yet for the library to be full of night owls who stay until the last minute. It *has* been a long day for Stephan, with classes and one of his TA sections that didn't have much interest in discussing this week's topic, and just generally feeling overwhelmed with all the work ahead of him for the semester. Jeff makes supportive noises and says the right things about taking it easy and reassures Stephan that he'll be fine. And if it all goes to hell, he can come see Jeff anytime, and Jeff'll do what he can to help figure out a solution.

It's the kind of quiet reassurance and guidance that Stephan's always subconsciously looked for in the older guys he dates. He only realized it a year or so ago when Scott pointed it out to him. He was a little disgusted with himself for being some stereotypical twink looking for a daddy substitute, so when Eric came along and was an awesome friend and the sex was good, Stephan decided to consciously break the pattern.

Jeff, though, he fits into Stephan's type as if he was the one the mold was made from. He's easygoing, encouraging, and has a great smile. He's got a pretty good body from what little Stephan's seen of it, and he likes outdoorsy stuff, evidently. He's also smart and interested in the same stuff Stephan's into, academically, which has never happened before. He likes coffee and agrees about the inherent boringness of historiography.

He also smells good, and as Stephan is following him up the steps as they board the shuttle bus, he has a brief moment where he wonders what Jeff's skin tastes like. But then they sit down next to each other, and Stephan sees the pale stripe of skin on Jeff's left-hand ring finger and remembers that the man is newly divorced and straight. *Damn.*

They're bombarded with the bad 1970s rock the shuttle driver has chosen—Blue Öyster Cult?—at beyond-full volume, and Stephan's amused that Jeff's kind of bouncing his leg to the beat. It's too loud to talk, and they're at the Faculty Housing stop in a few minutes. Stephan has this weird urge to, like, hug Jeff or touch him as they say goodbye, but thankfully he doesn't do anything other than grin and remind Jeff about their date for tomorrow.

He doesn't call it a date, of course. It's a *plan*. A drink. Maybe dinner. They're friendly academic colleagues. It's not a *date*.

And even if Stephan sort of wishes it was a date, Jeff's kind of like his boss. And *oh yeah*, Stephan has a boyfriend. While Eric has agreed that Jeff sounds pretty cool, he might object to Stephan actually *dating* Jeff. Although maybe Eric wouldn't veto a threesome…. That idea leaves Stephan half-hard, and when he gets off the shuttle to walk to his apartment, his jeans are uncomfortably tight.

It's just that Jeff is totally the kind of guy Stephan's always dreamed of, that his past boyfriends always fell short of being. The only guy who ever truly smashed Stephan's heart was, in point of fact, similar-looking enough to be Jeff's cousin. Stephan had been nineteen to Paul's almost-thirty, and still naïve about relationships, if not about sex. He'd honestly thought they would last forever and had been devastated when Paul dumped him after only three months for some brainless twink fresh out of community college, a twink who was clearly using the older man for his money. They'd already been fucking for a month when Paul had finally come clean.

He doubts Jeff would ever do that. Jeff had been married. Although that does raise the question of why he's divorced; maybe his wife *did* catch him screwing around with some young student-type or something. Jeff doesn't seem like the sort to throw everything away for a pretty face and perky tits, or he'd probably be flirting with Lauren a lot more. Hell, maybe his wife was the one screwing around. Or maybe they broke up for other reasons. Maybe they just drifted apart. Sometimes that happens, right?

After a long day, thinking about why relationships end is not really a place Stephan wants his mind to go right now. He unlocks the door to find the apartment empty, a note from Jamie on the whiteboard saying that she's kidnapped Jim for a few days and not to worry. And a note from Jim saying that if Stephan drinks the last of the beer he'd "better fucking replace it this time, asshole, or ELSE!"

He snorts and debates grabbing one, then realizes it's a little late at night for beer and he's probably too tired to stay up long enough to finish it leisurely, the way it deserves; after all, it's not Bud Light or some shit like that.

In his room, the answering machine is unblinking; no messages. Stephan checks his cell phone, and it's free of messages too. He could check his e-mail, but if Eric wanted to get a hold of him, he'd call or text. Then again, Stephan hasn't called Eric, either. He feels a little unsettled, a lot confused, and way too tired to think about Eric or Jeff or past relationships anymore. Lights off, he settles into bed a short while later, mentally listing the fifty United States in alphabetical order, and falls asleep trying to remember if he's said Missouri already or not.

IT'S hard to connect with Eric. Stephan texts him the next afternoon, asking what he's up to. When Eric calls back he says he's fine, if busy, and maybe they can get together on Friday if Stephan's free. Of course he's free; why wouldn't he be? Like he'd go off and make plans for the weekend without his boyfriend? But instead of letting his irritation out, Stephan takes a deep breath and suggests they get together for lunch or something before then; after all, it's only Wednesday.

There's a pause. "I want to, but I'm just kind of buried in homework," Eric says.

"We could study together," Stephan offers, suddenly thinking about sex.

Eric laughs. "Yeah, because that worked out so well last time."

"Hey! I can behave. You were just all stretched out on my bed and moaning and licking your fingers and stuff. A man has needs, Eric."

His boyfriend snorts. "I'm actually a man too, remember? I know all about your needs." There's a pause and then Eric suggests, "How about the library or Student Center or something? If we're in public, you can't grope me."

"I thought you liked it when I groped you," Stephan pouts, his tone suddenly a little more bitter than he meant to be, as he realizes that it's been a long time since they had full-on sex.

Luckily, Eric seems to miss it. "I do, just not when I'm studying. So, Student Center? They have those awesome fries…. And we can make some plans for the weekend, if you want."

There is either something really off in this conversation, or Stephan's having PMS, or… something. It's like their words match up, but Stephan feels like they're having two different conversations, and he has no idea why. They make a date for tomorrow afternoon and hang up before he remembers that he was going to tell Eric about his drink-slash-dinner with Jeff tonight. Ah well. It's not like it's a big deal; he'll tell Eric about it when he sees him.

THE pub is dim and reeks of a few decades' worth of smoke, despite smoking in bars having been banned in California for a while now. Jeff's got a stack of papers in front of him and a half-eaten ploughman's lunch at his elbow. Stephan throws his messenger bag onto the opposite bench and slides in, accidentally kicking Jeff as their feet tangle for a moment. It takes Jeff's eyes a second to focus on him, but Stephan just grins and grabs the beer menu, checking to see if they have his favorite microbrew.

"You're going to order the most expensive beer they have, aren't you?"

"Maybe. I hear professors make actual money, unlike starving grad students," Stephan points out. "Ooh, they have the Seabright Blur. That's seven dollars a bottle."

"So you just want me for my money?" Jeff teases, pushing his papers to the side.

Stephan blinks. "Uh." He has no idea how to answer that without saying anything incriminating, and he can feel his heart rate double, so he looks down at the menu and says, "Hey, they've got Arrogant Bastard."

"No kidding."

The waitress saunters over, and Stephan grins at her. "What's the most expensive localish microbrew you've got on tap?" He winks at Jeff in response to the older man's groan, and the girl giggles. She sets him up with an Anchor Steam from San Francisco, and Jeff has her bring a pitcher of it, along with food menus.

"So, Arrogant Bastard, huh? Guess you'll be expecting me to pick up dinner too." Jeff looks more amused than put-upon, fortunately, and Stephan's not above someone taking pity on his financial state. After all, he picks up the tab most of the time when he goes out with Danielle —so she won't have an excuse not to eat—and also Eric—or at least Stephan did when he was working and Eric was in school. Scott and Billy frequently get Steph's tab when he's a student. Everyone sort of takes turns buying, depending on who has a job at the moment. It all works out in the wash.

Apparently Jeff's in the circle now too.

"If you've got it, flaunt it," Stephan says, wiggling his eyebrows. The waitress helpfully brings over the beer as he says it, and she does a little wiggle that makes her boobs bounce as she smiles.

"God, you're all so damn young," Jeff groans, and downs over half his pint in one drink.

"Nah, you're not old; you're just tired," Stephan argues. "Long day? What're you working on?"

"Lecture notes, mostly. It's been a while since I taught the intro classes, but you know how it is. New faculty get the ones no one else will take." He shrugs. "And it's kind of fun, actually, even if the freshmen seem to get younger every year. But I was given a syllabus and outline just a few days before classes started, so I'm playing catch-up for a while, figuring out what I'm gonna say."

Stephan nods in sympathy, and they spend a while bitching about classes and how disorganized the university administration is and then get into talking about research projects they're both interested in. The beer helps, as always, getting ideas flowing, and soon it feels easy and comfortable to be hanging out with Jeff, as if Stephan's known him forever. At the same time, there's a little… spark or something, a feeling Stephan is totally going to attribute to the liquor and his apparent inability to stay sober.

Laughing, Jeff offers a steadying hand when Stephan lists to the left as he gets out of the booth. He guides Stephan out to the street and offers him a ride home. The bus always sucks when you're drunk, so Stephan accepts; besides, they're going to the same place anyway. He can walk home from Professorland, no problem. The night air'll be good for him, he proposes, and Jeff laughs again. Stephan likes the sound of it a lot.

The car window is cool where he rests his head against it, and Jeff's got some quiet music playing. They're not talking, but it's comfortable. He really likes Jeff. Like, more than a crush, maybe, but that's stupid because it's just a friend-crush anyway, even though he's attracted to Jeff. The guy's straight, after all, and it's okay to have a crushy-type-thing on a mentor-slash-friend. It's fine, right? Everyone has random crushes. It's a little embarrassing, but it'll probably wear off as he gets to know Jeff better.

Jeff pulls up to Grad Student Housing, and when did they get here, anyway? Stephan was totally going to walk. For a fleeting moment after he unbuckles his seatbelt, he thinks about leaning over in the car and kissing Jeff goodnight, wondering what the scratch of Jeff's stubble would feel like on his mouth, what Jeff's mouth would taste like. Then he opens the door, and the cool night air is like a refreshing slap across the face reminding him that he's an idiot.

Only idiots let crushes get out of hand when they already have a totally awesome boyfriend. Only idiots have stupid crushes on their straight professors. Only *drunk* idiots jerk off thinking about their new friend's dick.

Stephan's kind of an idiot sometimes.

Chapter 8
Ravioli and Wine

ERIC is late for their study session the next day, and when he's there, he's not really *there*, too focused on finding something interesting and new to say about some Alexander Pope poem before his class begins to pay much attention to Stephan. Eric does give him a decent goodbye kiss before shoving everything into his backpack and running off, but still.

They haven't seen each other in what feels like ages. Last year, when Stephan was working regular business hours, they saw each other probably three times a week and spent at least one weekend night together. Now Stephan feels lucky to get one weekend night with Eric. They're on the same campus every single goddamn day, but he sees less of his boyfriend than he did when they lived ten miles apart and had to make a special effort to get together.

He scowls as he gets a refill on his coffee and decides to stay at the Student Center and study for a while. There are some guys playing pool in the corner, he notices. One of them has a really great ass—round, firm—and he's sticking it out in a way that pretty much screams "newly-come-out-twink." Not a bad view, and it raises Stephan's spirits. After all, there's nothing wrong with looking, right?

Then again, his sex life does kind of suck right now. He loves Eric. He misses hanging out with him, and misses getting laid even more. One handjob last week, and only given out of obligation, just isn't okay. Everything feels so *wrong* ever since Eric got back to town after their summer apart. Eric's busy with school, and Stephan gets it, he docs; he sort of freaked out a little his senior year, too, realizing he only had nine months left before being turned loose on the world. It's a lot of pressure. So Stephan can't tell if he's being a drama queen or what, but *damn* he misses sex. And now that he thinks about it, Eric doesn't seem very interested in sex anymore. Or, at least, sex with him. Huh.

He knows it's normal for relationships to have ups and downs, and that long-term relationships go through lulls. That's probably what this is, only a lull. Of course some of the fizz and excitement are gone, but that doesn't mean it can't still be good, right? Rationally, this makes sense. Unfortunately, the only friends he has who are in relationships that have lasted beyond a year or so are Billy and Scott, and Jim and Jamie. No one he can talk to without being made fun of relentlessly. Well, maybe Jamie….

There's a crash of cues at the pool table, and he looks up to see a pretty girl sitting on the edge of the table with her legs wrapped around the waist of the guy with the great ass. They're kissing enthusiastically, and their friends are whooping and clapping as they laugh.

Great. Apparently Stephan's gaydar is broken too. Today sucks.

STEPHAN stops at home for dinner and a beer or three. He considers moping around the apartment and pretending to study, but he's got a lot to do, so it's going to have to be a library night if he wants to stay focused. His usual table in the basement is vacant, so he spreads out books, laptop, notebook, and pens, kicking his feet up onto the chair opposite. A girl with glasses wanders over to peruse the bookshelves he's sitting between, and he scowls until she goes away.

After an hour or two, Stephan's eyes are crossing, and it's hard to say what he needs more, a bathroom break or a coffee break. Luckily, he can have both, and if he's quick, he won't even have to worry about someone taking his stuff, although he does grab his laptop, of course. It's a bitch to juggle in the bathroom, but it's a helpful shield for hiding his coffee, since food and drinks aren't technically allowed in the library stacks.

Back at his table, he pulls over his notebook from Method and Theory and gets to work. Sipping coffee, he wonders what Jeff would think of their topic of the week, and if the older man is at the library somewhere too, or not. It would be nice to talk to him. Heck, he'd be a good study partner, Stephan bets, and thinks about proposing that idea for about two seconds before his brain shifts—somewhat predictably— to the other, better kind of study break. With Jeff. He bets Jeff would be up for a "study break" now and then, he thinks, feeling disgruntled and then a little ashamed of himself for being a dick who is mad at his boyfriend for not putting out.

Also? Jeff's still straight. Hot, sexy, smart, kind, and very heterosexual. So he might make a good study partner, but that's all. And with Stephan's stupid pseudo-teenage crush, that means studying with Jeff might be a little difficult and a lot frustrating. He's got sexy friends, he's got straight friends, and he's got friends who are both. But he knows by now that it's better to let the crush fade before he lets himself get too close and inevitably gets hurt.

And Stephan would never hurt Eric like that anyway. He's young, and has a sweetness and naivety that Stephan's always kind of, well, *cherished*, even though the word makes him feel like Oscar Wilde or something. Eric makes him feel sort of sappy. Not that they don't have typical guy-type fun, with beer and video games and burping contests, and God knows Eric's farts are things of legend and infamy.

It's been good for Stephan, being with someone younger. Eric looks up to him sort of, at least academically, and that's been really flattering. Eric's friends are sort of young and dumb, but then Stephan's almost always had older friends, as well as dating and fucking older guys. Or maybe that's the other way around. Whatever. Point is, things are different with Eric, but they're good. Or they were.

Yawning, Stephan shoves away his notebook; he's not getting anything done. His coffee cup is sad and empty again. Maybe he needs a short rest. He arches his back, then curls forward over the table, resting his head on his hands and closing his eyes. Once, last year, Eric was studying at the library, looking up some literary criticism for a book he hadn't read, and Stephan was hanging out with him in the stacks. He hadn't meant to be distracting, but Eric honestly hadn't taken much convincing to put the books aside and start making out. In fact, Eric might have made the first move, now that Stephan thinks about it....

Eric's big, strong hands had cupped Stephan's ass, squeezing and pulling him hard against Eric's solid body. A guy that much taller than Stephan was still a novelty, and arching *up* made him feel off balance, vulnerable, and a little submissive. Stephan's arms wrapped around Eric's waist, hooking his fingers into belt loops and guiding his boyfriend's hips into a slow, dirty grind as they kissed. The way Eric kissed when he was turned on just made Stephan fucking melt. Hungry. Like he couldn't get enough. The guy-sex thing was still new enough to Eric that it made him goddamned *wild*. Stephan wasn't Eric's first male lover, but he was Eric's first *good* male lover, and Eric seemed to be seriously reveling in being allowed to let his strength out, in manhandling Stephan without being so careful, without holding back or having to be gentle.

And Stephan fucking loved it. Loved the way Eric lost control, loved feeling like he made Eric so crazy that he couldn't hold back, didn't want to. That it was safe for Eric to lose himself in sex and lust, and just take what he wanted because Stephan sure as hell was eager to give it. Eric almost always topped, but Stephan didn't care, not yet.

Of course, just as things had been getting good and Stephan was fumbling with Eric's zipper, someone had walked past their aisle and gasped, then giggled and hurried away. Eric, breathless and sweaty, had pulled back. Stephan had suggested, in his dirtiest voice, that no one ever used the fourth-floor men's room and he'd love to suck Eric's dick there, but Eric had been too shy. He'd dragged Stephan out of the library, intending to drive back to his apartment, but Steph had grabbed the keys, tossed them into the backseat, and tackled Eric there in the car, in the parking lot....

Stephan sighs, shifting his head to face the other direction before he gets a crick in his neck, enjoying the memory. Of course, it would have been fucking *awesome* if Eric had let Stephan blow him. In the bathroom, or—even better—right there in the stacks. Where anyone could walk by and see Stephan on his knees, mouth and hands wrapped around Eric's dick, taking his cock and loving it. They'd have had to be quiet, of course; they were in a library, after all. It would have been delicious to torment Eric like that, since it was almost impossible for his boyfriend to hold back his moans, especially in the beginning. He had been so into it, relishing being able to thrust into Stephan's mouth like he'd never been able to with a girl, and fascinated with sliding his fingers and cock into Stephan's ass for *hours*.

God, it would have been so hot if Eric had fucked him, right there against the books. Stephan imagined their bodies rocking together, the hundreds of pounds of books on each shelf not enough to withstand the force of Eric fucking him deep and hard. Sliding the length of his dick in and out while Stephan held on to the shelves, unable to stop gasping and groaning, the books falling around them. People would hear the ruckus and come see what was going on, catching the two of them red-faced and out of breath, Stephan pulling his pants up and Eric looking pleased and smug and happily post-coital.

Man, that would have been fucking *amazing*.

Stephan palms his hard-on and contemplates jerking off in the men's room. It's still early; someone would probably walk in on him. Sighing, he rubs his eyes and pulls his notes back toward him and gets to work.

FRIDAY is a better day, as Fridays always are. He doesn't mind showing up for Jeff's nine a.m. lecture; it's a good, low-pressure way to wake up and get his mind going before he needs to be able to actually function in his French class. Madame Georges returns the Wednesday quizzes, giving Stephan the hairy eyeball along with his paper. He flushes, looking at his stupid mistakes, and resolves to make a little more time for French. Even if it *is* dumb compared to his "real" classes.

Danielle calls him and suggests that he meet her for lunch, so they meet at the taqueria to catch up and eat. Their Lit seminar is going really well; they're both excited about the readings and are having an enthusiastic debate about Anne Bradstreet when they walk into the classroom. It's awesome to be doing something he loves again—working at the podunk local history museum had *seemed* like it would be a great job for him, but had ended up being somewhere between annoying and brain-suckingly boring, depending on whether his tasks for the day were secretarial stuff like envelope-stuffing or manning the Admissions and Information desk for the handful of people who wandered in every week. School is *so* much better in comparison. If that was what "real life" was like for most people, Stephan is thrilled beyond belief with his plan to never leave the world of academia.

After class, he and Danielle head back to his place to steal Jim's good beer and hang out. There's a message on his answering machine from Eric.

"Hey, are you busy? I miss you," his boyfriend says when Steph returns his call, and Stephan can't help the dorky melty feeling he gets inside.

"Awww. Wanna come over? Me and Danielle are just hanging out."

"I was thinking of a real live date," Eric suggests. "Dinner and a movie? I pay, you put out?"

Stephan laughs. "How about if I pay and you put out?"

He gets a snort in reply. "Or we could split the bill and both put out?"

"I like the way you negotiate."

They make some plans for Saturday, and Stephan returns to the living room area to see Jim and Danielle on the PlayStation. He glares at Jim, who raises an eyebrow and gives him a stern look back. "Dishes," Jim says.

Rolling his eyes, Stephan heads to the kitchen, which is, yes, cluttered with his dishes from the last two days. Well, not *cluttered*; they're in neat stacks beside the sink, but not too much in the way. Still, Jim has a point, and it's better to just get them done now. He sighs a little and turns on the stereo, getting an eye roll from Jim and a cough that's a not-very-subtle cover of a laugh from Danielle.

Cleaning up doesn't take all that long; the warm, soapy water and the lemon-scented counter spray are soothing as he cleans the stove and microwave. Shakira is singing about breasts and mountains as he bops around the kitchen.

He realizes he's singing, too, and definitely dancing a little. His hips freeze mid-wiggle at the sudden applause behind him, and he holds a scrub brush in one hand like a conductor's baton. Jim and Danni are laughing their fucking asses off—she's doubled over, holding her sides, and he's clapping, leaning against the wall like it's the only thing holding him up.

"Oh my God, Steph," she wheezes, and she can't seem to say anything more.

Jim's doing a little better, grinning like he won the lottery and *still* clapping, that fucker. "Wow. I knew you liked dick, but I had no idea you could be so gay."

"Asshole." He throws the brush at Jim and marches out, stopping to switch off the stereo and head to his room to try to relocate his dignity.

He's making stacks of papers and books, trying to uncover the wood part of his desk, when Danielle comes in and flops on his bed. "Poor baby. Wanna go out dancing? Seems like you've got your boogie shoes on," she says with a grin.

"Bitch," he says, but he comes to sit down next to her. "I haven't been out in ages, though...."

"Me neither. Let's go out tonight," she says, poking him in the ribs until he giggles and grabs her fiendishly tickling hands away.

"Can't; I've got a date with Eric tomorrow, and that means I've got to get some work done tonight. Trust me, I'd rather go dancing with you than be stuck in the library, but I'm feeling way behind on my Method and Theory class."

Danielle pouts for a few minutes, and then shrugs. "Rain check, then. Want me to take off, or are you going to eat dinner first? I'll even cook, if I can raid your fridge," she offers.

That sounds like a deal to him; she's a great cook—when she can be bothered—and whips up some kind of pasta thing with ravioli and

ham and a bag of frozen pumpkin squash he didn't even know he had.
In fact, maybe it was Jim's or Jamie's.... He should probably ask.

Jim forgives the cardinal sin of eating a roommate's food when
he's invited to join them, and Jamie even contributes a bottle of wine to
make it all classy. It's so domestic and civilized—two boy-girl couples
at a dinner party—that Stephan almost can't stand it. Then Danielle lets
out a massive belch, and everyone laughs and it's all okay again.

Jamie offers to do the dishes, and Stephan packs up his notebooks
and laptop. He walks Danielle to the bus stop, ever the gentleman, and
kisses her goodnight before she goes. The walk to the library is chilly
but refreshing after the warmth from his wine buzz, and Stephan's
feeling relaxed, focused, and ready to get some work done. Which is
why it should be no surprise at all that someone's already at his favorite
table, making him grumble as he decides to head over anyway and see
if he can get them to leave. That is, until he sees that it's Jeff.

"WE'VE got to stop meeting like this; people will talk," Jeff says,
grinning up at him.

"You stole my table," Stephan snorts, putting his bag down and
pulling out his usual chair.

"I don't see your name on it."

Stephan leans over and points at a jagged ballpoint scrawl
embedded in the wood—"*Awesome Stephan's awesome table*"—from
his junior year.

Jeff's laugh makes him feel giddy; he must still be a little tipsy
from the wine he had at dinner.

"You little vandal," Jeff scolds. "It's a Friday night; what the hell
are you doing at the library?"

Stephan shrugs. "Got plans for tomorrow, and I'm behind in
M&T. Again."

"Method and Theory?"

"Yeah. I've *got* to find something interesting about it, or this semester is going to suck beyond belief. I can't get any work done if I just sit there, staring at my books and thinking about how much I hate it all the time."

Jeff nods in sympathy and shoves aside his own stack of papers and notebooks. He glances around, noting the relative soundproofing of the alcove they're in, and assumes correctly that if they're not too loud, they won't be disturbing anyone nearby. He puts on what Stephan thinks of as his "professor face" and starts probing. Jeff's good, making Stephan think about the subject differently, not just see the value in it, but find a few different angles that are noteworthy and even sort of appealing. After about an hour, Stephan's feeling like M&T might not be the most horrible class he's ever taken, and he's almost ridiculously grateful to Jeff.

When they break for coffee, Stephan insists on buying, since Jeff was essentially working for the last hour.

"You should be my advisor," he blurts, while Jeff is stirring pretend-sugar into his coffee.

Very smooth. Not that Stephan hasn't been thinking about it since the beginning, but still. What with his stupid crush, and Jeff being new and probably overwhelmed and maybe not even taking on grad students yet, it's a bit premature. And stupid. Really stupid.

Jeff grins. "I was wondering if you were gonna ask. I'd like to, but I'm not going to commit to any advising this semester. I'm still getting settled in, and I don't know the department's protocols and how it all works here. I don't think I'd be a very good choice, in a formal role. Not just yet." Stephan must look disappointed because Jeff chuckles a little. "That's my standard answer to everyone. Not that I'm changing it for you, because it's still true, but ask me next term if you haven't found a better faculty sponsor. I think we'd be good together."

God must hate Stephan; he can feel his face flushing with heat. Luckily, Jeff totally misinterprets both his blush and flustered silence while he tries to stop thinking about sex.

"Hey, it's not personal. I like working with you; I think it could be a lot of fun. I'm just really overwhelmed right now, to be honest. Getting settled into a new life and all."

Stephan nods. "Yeah, you've had a lot of changes. You're right. It can wait a while; the others said to make sure to get an advisor before the end of the first year, but that gives me until summer. It's all good."

The easy warmth in Jeff's smile makes Stephan feel all gooey again, and like, somehow, everything is going to be all right in the world. Which is an awful lot of weight to give a stupid grin, but there you go. And it's not just the grin, it's the way Jeff's eyes crinkle at the corners, the almost-laugh making his whole face light up. Damn, the man is gorgeous.

And Stephan? Well, he's smitten. Tonight, though, it doesn't feel angsty or particularly fraught with stupidity or unfaithfulness. Jeff's an amazing guy, and it's okay that Stephan's taken with him. It doesn't mean anything; it just is what it is. Jeff's great, Stephan's got a new friend-slash-mentor, and random sexual attraction doesn't by default mean anything bad. Everything *will* be all right. Stephan sighs happily, drinks his coffee, and they head back into the library together.

Chapter 9
Relaxation is Overrated

BY TUESDAY, the weekend feels like it was an eternity ago. Stephan is at his designated "office hours"—the time he has sworn to be available for students to drop in. He doesn't have an office, of course; those are reserved for PhD students, so he's hanging out in "his" corner of the Student Center coffee shop. He almost drops his pen when a kid comes up to him and actually wants his help, not just to borrow the napkin dispenser from his table.

The poor guy is seriously freaking out about the upcoming short-essay paper, even though he's got a choice of three out of five questions to answer. It was just assigned, and the TAs plan to go over it in section, but apparently this kid can't wait. Stephan manages to talk him down, take a few deep breaths, and forestall a freshman breakdown—at least for today. By the time the guy leaves, Stephan feels like he's just talked a jumper down from the Golden Gate Bridge: sweaty, jangly nerved, and drained.

A cup of coffee hits his elbow as Kristine pulls out a chair to sit down. She does her "office hours" around the same time as his, for the German language class she's TAing, and sometimes they hang out for a while.

"I thought he was going to cry," she says.

"Me too. I should add a package of tissues to my bag," Stephan notes. "And *thank you* for the coffee. You are a goddess. If I wasn't already promised to Danielle when we're thirty, I'd offer to marry you." His eyes close in reverence as he takes a sip. Ambrosia.

"I think Tina might kick your ass," Kristine answers with an evil grin. "Seriously, she does aikido. And Eric might be pissed too, no?"

"Eric understands that sometimes coffee trumps both love *and* sex." He pauses. "Well, love for sure."

"Slut."

Stephan grins at her, shrugging as they laugh, and then settle into studying while still "being available" for their students. He can't concentrate, Kristine's words buzzing around his head like annoying gnats. Because Eric *wouldn't* be jealous.

Not just because it's a joke, not just because the idea of Stephan married to a woman for anything but tax reasons is laughable. Stephan plans to die a heterosexual virgin—he's not even a little bit bi—so Eric's got nothing to worry about on that score.

But Eric has never been even slightly jealous except as a joke, like that night in the bar before the semester started. He thinks it's funny when he catches Stephan checking out other guys or flirting. It's like he doesn't think anyone is a threat to what he and Stephan have. Even when he gets a little pissy about Mike's innuendo, it's still just a big joke to him. The most jealous Stephan has ever seen Eric was when Stephan kissed Melanie at her birthday party a few weeks ago and made her swoon, and Stephan's pretty sure that was more the kind of jealousy where Eric wanted to be in her place rather than being angry at either one of them.

There's just none of that possessiveness, that feeling of ownership, to be found in Eric. And somehow that bothers Stephan. Not that he wants to be involved with a burly caveman with ownership delusions (been there, done that, thanks), but still. It would be nice if Eric wanted to hold onto him a little more.

Wanted him a little more.

Stephan slams his laptop shut with a bang, startling Kristine. She kicks him, swearing, then stops and tilts her head and gives him a penetrating look. "You okay?"

He has no idea, but no, he's probably not okay. "Yeah. I'm fine. Gonna go home and grab something to eat before section. Catch you next week?"

"Same time, same place," she says in a tone that lets him know that she's choosing to let him get away with lying, at least for now. He gives her a weak smile of gratitude and leaves.

The walk across campus does him some good. Stephan knows he's being an idiot. Eric is who he is, and Stephan *likes* him. Loves him, even. They had a great time together on Saturday, so why can't Stephan stop being such a demanding little drama queen and be happy?

As he walks home, he recalls their "date" over the weekend— dinner, a horror movie, and an unusually affectionate Eric. He'd touched Stephan casually all evening, kissing him as they waited in line for tickets, holding his hand and stroking his fingers during the previews. Eric had seemed to be in a great mood, like he couldn't get enough of Stephan, groping him in the dark theater, and the sex when they got back home had been good.

It was almost like things had been in the beginning. Eric's mouth on his dick was hungry and sloppy, the way he'd groaned around his mouthful as much of a turn-on as what he was actively doing. He'd been eager for sex, gently manhandling Stephan around the bed until he was where he wanted to be, on top, thrusting into Stephan's ass slow and steady. Stephan had been nearly out of his mind when Eric finally started giving it to him good and hard, biting his shoulders and making him plead for more. They'd both had a hand on Stephan's cock when he came, and Eric had followed with his own climax not long after.

They'd lain there, breathing hard, sticky and hot but unwilling to move. "I missed this," Eric had whispered into his hair. "Missed you."

"Me too."

With a sigh, Eric pulled back a little, and Stephan had shivered as cool air hit his sweaty skin. "I need to get a better handle on my schedule, see you more often," Eric apologized. "Sorry I haven't been making time for you. I thought it would be easier."

Stephan had nodded. "Yeah. It always was before."

"I'll try harder."

Twisting around, Stephan kissed his cheek. "Okay. Me too."

Eric's arms had wrapped around him, holding him while they dozed before getting out of bed to clean up. It had felt stifling, though, not comforting. It should have felt comforting....

Stephan trudges up the stairs to his apartment. What the fuck is wrong with him? Eric had missed him and is going to make an effort. The sex was good. Maybe he *does* have PMS or something. Maybe he's stressed out about school and is just taking it out on Eric, when nothing is actually wrong with them that can't be fixed by simply making more of a point to spend time together.

Their date had been good. Objectively, thinking about it now, it was great. Good food, a crappy but enjoyable movie, better-than-average sex. Eric had topped, of course, but whatever—it isn't like Stephan doesn't like getting fucked. In the morning they'd played video games and eaten pancakes and enough bacon that when Stephan has a heart attack at age sixty, he can probably point back at that single day as the cause.

Everything is back to normal.

RESOLVING to be happy is actually not all that difficult. Eric calls or shows up at Stephan's place every few days, and they eat together, hang out, and even study some. They have sex, they laugh a lot, and something inside Stephan relaxes. He hadn't realized how tight and clenched and miserable he's been making himself, and all it takes to make it better is feeling like he has one of his best friends back again. The orgasms don't hurt either, of course, but it's mostly just being around Eric and enjoying his idiotic and goofy side that Stephan has missed.

Eric is, in point of fact, maybe being kind of clingy. When Stephan gets home from class on the next Thursday, Eric is sitting in the stairwell, reading a book. "Did you eat lunch?" he asks, as Stephan unlocks the door and lets them both inside.

"Not yet."

"Good. Do you need to prep for TAing or are you pretty much free until then?" Eric is bouncing slightly on his feet and trying not to grin.

"I'm free," Stephan answers, grinning back. "Why?"

"We're going on a picnic!" Eric, face nearly splitting with his joy, goes outside and pulls an honest-to-God wicker basket out from under what had looked like a pile of dirty laundry outside the front door. Less than ten minutes later, they're sprawled out on the paint-stained sheets and blankets under the redwoods behind Graduate Student Housing, eating sandwiches.

"You're awesome," Stephan mumbles around a mouthful of apple and cheese.

"Yeah, you're lucky to have me." Eric raises his beer in a salute to himself and drinks deeply while Stephan snorts and then tries not to choke to death on a chunk of apple. By the time his airway is cleared, tears are streaming down Eric's face and he's fallen onto his side, laughing so hard.

"Nice, asshole. I could have died," Stephan wheezes.

"Aw, poor baby." Eric wipes the tears off his face and wiggles over to press against him. Stephan shoves Eric away in a token protest, but relents and lets Eric pull him down to lie on his back. They make out for a while, trading kisses that taste like beer and sweet apples, and Eric's on top of him grinding their erections together and kissing the air out of him, until there's a distinctive ringing, and Eric launches across the blanket to his cell phone in his backpack.

It doesn't seem to be anyone important, so Stephan just wipes the kiss-slobber off his chin and goes back to eating while Eric talks to whomever. There's an awkward moment when Eric hangs up, and Stephan raises a questioning eyebrow until Eric says, "My sister's having some problems with Mom," and then Stephan wonders what was so goddamned important about a pre-teen arguing with her mother that Eric interrupted making out with his boyfriend. But then he gets over himself because the picnic is a sweet gesture and it clearly took some planning, and while the making out was nice—really nice—

Eric's not exactly the *al fresco* sex type, anyway. So there's no point in Stephan getting his panties in a twist about it.

They clean up when they notice how much time has passed, and Stephan leaves Eric in his apartment, barely making it on time to the classroom where he has his TA sections. The students are all seriously freaked out about the paper assignment now, but he manages to break it down into small enough pieces that none of them seem overwhelmed by the end of the hour. Or, well, at least not overwhelmed to the point of simply staring at their laptops in a dazed stupor.

Stephan returns to find both Eric and Jim in the living room, studying like good little boys. He makes a few comments and gets a throw pillow thrown at him, and then shrugs and makes Eric scoot over to share the sofa. It's quiet and peaceful, the squeak of Jim's highlighter and Eric's occasional hums as he reads something more a pleasant background noise than distraction. He's going through his flashcards, drilling vocabulary and irregular verbs in preparation for tomorrow's French test. Madame Georges had looked directly at him on Wednesday when she reminded them to study.

It's not like he's that far behind, or behind at all, actually. The problem is that he's been plowing through the grammar assignments, finishing them quickly and then moving on to his other "real" classes, and not spending enough time memorizing. It's just so fucking boring, and he could be spending that time on more important work, to be honest. But still, he's going to be graded on this class no matter how lame he thinks it is, so he'd better get over himself and find a way to fit this into his schedule more often. Maybe he can review cards while he's on the elliptical at the gym....

By the time Stephan is about ready to throw his pile of index cards at Eric and demand that he entertain him, Jim lets out a huge yawn and slams his heavy textbook loud enough to make the others flinch.

"Pizza?" Jim asks, standing up and stretching up to the ceiling without effort.

"Brilliant," Eric agrees. "I think my eyes are about to permanently cross. This class has more reading than any I've ever taken: twenty novels in fifteen weeks! What was she thinking?"

"That you're all masochists?" Stephan suggests, and then he dodges the hand Eric's trying to smack him with.

"Sit down and shut up, you two. Order pizza first, then you can play your kinky sex games. Meat lovers? Pepperoni? Or um—" Jim pauses to scan the coupons stuck to the fridge. "Veggie delight?"

"Pepperoni," they chorus, and Jim just shakes his head as he pulls out his cell phone. Stephan kicks him and adds, "Caesar salad too. For Jamie."

"For Jamie? Right. You watching your figure again?" he scoffs.

"Nah, I'm watching it for him," Eric says with a leer and eyebrow wiggle.

Jamie shows up while they're paying the pizza guy, rolling her eyes at the way the guys are salivating just from the smell. She changes into casual clothes and joins them, splitting the salad with Stephan, who is *not* watching his weight, just trying not to die of high cholesterol, thank you very much. It's not like he's getting a whole lot of exercise lately, unless you count walking around campus. Two measly sessions at the gym per week are maybe keeping a beer gut at bay, but that's all. He needs more vegetables in his diet, less fast food. Vitamins and minerals and stuff.

Also? He's maybe drinking a little too much coffee if he's freaking out about his health even while shoving a slice of pizza in his mouth. He's not even in his mid-twenties yet. So why does he feel like he's having an aneurism?

He takes a shower after dinner, leaving the others to clean up when Eric turns down the request to wash his back. The hot water helps some, but he's still twitchy, and the only things he can think of are caffeine withdrawal and his French test tomorrow. He's fairly prepared, but feels like he might just randomly blank out and forget everything he's learned, as if he was suddenly taking a test in Arabic or something.

Throwing on some loose track pants, he finds Eric on the sofa, still reading, and Jamie setting up the DVD player with one of her yoga disks that she does when her back is hurting.

She gives him a critical look, then gestures to the empty space she's made by removing the coffee table to the kitchen. "Join me. There's room for two."

Sighing, Stephan nods. "Can't hurt, right?"

"Well, it can if you do it wrong," she teases, and he sticks his tongue out in reply.

She selects the "Stretch and Relax" routine and the program starts. It's not that difficult to follow along, breathing, slowly bending in different patterns, and it feels really good despite some of the cracks and pops his spine makes. Jamie suggests he raise or lower a body part a few times, helping a little but not intrusively.

About three-quarters of the way through, when he's feeling good, relaxed and pliant and the poses are getting easier, he gets a weird feeling on the back of his neck. The next time he's upright, he turns to see Eric watching him. He quirks an eyebrow.

"I had no idea you were so bendy," his boyfriend says.

Stephan grins as he follows Jamie into the next move, folding forward at the waist and hugging his ankles. "Supple?" he suggests, pressing his ass upward just a little more.

Eric clears his throat. "Yeah, that." His eyes have a kind of glazed look, a look that Stephan likes. A lot. The program seems to be ending with a lying-down meditation thing, but Stephan's got a better idea. Eric's on the same page, tossing his book down and pulling Stephan into the bedroom, kissing Stephan like a starving man as Jamie's amused laughter comes through the door.

It's a quick and dirty fuck, perfect and so hot, and Eric is apparently in a super-dominant mood, all but growling as he peels the track pants off of Stephan and pushes him down on the bed. He's biting and licking Stephan's ass, murmuring about how fucking gorgeous it is, how he wants to just eat Stephan alive sometimes, and Stephan thinks maybe Eric's actually going to rim him for a minute. But then wet fingers are pressing inside, and then Eric's cock is slamming in, and it's rougher than it's been in ages, and it's So Fucking *Good*.

Stephan's eyes roll back in his head at the feeling of Eric's hand wrapping around his dick, and before he knows it, he's coming, soaking the bedspread and shouting, totally forgetting everyone else in the building can probably hear them. Eric's loud, too, grunting as he jerks against Stephan's ass, thrusting in deep enough to make Stephan's spent dick spurt a little bit more, until finally he comes with a gut-deep groan.

After a little while, he catches his breath and wiggles into a position where Stephan can actually breathe. "Holy fuck, that was good," Eric pants, eyes still closed.

"Mmm hmm. Gonna start doing yoga every day," Stephan says, and lets Eric wrap his arms around him, laughing weakly.

Seriously, that was fucking awesome. Stephan is through comparing Eric to some impossible standard, like Jeff. Jeff is his straight professor and just a crush. Eric is great. The sex is great. He has a good thing here, and he's going to appreciate it more.

Chapter 10
Ecstasy

THIS is the *best* fucking party Stephan's ever been to. At least, it's the best one in ages; he's maybe a little too messed up to objectively decide if it's truly the best ever. Still, it's awesome. And he's not just saying that because of the drugs. No, the music is great, and someone with good taste is DJing rather than the usual dick trying to prove how cool he is with obscure techno-pop world music. People are actually dancing in the main room, rather than just milling around looking for somewhere quieter to talk.

The party is at a friend of Eric's, at a huge house up in the hills outside of town. It's isolated enough that the events they have are pretty big, drawing a couple hundred people, and they go all out with themes and stuff. They decorate the house, provide a keg, and have a bar for cocktails. People bring stuff to share and it's always great. Eight people live there, mostly students or recent graduates. Tonight is probably someone's birthday, and the theme on the e-mail invitation demanded that everyone dress as Greek gods and heroes. It's only September, but it's never too early for a costume party as far as Stephan is concerned.

Which doesn't mean he came up with anything more interesting than a white bedsheet toga and a crown-type thing spray painted yellow to look like the sun. Eric is way better at this shit than he is, in costume as a modern-day Hermes-as-bike-messenger, with cardboard wings attached to his helmet and sneakers. He's such a geek, but so gorgeous Stephan can't help but love him.

His boyfriend wanders off once Stephan starts dancing, talking to people he knows and enjoying himself in his own way. Stephan is a little tipsy, shaking his groove thing on the crowded dance floor with two girls and having a blast that's only a *little* bit influenced by the pill he took. Chad gave it to him, passing around drugs like candy and wandering around in a fig leaf G-string that Stephan is ashamed to admit actually doesn't look that bad on the jerk.

A short while later, Stephan is feeling incredibly good, a little hyper and kind of like the edges between himself and the rest of the world are dissolving. Nice. It's been a long time since he's done anything harder than pot, and the feeling of euphoria is, well, euphoric. He's high as a kite, basically.

He has no clue how much time has passed when Eric comes up to him, a smirk on his mouth and a hint of worry in his eyes. Stephan is a little surprised to find that he's kind of grinding against one of the girls, and blames it on the sultry beat of the music; God knows it's got nothing to do with the soft breasts and smooth arms pressing against him. He lost his toga at some point and is now wearing only a white T-shirt and boxer briefs, both of which are damp with sweat. And his crown, of course.

"Let's get you some water," Eric suggests, and that sounds like a fantastic idea; it's really fucking hot, and Stephan follows as he's led outside.

It's quieter out there, although the throbbing beat of the music still seems to be controlling Stephan's heartbeat. A sudden wave of vertigo makes him stumble, and Eric presses him against the wall, reassuring and steady and so, so firm. All over. Stephan's hands stroke over the weird textures of Eric's clothes, his hair, his skin. He feels amazing.

Eric chuckles against Stephan's mouth, more breathing against his lips than kissing. "You do too. God, you're so gorgeous, Steph. So sexy, the way you move...."

He pulls Eric down by the ears, kissing him deeply. He's totally peaking, inundated by the sensation, overwhelmed, and at the same time he wants more. He *wants* to be overwhelmed, and wow, this is doing it. Maybe not in a good way, but... the feeling of their lips meeting and tongues merging, melting into each other, is too much. Stephan is shaking from the sudden overload, but he can't tell if it's in a good way or a bad one. He pushes Eric back, moaning as he licks his own lips; even that sensation is almost too much to handle.

So touching is good—Eric's body feels fantastic—but something about kissing is just too intense, too overwhelming for him. His lips feel too much. On the other hand, Stephan is unbearably hard. He's panting for it, rubbing his dick against Eric's leg almost unconsciously, and starting to throb in need. Sometimes E makes it hard for him to come, but he feels like he *needs* it, all of a sudden, almost frantic.

"Hey," Eric says, pushing himself away from Stephan's grasp. "What're you on?"

Stephan shrugs, closing his eyes. "Just normal stuff." He doesn't want to get into a fight; he wants to fuck.

"Who gave it to you?"

"Your buddy Chad," Stephan answers, and he can't help rolling his eyes.

Eric sighs. "Well, at least it's not one of Mike's experimental things."

Stephan tugs him back close, so their bodies are pressed together. "God, you're such a downer, man. Just come on, touch me…."

He hears Eric chuckle a little, breathing on his temple. "Yeah? What do you want, Steph?" Eric's hands are resting on Stephan's shoulders, body pressing him against the wall, and Stephan's grabbing Eric's ass and grinding against his crotch.

"I want you to touch me, babe, come on. I want to feel your hands everywhere," he mumbles, breathless and shaking with lust.

"Everywhere?"

Stephan nods. "Everywhere. Fuck, please, come on." He grabs Eric's hands, drags them down his body, moaning and arching as fingertips rub his nipples through the thin fabric and go down even further. Without inhibition—not that he usually has much—Stephan groans, "God you have the best fucking hands." He presses them against his dick and grinds up against them. "I love the way your great big paws wrap around my dick, the way your fingertips rub my balls when you're fucking me with the other hand. Come on, babe," he pleads. "I *need* it."

"Yeah, all right. You're going to come in your shorts if I don't help you out, aren't you?" Eric says, sounding a little weird, but Stephan doesn't care, moaning his agreement. He's about to get off on Eric's hands and body whether he participates or not, but God, he wants Eric to do it.

He whines a little as Eric pulls away, grabbing Stephan by the hand and leading him over to a spot in the yard where there are a bunch of blankets, leftover from the barbecue stage of the party earlier in the evening. It's dark, but they're not that far away from the house, and it's not exactly private, but Stephan couldn't care less. His hands are fumbling uselessly with his underwear when the world tips and he's falling for what feels like ages but is probably only a moment, and then Eric is on top of him, pushing his hands out of the way.

Shit, it's so fantastic when Eric is with him like this. He's got one hand busy with Stephan's clothes and is offering the other to Stephan, who is holding it and licking Eric's fingers, moaning as he sucks them. "Jesus, I can't believe you're getting off on this so much," Eric says in a stunned voice, but Stephan doesn't care. The salty taste of Eric's skin is superb, and yeah, sucking his dick would be better, but this is *so good.*

Honestly, he should have remembered. When he's on Ecstasy, anything against his mouth just completely melts his mind. Unfortunately, it also kind of makes time jump around, and the next thing he knows, there's a hand on his dick and fingers are sliding into his ass and Stephan feels like he wants to come already but his body is just *not* going to let that happen. Every stroke of Eric's fingers inside him and every pull on his cock makes him feel like he's going to totally fall apart. His hands are clenching Eric's shoulders, his hair, and finally the grass under the blanket when he notices he's pulling Eric's hair too hard. The sensations keep building and building *way* past the point where he should have come already; tears are sliding down his face with how much he needs to come and can't.

"God, come on, come on, *please....*"

"I've got you, right here, in my hands," Eric whispers, his lips tickling Stephan's. That's it; it's too much and just enough. The slight pressure of their mouths together and hands everywhere, inside him and all over, and finally Stephan explodes, coming and coming and coming for what seems like an eternity even though that's probably the drugs.

It seems like he still hasn't stopped coming by the time he notices that Eric's hands are gone, and Stephan pulls it together enough to spread his legs and lift his knees. "Come on," he says, reaching for Eric's cock, which is hard and straining against his bicycle shorts. "Come on, fuck me."

Eric buries his head in the side of Stephan's neck and huffs, "Can't. No condom. Probably couldn't last anyway," he admits, reaching for his waistband at the same time Stephan does. They struggle to get them down, not all the way but enough, and Stephan manages to get Eric's cock out. Eric's giant dick is sliding through the mess on Steph's stomach and their hands are tangling together. Stephan gets his useless, awkward hands out of the way, overwhelmed again. Feeling the pressure of Eric's cock on his stomach is sooooo good, about a billion times better than it's ever felt before, like his *whole body* is being fucked. Stephan idly wonders if he can come again as Eric's hips stutter and he curls around Stephan's body, pressing down hard as he releases his own fluid into the mess covering Stephan. The sensation of Eric losing control on top of him, of his cock against Stephan's belly and his come all over him, makes Stephan moan and twist up again, pressing his still semi-hard dick into warm flesh and wanting to come but knowing he can't.

This is the best sex Stephan has ever, *ever* had.

It takes him a long time to come down. Eric's wrapped up around and beside him, having used the blanket to clean them up and tucked them both back into their clothes, so they'll at least be respectable enough to drive home. The stars overhead are really bright, and Stephan thinks he might be able to touch them, they're so close, but he can't be bothered to stand up and find out. Some girls he doesn't recognize come outside and join them, smoking clove cigarettes, and soon others come outside, too, to get away from the noise and music, and mellow out as they sober up.

Eric coughs.

With a sigh, Stephan struggles to get up, knowing that's his cue. He likes the smell of clove smoke; Eric hates it. Probably doesn't like the way Stephan is kind of snuggling with one of the other guys, either, but whatever. It's just cuddling, and he's still a little touchy-feely. He's tired, more wiped out than burnt, but bed sounds good, and he's happy enough to go home.

THE next morning Stephan has no memory of how he got into Eric's house, and his head feels like... something. Sandy, maybe—like sandpaper. Or like something that *needs* sandpaper because it's all rough and splintery. It doesn't suck as much as a tequila hangover, but he still doesn't feel good.

He finds Eric downstairs, a full pot of coffee on the counter and a book in his hand. It takes him two cups and a piece of toast before he notices Eric's not talking to him. He got a cursory kiss on the cheek and a grunt in response to his questions about food and drink, but otherwise Eric is ignoring him.

"Uh. What's wrong?" he asks, because he's way too drained to figure this out without some help.

Eric closes the book and lays it down on the table, lining it up precisely with the edges. "I know you were pretty messed up last night, but... I don't like having sex in public."

Stephan blinks. "It wasn't in public; it was in the backyard. There wasn't even anybody else out there. I think."

"I know, man, I *know* you don't think it's a big deal," Eric says. "But it is to me." He pauses for a breath. "I don't like it when you do drugs. And you were so... I mean, you were hot, okay? It's not like you forced me. But I couldn't really tell you 'no' either."

There's a silence while they both chew on that, and Stephan starts to get a really awful feeling in his stomach that has nothing to do with recreational pharmaceuticals. He knows Eric doesn't like drugs, but he didn't realize it was such a big issue. When the hell did that happen?

And he remembers having fucking *amazing* sex. He was so turned on, and yeah, he was probably begging and whining for it, but... Eric could have said no, right? Was he *that* bad?

"I'm sorry. Okay? Really, Eric, I didn't mean to make you do something you weren't comfortable with." He doesn't know how to say he's sincere without it seeming like he's not, and hopes Eric can tell by his expression.

Which apparently he can, because Eric sighs and nods. "I know you didn't. I just... I don't want to disappoint you." He bites at the corner of his lip.

Stephan doesn't know what to say to that, other than the required response. "You don't." But the taste of the lie lingers in his mouth for the rest of the morning because sometimes, Eric does.

Chapter 11
Nausea

"SO WHAT'S up with you and Eric?" Billy asks, passing Stephan a beer and settling down on the sofa.

Scott nods. "Yeah, where is he? I thought he was coming over with you." It's Sunday and the Cowboys are going to beat the shit out of the Vikings. Billy and Stephan are Dallas fans; Scott will root for whoever is playing against them, just to drive Billy insane.

Taking a drink, Stephan shrugs. "I don't know. I didn't ask him." Billy gives him a look heavy with significance, but Stephan has no idea how to respond. He didn't ask Eric because, well, he didn't want to see him tonight. He's still reeling from their talk this morning and not quite sure what to do. Or how he feels. He also might still be sort of hung over.

He drinks and eats and shouts at the idiots on the field along with his buddies and generally does his best to forget all about his real life for the next few hours. Things get a little uncomfortable again at halftime when Stephan gets a text message, but it's just Will reminding him about the TA planning meeting tomorrow. Billy and Scott both look at him expectantly until he says it wasn't Eric, and then the game starts again.

The problem is that all of Stephan's friends like Eric. Not that that's a *problem*. He's glad everyone gets along; he doesn't like drama in his circle of friends. And he respects their opinions; they're usually only too glad to point out when Stephan is dating a jerk. Eric's been a little more distant with *them*, partly because they're all older and, probably, partly because of the drug thing. Or something.

In fact, Mike and Billy are the only two who have been a little standoffish with Eric. Mike because, well, the drug thing for sure. He might be a big stoner, but he can tell when someone disapproves of him. So that's not surprising. And Mike can be kind of hard to take; he's batshit crazy, and not always in a good way.

Billy, though, that's more difficult for Stephan to figure out. Then again, Billy is a hard-ass and doesn't like anybody too easily. He's always been a little protective of Stephan, kind of like an older brother almost. Billy never likes anyone Stephan dates, which has made sense because everyone he's dated before Eric has ended up being a dick.

Huh.

The Vikings manage to win, which at least gives Stephan something external to be emo about. It's getting on toward evening now, and he's getting his shit together to head back home when his cell phone rings again. This time it is Eric, calling to cancel their lunch plans for tomorrow. The conversation is awkward, full of pauses and too-rushed assurances that everything is fine. By the time he hangs up, Stephan has never felt like things were *less* fine. It's fucked up.

Billy isn't even pretending not to have been listening.

"So, you want to talk about it?"

"Not really, no."

"Dick. I'm trying to be a sensitive friend here."

"I know," Stephan sighs. "I just... I don't know. I don't really know what's going on. It just sucks."

Billy nods. He taps his fingernail on the glass beer bottle for a minute, thinking, and Stephan waits. What eventually comes out is a little bit of a surprise. "Eric's a nice guy, Steph. The nicest guy you've ever dated. He's a good kid. Smart. And hot."

There's a pause there, and Stephan can feel his insides twist into a knot, waiting for Billy to finish.

"Too bad he's kind of boring."

Stephan snorts and tries to laugh. "Fuck off; he's not boring." He ignores Billy's raised eyebrow and punches him in the shoulder. "You're an asshole."

"Yup." Billy nods. "But I'm right too."

There's nothing he can say to that, and since he's standing with his hand on the doorknob, he leaves. Because to be honest, right now Stephan kind of agrees.

THE next day is a fog, moving through classes, studying, avoiding thinking about Eric. He feels upset, which is way more annoying than feeling angry or guilty or disappointed. He's not sure if he's mad at Eric or at himself or just sad or what, but he's sick of feeling like an emo little bitch. He's just going to stop thinking about it. Right? Right.

The TA meeting goes pretty well. Lauren is having a lot of trouble getting her groups to participate in discussions, and Will and Stephan suggest a few different tactics to get the kids talking. Mostly, it's just that they're all five weeks into the semester and everyone is stressing out about how much work they have to get done. It's extra frustrating to have to deal with sort-of teaching on top of the already overwhelming classes they're taking, but hey—that's why grad students get paid.

"I'm such a fucking wreck," Lauren moans, rubbing her neck as she slumps forward on the table they're sitting around at the Student Center.

Stephan nods, his coffee cup sadly empty and his caffeine levels down into the dangerously low zone. "Me too. You know what? Screw it. I'm going out tonight. I need a fucking break from this shit."

Yes, it's irresponsible. There's work he should do. There's *always* work he should do. He's sick of work, sick of being emo, sick of everything. Of being responsible. So screw it.

Lauren's nodding, while Will looks scandalized. "It's a Monday night!"

"Exactly—it's Ladies' Night at the Red Room," Lauren points out. "A dollar off drinks for every inch above my knee I show. Come on guys, be my wingmen. Protect me from the losers." She winks at Stephan. "I'll even let you have a few of the less-sexy ones."

"I'm still taken," Stephan reminds her, rolling his eyes, but it's just for show. He's totally in, even if the Red Room is one of the grosser meat-market bars in town. Not so queer friendly, but it's not like he'll be cruising. He'll just go, have a few drinks, maybe dance a little, and forget about everything for a while. Hell yeah.

They make plans to meet up later, and Will even lets himself be cajoled into joining them for a beer. Stephan has a few hours to shower, eat, and even get a little studying done so he doesn't feel *totally* guilty. He knows the guilt will come, especially if he has a hangover tomorrow, but it's a price he's willing to pay to get the fuck out of his head for the night.

Lauren picks him up since she lives on campus, too, and they meet Will at the Red Room. Neither guy can stop staring at her legs, although more in amazement than in lust. Stephan has no idea where she found a skirt that short; it barely seems to cover her crotch, let alone her ass. Even if it wasn't Ladies' Night, he doubts she'd have to pay for a drink herself, wearing that.

The beer on tap is awful, but the music is good, or good enough to dance to, at least. Stephan switches to drinking Jameson's and gets thoroughly trashed in less than an hour. Will has his one beer, looking uncomfortable the whole time, and dashes out like the police are about to raid the speakeasy. Lauren is flirting with five—no, six—guys, and seems to have things under control. Steph raises his glass to her in both a toast and question. She grins; she's fine, so he downs the last of it. She can always come find him on the dance floor if she needs him to act manly or something, but he's pretty sure she can take care of herself.

It's good to lose himself in the beat of the music, let his eyes drift mostly shut and just move. Let go. He doesn't care that there are only a few guys dancing, that he's surrounded by drunk, giggly girls while the guys line the walls, watching and salivating like hungry dogs. Whatever.

The world is spinning, and he can only blame the strobe lights a little; he's drunk. He's out without his boyfriend even knowing, on a fucking Monday night, and he has class tomorrow morning. He laughs manically, twirling one of the girls he's sort of dancing with and then lowering her in a dip as if they were doing the tango. She gasps breathlessly, then grabs him by the arms and plants her lipstick-sticky mouth against his, squeezing his biceps through his thin T-shirt and pressing her tits against his chest.

Oh shit.

"Uh, hey," he says, pushing her back and wondering how to get out of this. "I, uh…." She gives him a sultry smile, and suddenly he's way too hot and dying for some water and some air that's not thick with the stink of sweaty bodies and perfume, and he has to get out of there. She doesn't need an explanation; he doesn't *have* to tell her he's gay. It's not like he led her on, and if he did, well, he's drunk and she'll get over it.

"Sorry." He shrugs and pushes past her, heading toward the door. He tries not to hurl as he shoves through the crush of people.

"Asshole," he hears behind him.

He shrugs again. Maybe he *is* an asshole. Maybe he shouldn't be out, feeling vindictive and naughty and like he's doing something his boyfriend wouldn't approve of. Maybe Stephan is just a huge jerk, never satisfied, always wanting a nice guy, and then when he gets one, wanting someone more exciting. Maybe he's clinging to the shreds of his youth, rejecting a perfectly wonderful relationship—and friendship—in favor of partying and drugs and drinking and wild sex. Stuff that's not supposed to be important, right? Yeah.

But it kinda is. Because Stephan? Is an asshole.

The sidewalk under his feet seems to be tipping and lurching, and his nausea is actually forestalling the panic attack, rather than encouraging it. It seems he'd forgotten that booze and angst don't mix so well for him; the combination tends to make him hurl. He staggers toward the curb, barely making it to the gutter in time. Whisky and beer taste *really* awful on the rebound.

He's got his hands braced on his knees, panting and thanking God for the cold, fresh air when a car pulls up next to him. It idles. Finally he glances up and feels another wave of nausea as the window rolls down.

"Stephan?"

He closes his eyes for a second, praying that he's so drunk he's hallucinating or something, but no, he's not that lucky. When he opens them again, it's still Eric. Looking at him with faint disgust, although that could very well be because Stephan is still hocking up vomit-flavored saliva and spitting into the gutter.

"I thought that was you…. Chad got wasted and demanded that I come pick him up," Eric says, jerking his head toward the backseat, where his housemate is sprawled, passed out and reeking of tequila. "Get inside; I'll take you home." It sounds like a decent offer, so Stephan gets in, wishing he could be unconscious too. He's barely finished buckling the seatbelt when Eric asks, "Don't you have class tomorrow?"

Stephan makes a noise that sounds mostly affirmative and closes his eyes, leaning against the cool window. The ride seems like it takes forever and the silence is oppressive, but Stephan's in no state of mind for conversation, and at the very least, Eric seems to respect that. His disapproval or disappointment or whatever is almost tangible, but there is no way on earth Stephan can deal with that right now. It's honestly all he can do to not puke all over the inside of Eric's car.

When the car stops and stays that way for longer than at a red light, Stephan opens his eyes to see that they're outside Grad Student Housing. He smiles feebly at Eric and goes to get out of the car. It takes a long moment to disentangle himself from the seatbelt. Embarrassing, but what are you going to do?

"Good luck surviving tomorrow," Eric says, mustering up a sympathetic half-smile. "I'll give you a call." He leans in for a kiss, which Stephan abruptly jerks back from.

"Better not; puke breath." He tries to smile to take away the harshness of his rejection, but it's probably more of a grimace.

"Right." Eric pauses. "Okay then, well…."

"Yeah." Stephan gets out, but then leans back in before he closes the car door. "Thanks for picking me up."

Eric gives him a smile, but there are no dimples, and even a totally wasted Stephan can tell that his eyes seem sad. "Of course; what was I going to do, leave you there throwing up in the street? Good night."

"Bye." The car pulls out, and Stephan lifts a hand to wave for a moment before turning to tackle his immediate insurmountable challenge—the stairs up to his apartment. One damn thing at a time.

Chapter 12
Food Therapy

THE next morning Stephan wakes up feeling like death and goes to the gym before Method and Theory, trying to wake up and maybe repair some of the damage done to his system. He's on the elliptical with his headphones, hoping to reach that endorphin-high state where his head stops pounding and he zones out and doesn't think about anything at all. It's easier to get there on the treadmill, like a Real Man, but Stephan blew out his knee playing baseball in high school and it hurts today. Along with every other joint in his body. And his skin. Anyway, he's okay with not being a Real Man; today he barely feels human. A nun could beat him up. So the elliptical it is.

Near the end of his program, someone comes up behind him and wolf whistles loud enough for Stephan to hear over his music, commenting, "*Damn*, look at that fine, tight ass. Apple bottom juicy booty, indeed."

Stephan twists a little, looking over his shoulder, and manages a laugh. "I thought I recognized your voice and the lame pickup lines. What's up, Mike?"

"Your perky buns?" Mike leers, reaching up to grab the ass in question as he leans in to look at the readout on Steph's machine. "Oh good, you're almost done. And you've burned off enough calories to come over tonight and let me feed you. It's been ages, man; I'm beginning to think you don't love me anymore."

Stephan snorts, pushing the button to stop, and walks over to the mats to do some cool-down stretches. "How could anyone not love that face? But you're right; it's been a while."

Mike flops down next to him and rolls onto his side, openly ogling Stephan. "Damn right; come over tonight and bring beer."

Shaking his head, Stephan lets himself sprawl backward, the ceiling fans cooling the sweat on his body as his heart rate slows. "Yeah, I dunno. I might have to be a teetotaler for a while; I got pretty drunk last night. I think I'm still sweating out the booze. And I should stay in and do work."

"Ah, so that's what that smell is: filthy acetaldehyde. That's why pot is better. But all work and no play makes Stephan a very dull boy, even with that truly fine ass. Do you have a paper due or a test?"

Stephan thinks, then shrugs. "No. Just feeling guilty. I could come over for a while, yeah, sure. When?" He misses his friends; he's allowed to see them, right? So long as he gets his school stuff done, it's fine if he fucks off a little. Besides, it's not even midterms. Yet.

So they make some plans, and when Stephan shows up at Mike's that evening after his TA sessions are over, the single apartment his friend has somehow talked Grad Student Housing into letting him live in for the last six years smells invitingly like spaghetti sauce.

One weird advantage of so much schooling is that somewhere along the way, Mike decided cooking was chemistry too. He's a better cook than Danielle, even, not that Stephan would ever tell her; he's not stupid. Never insult anyone who is a halfway decent cook if you ever want them to make food for you again. In fact, a lot of his friends are pretty good cooks, he muses. Must be some truth to that cliché about the way to a man's heart being his stomach... for friendship at least. Maybe he should learn to cook one of these days....

A dish towel hits him in the face. "Dude. Stop zoning out and come make the salads." Stephan snorts, but tucks the towel into his waistband and heads to the counter where Mike has carrots and mushrooms and a cutting board and knife all ready to go.

They catch up over the events of the last few weeks, Stephan's classes and Mike's research, gossiping about friends in common, and generally harassing the hell out of each other. It's flirty, yeah, but it's comfortable, not crossing any boundaries. This is just how they are with each other, a thing that Eric never seems to understand, even if he isn't exactly possessive.

"Go set the table, bitch," Mike orders, smacking Stephan on the ass with a—thankfully clean—spoon.

"What do I look like, Suzy Homemaker?" he protests, but he grabs the plates and silverware anyway, carrying them all of six steps across the room to the small table.

"Hey, if the apron fits...."

With a theatrical pout, Stephan pulls off the dish towel he'd forgotten about and sticks his tongue out at Mike. They both crack up, and Stephan feels better than he has in ages.

The meal is fantastic, of course. Mike's family might be Jewish, but he's fantastic at making anything Italian. He claims it's because pasta is cheap and he's been in college roughly since the dawn of time, so of course he's good at sauces for it. Mike is also the only guy Stephan knows who eats vegetables regularly, even going through the occasional vegetarian phase. It's partly because he feels sad for the animals and disgusted by factory farming and other hippie shit that Stephan finds himself agreeing with, but more honestly it's because Mike likes to clean out his system every now and then so the drugs he takes are more effective. Or that's what he says, anyway.

Stephan is slouching back in his chair, drawing abstract designs in the smear of red sauce left on his plate, feeling full and content and pleased with life. Mike gets up and clears away some of the dishes. Warm hands fall on Stephan's shoulders and start to rub. It feels good, for a few minutes, but then starts to seem a little weird, so Steph reaches up, batting Mike's hands away.

"You're totally stressed out. I have just the thing.... Lemme get the bong," Mike suggests.

Snorting, Stephan shakes his head. "No way; that's kind of the source of all my problems lately."

"Oh yeah? You overindulging lately? Tell Dr. Mikey all about it."

Stephan shrugs, and Mike's hands go back to work, soothing the story out of him. "Got totally wasted at a party over the weekend and kind of molested Eric, I guess, or something. And then I went out last night with the other TAs and drank way too much. I was puking in the gutter when Eric drove by and stopped to pick me up."

"Ouch." The sympathetic squeeze on his shoulders does nothing to alleviate the clear realization of how fucked-up things are, and that it seems to be all Stephan's fault. Somehow.

"Yeah."

"So things suck right now?"

"Pretty much."

"Bummer."

That, at least, gets a chuckle. "Do us all a favor and don't go into psychology, Mike."

Mike makes an offended noise and tickles Stephan in retaliation. Shrieking, Stephan tries to bat away his friend's evil hands, but gets his wrists grabbed and held tight behind his neck for his efforts. Pinned. He freezes.

"Let me go."

To his credit, Mike does, instantly. "Sorry." He comes around and sits down at the table again, giving Stephan a probing look. "I thought you used to be into some of the kinkier sex games, didn't you? I remember you asking me and Jim stuff about how to play safe, way back when you were just a barely legal little twink."

Stephan rolls his eyes, self-consciously rubbing at his wrists. No harm done, of course; Mike was just being, well, Mike. "Yeah. Not in a while. Not anymore."

Mike gives him a hard look. "Ah. Eric's not into it?"

Okay, maybe Mike wouldn't be a horrible therapist after all, but still. "Dude, I'm way too sober to talk about my sex life with you."

Mike grins. "Hey, that's not my fault; I offered you the bong."

Shaking his head, Stephan gets up and grabs two more beers from the fridge, tossing one to Mike. It's all he can have tonight—by his own rule—but he sure as fuck needs it if he's really going to talk about his sex life. It's been a while, he thinks, as they relocate to the "living room," Mike on the utilitarian sofa, and Stephan sprawled on the floor, wondering when he got so inhibited that he can't talk about sex anymore…. Maybe it was somewhere around the time he figured out what he was doing in bed and didn't need to ask his friends stuff like which lube was the best if you're going to end up tasting it….

He drinks half the bottle, then starts picking at the label. "No, he's not into it."

"It?"

"Kinky shit. Or, well, playing around much," Stephan says.

"So the sex is bad?"

Stephan makes a face. "It's not bad. It's good, actually, really good most of the time. It's just… almost always the same."

"So it's good, but he's boring in bed?" Mike clarifies.

Taking a moment to think about that, honestly considering, Stephan finishes his beer. "Not boring. Just not… exciting…." There's a pause while he thinks. "But that's normal, right? We've been together for almost a year. It can't be crazy porn sex all the time."

When he glances over, Mike's got a scrunched-up look on his face. "Dunno; never 'dated' anyone that long. But I think sex is pretty important, and if he's not giving you what you want, maybe you should show him what you want, or—God forbid—talk to him about it. Maybe he's just inhibited."

Hm. Maybe Mike's got something there; he could just show Eric what he wants. If they, you know, ever fuck again. Or even just talk. Stephan sighs.

"Don't you think sexual compatibility is important?" Mike asks.

"Yes. Duh," Stephan snorts, tossing balled-up bits of the paper label at his friend. "It just seems stupid to break up with someone because he's not, you know…."

Mike kicks him when the pause lasts for too long.

"It just... it's like he's always holding back, sort of. He doesn't let go anymore. Get wild. You know." Stephan's got his arm over his head so Mike can't accuse him of blushing or some shit.

There's a bit of a silence while those words linger in the room. He's never put it in words before, but yeah—Eric doesn't let go. He used to, at first, when they were fucking all the time and Eric was so goddamned excited to be with a guy who was as interested in sex as Stephan. And good at it. But maybe that wasn't about Stephan, himself. Maybe it was just about the sex.

"Do you top or bottom?" Mike asks out of nowhere.

Stephan lifts up his arm to shoot Mike a confused glare. "What? Both. You know that."

"I mean with Eric, you idiot."

"Fuck off."

"Answer me," Mike insists.

"I guess I mostly bottom. Why?"

"Why do you think that is?"

"Stop fucking analyzing me, dickface, and tell me what you're getting at."

Mike shrugs. "I just think it's interesting. You used to be kinky; now you're not. You used to be a switch, now you're a bottom. You don't seem happy about it, so I wonder if Eric is happy with things like they are. Seems like he must be, if those are his preferences, and you're just going along with it because you don't mind."

Another, even more puzzled look is all Stephan's got in reply to that.

"Is he really even gay? Does he like to be fucked?" Mike asks.

"He's bi. And he's sure as hell liked it the few times he's let me fuck him. But he is... kinda inhibited about it."

"Oh?"

"Well, like, I'll ask or whatever, and he'll say he doesn't have time or just, you know, roll me over and do me instead. Plus not all fags like to be fucked, you know," Stephan points out. "Doesn't mean they're secretly straight."

Mike's getting an evil grin on his face, the kind that lets Stephan know he's really not going to like whatever Mike's about to say about his boyfriend. "Maybe your boy has issues about his asshole, Steph. Maybe he thinks it's diiiirty. Maybe he thinks it's *wrong*."

"Fuck off. He doesn't think it's wrong. He's not like some self-hating homophobe or something."

"Mmhmm. Sure. Well, maybe he's worried about shit, then. He thinks his body is unclean."

"It *is* unclean," Stephan points out.

"Filthy, dirty faggots," Mike says, wiggling his eyebrows. "Seriously, maybe your boy's embarrassed about it. You're only, what, his second dude?"

Stephan thinks for a moment. "Huh. You might have something there. But still, it's been almost a year; you'd think he'd be over it by now."

Mike flops back onto the sofa, arms spread wide. "That's all I've got, man. I'm sorry, but your time with Dr. Mikey is over for the week. Oh, and this is a cash-only office. Please pay the receptionist on your way out."

Rolling over, Stephan gets to his feet and smacks Mike on the head. They tussle a little, and Mike hugs him for a long moment, reassuringly. Then he air-kisses both Stephan's cheeks and escorts him to the door, waving him off like the Queen of England.

He's fucking nuts, but he's a good friend. Stephan's glad he has him.

Chapter 13
Falling Down

ERIC texts on Tuesday night, checking that Stephan's still alive. He replies with an affirmative and a totally fake smiley face, then sends another message thanking Eric again for the ride. He doesn't get a reply to that, but he doesn't get a phone call, either, which is good. Well, it's not *good*, but he doesn't want to talk to Eric, so, yeah.

They manage to avoid each other for the rest of the week. Wednesday afternoon, there's some good-natured ribbing from Lauren about him being a pansy-assed lightweight who can't hold his liquor and how he got picked up in a car by some hot guy and Lauren had to go home all alone. Stephan protests that he slept alone that night.

"Aw, that's so sweet. Did your boyfriend stay up all night taking care of you?"

"Uh. He had an early class," Stephan mumbles. "He just gave me a ride home."

Lauren laughs, shaking her head. "You're so domesticated. I bet sometimes you two just curl up in bed and cuddle, don't you?"

"Hey, I like to cuddle too," Will argues. "It's not a gay thing."

"I'm just jealous," she answers, shaking her head. "Someday I'd like a little more than a quick fuck.... Straight guys either just want a booty call or to get married. I wish I could find something in between."

"Not just straight guys," Stephan mutters, but then he stops. The other two are commiserating about how hard it is to find someone who's serious but not *that* serious, and he feels his guts tighten up. He *feels* married, kinda, maybe. He thought he was supposed to like this, being in a long-term relationship, but... he doesn't, not right now. He likes feeling settled, but it *is* kind of boring. Is security always boring? Does it have to be? He has no idea.

Before that party and the drugs, things with Eric had been comfortable, relaxed. Easy. Well, once they decided to start making more time for each other, anyway. But that's beside the point. It was nice to have a relationship that wasn't always difficult and full of drama. But maybe that's Stephan's problem—maybe he thinks stuff with Eric should be harder, more of a struggle. Maybe that's the kind of excitement he wants.

Maybe he's just an immature stereotypical asshole male, like Lauren's bitching about. It's possible. He does miss the hot sex. He's not a saint.

But he's fucking tired of expecting it to be easier. Even if the last month with Eric has been mostly drama-free, it still *feels* like a hell of a lot of work. It's exhausting, and Stephan can't figure out why, can't see what's really going on. He just wishes it was over.

"Fuck," he says, spilling the rest of the coffee left in his cup. He apologizes, cleaning up the mess with a fistful of napkins, then makes his excuses and runs off to his American Lit class. He has no idea what he meant by that last thought, and he doesn't want to know.

DANIELLE tackles him after their class and demands that Stephan schedule a study date with her, joking that she'll put out if he will. The class is his favorite, and it's managed to put him in a much better mood, so he dredges up a smile as he reaches for her tits, almost getting in a grope before she smacks his hands away.

"Such a tease, Burke. Not until we're married; you know I'm saving myself for our wedding night."

Stephan snorts. "That's not what I heard—through the *wall*."

She fails to rise to the bait, shaking her head. "What can I say, I like to fully enjoy myself."

They head to the coffee shop and brainstorm ideas for their project proposals. They've done this together a lot and they're good at it, each coming from a different perspective, which, in the end, makes for much more well-rounded research papers. Friday night seems like the best night to try to get some work done over the weekend; Danielle's got a date on Saturday, and Stephan's planning to throw himself into his Method and Theory reading. He doesn't have any plans with Eric, but he doesn't want to make any plans either. Just in case.

They're not the only ones freaking out about schoolwork; midterms are coming and his TA sections are packed with kids he's never seen before, panicked about the paper due on Monday and needing some serious hand-holding. He has the group go over each of the proposed questions, and is smugly pleased that a small percentage of students are already finished. It's nice to know he's not the only one who gets his work done with more than four days to spare. Being a goody-two-shoes pays off in managing academic stress, he knows. Some of these kids are definitely going to be pulling all-nighters, dropping off shitty papers Monday morning and thinking they can get away with it. And the sad truth is that they will; it's only an intro class for undergrads. He can't be too hard on them, although he is relying on Jeff's "grading party" next week to help him figure out how high—or low—the bar should be set.

The library is pretty crowded for a Friday; Stephan has to glare at a guy sitting at *his* table until the interloper leaves. Danielle joins him and they spread out all their books and notes and laptops, working fairly quietly together, with the occasional short discussion about an idea. Writing a proposal is new to Stephan, and while he usually drafts an outline for each of his research papers, he feels rusty. He was only out of school for one year, but he feels like his mojo has gone missing. Danielle does a good job of both reassuring him and giving him shit for being so neurotic. Anyway, they end up having a productive late afternoon and evening, breaking for "dinner" from the coffee cart in the lobby. He's got his proposal pretty well finished and she's satisfied with her work, too, so they call it a win and head home a whole hour before the library closes.

Saturday is utter hell. He studies at home until he feels restless, like he's going to jump out of his skin, and agrees to join Jim for a "short jog." An hour and a half later, he gasps some obscenities out at Jim, and turns back toward home, cursing that fucking bastard's three-inch longer legs and evil fucking laugh. He should have known better, he thinks, as he downs some Gatorade.

Despite his conversation a few weeks ago with Jeff, there are just some parts of Method and Theory that are still as dull as concrete. He can wrap his head around why it's useful, see the interesting aspects of how opinions sneak in no matter how objective a historian attempts to be, but *shit*—there's simply no getting around the fact that studying about how people study is *boring*. He tries reading at his desk, on his bed, on the sofa, and at the kitchen table. By the time the sun goes down, he's got a pounding headache, knots in his shoulders, and wants to kill someone. A hot bath might help....

Grad Student Housing is way sweeter than the dorms, despite being decorated with the same rock-solid furniture. The apartments are designed to house only two students, giving each one a small bedroom but a decent-size desk in each room. The kitchen and dining area are tiny but adequate for two, and it's not like they spend much time hanging out in the living room except to watch TV or play games. But the really good part is that the bathroom has a tub, and a nice long one at that. Since both he and Jim are over six feet tall, that means it's actually possible for them to fit into the tub. Jim doesn't use it—aside from the occasional bath with Jamie, and Stephan usually leaves when he hears their splashing and her giggling—but Stephan fucking *loves* the tub. When he has a house of his own, he's totally going to have a hot tub.

Jamie's left some bubble bath on the edge of the counter—along with a pink razor and some ultra-slippery soap that smells like flowers—and Stephan may or may not have accidentally spilled some into his bath. It's citrusy and woodsy-smelling, and he sinks into the hot foamy bath with a sigh. It's been a long fucking day.

A long fucking *week*....

The only high point was having dinner with Mike. Not that a productive afternoon with Danielle is anything to disregard, but it wasn't exactly fun, per se. Then again, he's not sure "fun" is the word he'd use to describe his dinner with Mike, either.... Good food. Weird conversation. Good though....

Mike's a giant weirdo, but he's actually not bad to talk to. He's patient, lets you spill things out at your own pace, listens, asks good questions, and can be counted on to punch you before you get all weepy and cry or some shit. In fact, Stephan remembers that he talked to Mike a lot after his last—okay, only—major relationship ended. Mike listened to him whine about what was wrong with him and how come he always ended up with assholes like Paul, said some insightful things, and then took him out to kick his ass at basketball.

Why hadn't he remembered that talking to Mike was good? Oh right, because Eric doesn't like Mike. Huh. Well, screw Eric.

Stephan ducks his head under the water, a futile gesture at washing away his ugly thoughts. He's so angry, but tired-of-it angry, not energetic-rage angry. He's tired of how he feels, tired of being frustrated and feeling guilty. He's not a drug addict or an alcoholic, and he gets his schoolwork done before it's due and pays his bills on time; he's a responsible adult. But Eric disapproves, and when the hell did that even happen? How could this have not been an issue for the first six months, when Stephan was seeing Mike and Jim and Billy and Scott every couple of days, hanging out drinking and smoking pot and doing all the stuff Eric apparently disapproves of?

What the hell happened to the guy who was relaxed and easygoing and funny as hell and a good lay? When did Eric get so uptight and boring?

Stephan flips over to lie on his stomach, feet sticking up out of the tub. No, that's not fair. That's just the anger speaking. Eric's a great guy. Sweet. But maybe that's part of the problem—he's too sweet. Sometimes Stephan wants sex to be dirtier, raunchier. More raw. Not just to be topped, but dominated.... He hadn't noticed how much he'd missed that stuff until Mike made him think about how long it's been since he had anything resembling kinky sex.

Stupid Mike.

Stephan wants a boyfriend who's committed to the sex part, not just a best friend to hang out with—he's got those. He wants someone who wants to fuck him the way he wants to be fucked. Someone who will let him top sometimes, someone who likes kinky sex, someone who is apparently more sexually compatible than Eric is, who wants it as much as he does.

Maybe that makes him a jerk or something, but sex is kind of a big deal. And he likes Eric, maybe he even loves him, but if this one piece is missing, then it doesn't feel like it's going to work out. Unless he's being totally shallow, which is a possibility. Maybe he's asking for too much.

Maybe Stephan can just drown himself in the bathtub....

STEPHAN is taking a study break, wandering aimlessly through the stacks in the library, trying to re-focus his eyes and loosen up the knots in his back. He finds himself in the French literature section and casually begins to browse. He finds *Justine* and pulls it off the shelf. He hasn't read it, and from what he knows about de Sade, doesn't get what all the fuss is about. The man seems like a genuine fucked-up weirdo, more of a sociopath than into kinky sex. Still. He thumbs through a few pages, mentally shrugs, and takes it with him back to his table.

And because his life really can't get any more fucking perfect, Jeff is sitting there, making himself at home, using Stephan's laptop to hide his coffee cup. Stephan almost says something snarky when he realizes there are *two* coffee cups there and remembers that he had sheepishly tossed his out under the stern glare of one of the librarians passing through his area an hour ago.

Jeff brought him coffee. "No greater love hath man," Stephan croons, reaching out to the still-hot cup and cradling it tenderly.

Jeff laughs. "Anyone ever told you you're easy, kid?"

"For coffee, I'm the biggest whore around," Stephan agrees, closing his eyes and taking a reverent sip.

"So what are you working on? I see historiography books and Twain and Parkman and... what have you got there?" he says, reaching for the book in Stephan's hand.

Stephan holds on to it a bit longer than he should, getting a slightly puzzled look from Jeff, which morphs into a seriously raised-eyebrow expression once the cover is visible. He tries not to fidget or act embarrassed; it's not like it's anything he should be self-conscious about. It's just a book. A notorious *sex* book, but still. It's not like it's *porn* or anything.

"Doing some extracurricular studying?" Jeff asks.

Sitting down, Stephan busies himself with the stacks of papers and books. "I was just wandering around the stacks. Wondered what the big deal was about the guy. Have you read it?"

Jeff nods, flipping the pages. "Yeah, ages ago. Sadly, it's not very interesting, or at least, I didn't think it was. I've read much better kinky porn and far better writing on the psychology of sadomasochism."

Stephan tries not to choke on his coffee.

"I read it for the titillation factor," Jeff smirks, "but it's more political and social commentary. Well, that and rape fantasy." He shrugs. "That's just what I remember, though; you may have a different experience with it."

"Huh. Maybe." Stephan desperately wants to ask Jeff what he would recommend instead, but doesn't. "So, uh…."

Under the table, Jeff gives him a light kick. "Everyone's interested in kinky sex, Stephan. Even us old guys. Nothing to be embarrassed about."

"You're not old," he refutes automatically. "And I'm just out of it from studying too much. Writing a research proposal, an essay, reading this M&T crap, not to mention stupid French memorization, discussion topics for section, and office hours. I hate this part of the semester; it seems like it will never end."

"Well, good thing you've found something to take your mind off school for a while," Jeff teases. He reaches over to Stephan's backpack and slides *Justine* inside. His thumb lingers for a moment on the pink triangle button on Stephan's backpack. Stephan licks his lips; he's always been pretty open about being queer, but has it come up in front of Jeff before? He can't remember.

"It's just been a long week. Too much studying," he says.

"And not enough sex?" Jeff asks, winking.

"Shut up," he snorts. "It's just been all work and no play this week, I guess." He takes a breath and adds, "Haven't seen much of my boyfriend lately."

Wiggling his eyebrows, Jeff asks, "Literally?" and they laugh. "Well, you *could* study the history of sex, or sex in America, or something. Not everything is black and white: interesting/boring; school/work; gay/straight. Sometimes interests overlap."

"Huh. No, yeah, you're right," Stephan agrees. "Lots of things aren't that clear." Like this conversation, for example. Did Jeff just imply that he isn't straight? But he was married. Or maybe he was saying he is okay with Stephan being queer? What?

Thankfully, Jeff interrupts Stephan's confusion after just a few moments. "Hey, not to change the topic, but I saw a flier by the coffee cart for some local band called the Westward Hos. They're playing at a club this Tuesday. Have you ever heard of them?"

"Yeah, actually my friend Scott used to be in a band with their drummer for a while. You thinking of going to the show?"

"Thought I might. You free or are you too buried in schoolwork?"

Stephan thinks about it for a few seconds. His research proposal is pretty much finished, the essay isn't due until Thursday, and everything else is current. "Sure, why not?"

They make some plans to meet up at Jeff's place Tuesday night and grab dinner somewhere before the show. It turns out they have similar tastes in music and food, and Jeff even says he likes to cook and Stephan should come by sometime for his signature salmon dish. They work amiably together for the rest of the afternoon.

STEPHAN'S jerk-off fantasy that night is full of dark rooms, black leather, and the sweet sensation of submission. He imagines himself kneeling, being commanded down by a man with a gravelly voice and rough stubble. Of his face being held while a thick cock fucks his mouth, gently, but unrelenting. Of being bent over a hard surface, his pants yanked off, fucked hard and deep until he's gasping for breath and coming all over his hands.

He misses being *taken* like that, being treated like he's so sexy and desirable that his lovers can't control themselves. Like he's so hot that they *have* to push him around a little—or a lot. Misses feeling like he can let go, *has* to let go, and that someone will catch him before he falls too far.

He wants to fall again.

Chapter 14
Under Stars

THE next two days are busy but largely uneventful. Stephan's all dressed up for his TA sections Tuesday afternoon because he's going over to Jeff's as soon as they're finished, and some of the girls make moony eyes at him. He tries not to preen too much, but he knows he looks good. His clothes are nothing special—jeans, work boots, and a fitted white button-down—but somehow it all comes together with a little bit of stubble and hair gel, and he looks, well, "ravishable" is the word Eric has used.

Back when he was talking to his boyfriend.

Stephan's not thinking about that, though, as he walks through the Professorland complex and finds Jeff's condo. There's a shout to come on in, and the door's unlocked, so Stephan does. From upstairs Jeff yells that he's looking for his goddamned shoes and he'll be down in a second and that Stephan should make himself at home.

Jeff's place is all weird 1970s angles and white stucco walls, lined with a ton of built-in bookcases, which makes sense for university-built housing. Every shelf is full of books, but they're deep enough to have knickknacks in front of them, too, mostly lots of candle holders and statuettes. Stephan notes with amusement that the books are semi-sorted by geographic area, and the statuettes match: the Mercury figurine and Greek vase are by the Greek and Roman history books, the Buddha statue is with the Asian collection, and there's a set of Mount Rushmore bobbleheads with the American stuff.

Jeff comes downstairs and catches Stephan poking at Teddy Roosevelt's head. Stephan grins but then almost chokes as he takes in the sight before him. Jeff is fucking *gorgeous*. He's dressed fairly simply, too, but *damn* he looks good. His clothes are nothing special at all, but his sleeves are rolled up, and Stephan can see tattoos peeking out by his elbows. He's wearing a thick silver wristwatch and some bracelets and a few silver rings, and that much jewelry would look totally stupid on most guys, but somehow Jeff pulls it off without looking like either a mobster or a major douche. His stubble's a bit longer than usual and has more than just a touch of gray, but it's sexy.

Dear God is it sexy.

Stephan swallows, trying to figure out if he's allowed to say anything complimentary or not. They're just two friends going out to see a band and grab dinner, and although that sort of *sounds* like a date, it's not. Jeff's his friend, but he's also Stephan's professor, and Stephan needs to stop thinking about what that stubble would feel like catching on his own or—better yet—against his shoulders as Jeff slams into him from behind, fucking him hard.

"Ready to go?" Jeff asks.

He has to clear his throat and his "Yeah" is a little raspy, but Jeff doesn't seem to notice. Either Stephan is the master of subtlety or Jeff is super-oblivious, and Stephan knows it's not the former—a *child* would have noticed the way Stephan just checked out his professor. But maybe Jeff docsn't pick up on guys checking him out because he's not wired that way himself. He's not looking for it, so he doesn't see it. That's both handy and a little sad, but whatever. It's not like Stephan expects anything to come of his stupid crush anyway, so he should be glad that Jeff's clueless.

Plus, that means once he stops freaking out so much about getting caught staring—okay, *drooling*—Stephan can just relax and enjoy it. He's got a night out with a really cool, interesting older guy, who also happens to be so goddamned sexy Stephan can barely keep his hands to himself. Sure, it sucks to only be able to look but not touch, but it's better than sitting at home studying and fretting over Eric.

"How do you feel about barbecue?" Jeff asks as they walk to his car. "I surfed around online and there's a reasonably new restaurant downtown. I mean, it could suck, but the reviews were pretty good and at least it would be new, so you won't have the advantage over me," he says with a grin.

"Sounds good. What kind of barbecue?"

Jeff's smile grows as he lightly smacks Stephan's shoulder. "A California boy who knows there're different kinds of barbecue? Color me impressed. The website with their catering info says it's Texas style."

"Cool," Stephan nods. "My dad's folks are from the South, so he does barbecue Memphis style. It's practically a sin not to have ribs with my grandpa's sauce for the Fourth of July at our house. I bet this place has a good brisket, though. Man, just talking about it's got my mouth watering."

"Me too. I did some postgraduate work in the South and developed a thing for barbecue. Memphis ribs are the best for pork, but you just can't beat a good Texas brisket, in my opinion. Living in Seattle and now in California, I was worried there wouldn't be any good barbecue without getting on an airplane."

"Well, don't count your chickens," Stephan cautions him.

"True enough. If the food sucks, we'll just have to have more beer."

The drive is short, and the new restaurant turns out to be walking distance from the club where the band is playing later, so they park in-between. Jeff's on an amusing tirade about how bastardized barbecue has become with the introduction of chain restaurants all over the country, and how it took him ages to find a tiny hole-in-the-wall in Seattle with displaced Texans as the chef and owner.

Stephan makes a stab at defending California barbecue, and they get diverted into a semantics discussion of "barbecue" versus "grilled food." Stephan can't stop smiling, and it's so easy for him to reach over and steal Jeff's beer when his runs dry that he doesn't think anything of it. The small table is a disaster of napkins and wet wipes, and they're both kind of a mess. It doesn't seem weird when Jeff holds out a fork with pulled pork for him to try; they're passing small sampler plates back and forth, discussing vinegar versus tomato-based sauces and dry rubs and so on. Jeff is apparently *really* into cooking, and barbecue in particular, although he says he's a better eater than cook, since he doesn't think anyone can do "real barbecue" without a pit.

He's having such a good time, so caught up in Jeff's enthusiasm, that he doesn't even realize what he's doing until his hand, holding a napkin, touches Jeff's mouth to wipe away a smear of sauce, and he suddenly realizes he's crossed a line. *Shit.*

There are two ways to play this, so he goes with, "Can't take you anywhere, can I?" and a mother-hen "tsk."

There's something in Jeff's eyes that seems to not be buying it, but he lets Stephan off the hook with a grin and a shrug sticks out his tongue. "Guess not. You'll have to hang around to keep me presentable, huh?"

Before he says something lame like *"I'd like that,"* Stephan looks at his watch and notices it's time to go, unless they want to stand all through the concert. The venue is small and set up like a café with lots of tiny tables, a small elevated stage, and about ten square feet of space intended for a dance floor. The musicians are setting up and Stephan greets them, making small talk with Jan-the-drummer for a moment or two and congratulating her on the gig while Jeff gets a pitcher of a nice dark beer and some glasses.

They've got a little under an hour to let their dinner digest while they stake out their table, and the place begins to fill up pretty quickly; the locals know to get here as soon as the doors open if they want to sit down. He's telling Jeff about other shows he's been to here, about Billy and Scott and all of the bands they've been in, and he mentions the song Billy wrote for Scott's birthday.

"Aw, that's sweet," Jeff says, and while it could be a put-down with the right emphasis—two fags writing lovey-dovey songs for each other—Stephan can tell that it's not. Jeff seems genuinely touched.

"Yeah. Eric got a little misty-eyed," Stephan smirks.

"Eric, huh? So what's he like, this boyfriend of yours? How come I never see him studying with you at the library or anything? You sure he really exists?"

Stephan takes a long drink, trying not to wince. "Eric lives off campus with some friends; we don't study very well together. And he's... well, I guess he's been busy. We haven't been seeing a whole lot of each other lately." He shrugs, not sure whether he's *acting* nonchalant, or genuinely *is*.

Jeff gives him a questioning look.

"I don't think things are going very well," Stephan admits. "I don't know. I thought relationships and stuff were supposed to get easier as you got older."

Jeff laughs, amused. "What did you say you are again, twenty-two? You're still a kid."

"Twenty-four. I took a year off before grad school, and I was a five-year senior."

"That's still pretty young, I think."

Shaking his head, Stephan kicks Jeff's chair. "Don't call me a kid, old man."

"Well, lately I feel old, then," Jeff acknowledges. "So, tell Grandpa all about your love life. I'll try to find some words of wisdom for you."

With a shake of his head and a little bit of a smile, Stephan tells him about Eric, that they hooked up at a New Year's Eve party and it just went from there. Easy, relaxed, and fun. Then Eric went home for two months over the summer and Stephan missed him a lot, but things have been kind of fucked up to varying degrees ever since school started this fall, but he can't figure out *why*. Jeff doesn't have any suggestions for him other than to talk to Eric, and unfortunately Stephan knows that's the only real solution. There's no magic fix; they're going to have to be in the same room and figure out a way to resolve things together.

"I thought love was supposed to be easier than this," Stephan sighs, swirling the dregs of foam around the bottom of his glass.

Jeff snorts. "Love *is* easy; it's the relationships that are work." He gives Stephan a probing look. "Tell me, when was the first time you fell in love? When did you know you were gay?"

Stephan wrinkles his nose. "I always knew. Lost my cherry in high school. Older guys had a thing for my pretty little face, I guess, and I had a bad history of crushing on straight boys and having meaningless sex with whoever was handy."

"I bet," Jeff says, grinning.

With a wink, Stephan continues. "Guess I was a bit of a slut, but at sixteen, who isn't, if they have the choice, right?" He shakes his head. "Luckily, I was always good about being safe. Eventually I got over that in college, and fell in love with an older guy, Paul. We were only together for about three months, and he was cheating on me for the whole last month, it turned out."

"Sorry," Jeff offers. "Being betrayed like that really sucks. Was it a long time ago?"

"Few years," Stephan agrees. "Doesn't really seem like 'love' now, but I thought it was at the time. I played the field for my last couple years of school, then met Eric during my year off. It's been... good. I mean, I have a bad habit of dating jerks, so it's best that they were all pretty short affairs. But it was never...."

"What?" Jeff presses when the silence goes on for too long.

"Well, you know. I mean, when everything is new and you break up before it has time to get old, it doesn't have time to be boring, right?" he asks. "I mean, not that being with Eric is *boring*, really. It's just... not exciting. But, I mean, that's how it goes, right? You said you were married; it's supposed to be easy companionship, right? And I guess the hot sex kind of declines over time, then, right?"

Jeff nods. "Generally, yeah. But if you're not happy, kid, that's okay. You're *not* married. And sometimes things just don't work out. People drift apart. Or they look for passion elsewhere."

They both finish their pints, surrounded by noise but silent. Jeff offers to get another pitcher, but Stephan remembers he's got an early class and does the responsible thing and says no. Jeff rubs it in that he doesn't have class until midday so he's getting one more and Stephan can drive them home if Jeff's not sober. He brings Stephan a Coke, along with the pitcher, and barely makes it to his seat before the owner steps up to announce the band.

The Westward Hos put on a pretty good show. The music is fairly standard Americana/folk, which isn't Stephan's favorite, but the singer has a nice voice and the lyrics are intriguing. It's mellow, people milling around, but respectfully, and conversation is a dull murmur that the music doesn't have to compete with.

At the break, Stephan lets Jeff have the first go at the head while he holds the table. By the time he makes his own way to the bathroom, and stands in the unisex line forever, the band has already started again. They're warming back up with a cover by Garbage, which amuses Stephan. He's got a smile pulling at his mouth as he makes his way through the crowd, humming along as his eyes search for Jeff and their table. The singer's put her own twist on the familiar words, of course, but Stephan's still surprised when they grab at him. *Don't let a soul mate pass you by.*

Jesus. He spots Jeff at the same time, and it's like a divine light shines down on the guy or maybe it's just a spotlight, but Stephan's heart suddenly pounds in his chest, and he can't quite catch his breath for no apparent reason. It's not like he didn't know he had a crush on Jeff—duh—but, well. It's like something shifted in his head, and it's not just lust, it's not just admiration or hero worship or whatever. He's not going to put it into words, even if he could, but Stephan has *feelings* for Jeff. Real ones.

Holy fucking shit. *So* not good.

He practically falls into his seat, staring at Jeff and trying to remember how to breathe. With shaking hands, he refills his glass from the beer pitcher and downs half of the pint in one go. Jeff gives him an inquiring look, but Stephan can only look away and try not to flush. He realizes he's hard about halfway through the next song, and is mortified, wondering if he was like that as he walked back to the table, and if Jeff noticed.

By the end of the set, Stephan's managed to get himself back under control and stop freaking out. The beer's probably helped him mellow out, and either he's more drunk than he should be or the music is getting better, because he's starting to get really into the lyrics by the end. He likes when people sing about real things, real emotions, not just sappy head-over-heels love bullshit or suicidal breakups.

Jeff says he's sober, but Stephan cajoles him into a short walk around outside before they go back home, saying he wants to get some air but really to observe for himself Jeff's state of intoxication.

"So, what'd you think?" he asks.

Jeff ponders for a minute before answering. "They were good. The music wasn't anything fantastic, but I liked the singer and the words." He smiles self-consciously. "I don't really know much about music, I guess; words are more my thing."

Stephan nods. "I liked the lyrics too. It was nice to hear something that wasn't all emo."

Laughter colors Jeff's reply. "Yeah, it's good sometimes to hear someone sing about real relationships and love. Even if it does make you think too much," he adds.

Stephan isn't sure if it's okay for him to ask, but he figures what the hell; Jeff asked him about his love life, so it's only fair if he asks too. "So, what's the deal with you? When did you and your wife spilt up?"

Jeff's silence lasts for a few long minutes, long enough that it seems like he isn't going to answer, and Stephan is trying to think of something else to say when Jeff finally speaks. "We signed the divorce papers just before I moved here. She moved out about six months before that, but I guess things were fucked up for a long time."

It's clearly a touchy subject, but Stephan is nosy and hopes Jeff will just tell him to fuck off if he honestly doesn't want to talk about it, and, well, he's nosy. "How long were you together?"

"Seven years," Jeff answers, then he gives a bitter laugh. "Guess what they say about a seven-year itch is true."

Stephan's hand comes up to rest consolingly on Jeff's shoulder for a moment. "Hey, I've never even made it to seven months, until Eric," he offers. "And now that's all screwed up, anyway."

Jeff stops, raising his head to look at the moon for a moment, a thin sliver barely peeking out above a cluster of eucalyptus trees. "Well, I hope you work it out, however will make you most happy. Love shouldn't be boring, but sometimes it's hard to tell whether you just want more than you should or not. And I don't have any answers for you on that score," he says, shaking his head.

"Yeah…. Settling down would be nice, though," and it's not Stephan's fault that he sounds a little wistful. "I want something steady and solid that I can count on, you know? But I still want it to be fun and for the sex to be hot."

Jeff snorts. "Me too. Seems like there should be some middle ground between a responsible but passionless marriage and a sinfully hot affair."

"Yeah. There must be, right? I mean, Billy and Scott have that. They're together in all the married ways, and they still leave their own parties to go fuck each other senseless in their bedroom," he says, smiling.

"Absolutely. Keep the faith, man. Who knows? Maybe it's easier for two guys to make it long term than for straight couples. Their sex drives match better, maybe. It's been ages since I dated anyone, but I recall it being easier," Jeff says, as they reach the car and he digs out his keys.

Wait, what? Stephan's head circles around like he's missed something, but he's not sure. Dating is easier, or dating guys is easier? Jeff has dated guys? What?

Jeff's chuckle breaks him out of his stunned reverie. "Time to go, sweetheart. Let me take you home."

And even though it's not *all* he wants, there really isn't anything Stephan would like better, so he gets in.

Chapter 15
The Talk

CLASSES go by in kind of a blur. He can't stop thinking about what Jeff *maybe* said but probably didn't, no matter how much Stephan wishes he had. It's a puzzle, and he sits in the Intro to American History lecture the next day, watching Jeff and wondering. He knows he's obsessing and should really stop it already, because his crush is getting kind of epic. He also knows that a big part of the reason that's where his mind keeps going is because it's a hell of a lot more pleasant than where his thoughts *should* be—on Eric.

He's *got* to have a talk with his boyfriend. Stretching it out and trying to avoid it is just making him miserable. But goddammit, Stephan *hates* talks like that. He can't see any way out of this fucked-up mess than them breaking up, and he doesn't want that. He wants to make this work; he doesn't want to fail at a relationship again. Eric is a good guy, a good boyfriend. Things were great between them. Even the sex was good, or used to be. If he tries hard enough, Stephan is sure he can figure out what went wrong between them and how to fix it. Maybe Eric will know....

He finally breaks down and texts Eric, because he's a pussy. He's afraid to call his own fucking boyfriend. Or, well, to be brutally honest, he's afraid to call and find out that he doesn't *have* a boyfriend anymore. He doesn't want to break up over the phone, for fuck's sake. How lame and high school would that be?

Hey you. Can you come over tomorrow?

An hour goes by with no response, and then Stephan's phone finally buzzes. *Sure. How about lunch?*

Palms sweating, Stephan texts back. *Dinner's better. OK 4 U?* Everything inside him feels clenched up; a few months ago, they would always call each other back when one of them texted, unless they couldn't talk because of where they were—in class or at work or something. But it's evening, so Stephan knows there's no good reason that Eric's not calling him back. He just doesn't want to.

But then, Stephan's not exactly dialing Eric, either.

Sure. 7?

Sounds good. Been a while, he can't stop himself from adding.

About five minutes pass before Eric answers. *Yeah.*

OVER the course of Friday, Stephan is sure his insides are being replaced with concrete. It's not that he can't breathe, it's that he feels like gravity is pulling on every molecule in his body about a hundred times harder than usual—the elephant isn't standing on his chest; it's trampling all over his body. He couldn't sleep the night before, and he has no clue at all what happened in French today. He thinks they took a quiz, but he can't actually *remember* it, which is a little scary. He started off his morning by spilling the whole pot of coffee all over the floor without actually getting any in his mug. He's a complete fucking nervous wreck, basically.

It's been ten days since he's seen his boyfriend or conversed with him in any way but last night's short texts. Maybe this isn't a big deal in the real world, but in the world of Stephan's head, it's forever. He's seen Jeff twice in that time, hung out with Mike, called Billy, seen Danielle and Tina in class and after, and Kristine during office hours. But not Eric.

Fuck. This is so bad.

Should he clean up the place? His room is kind of a mess, but it's not like Eric will mind. Or, he wouldn't have, in the past. It would be weird if he cleaned up, Stephan decides, but then finds himself scrubbing the kitchen half an hour later without even realizing it. Jim gives him a puzzled look when he gets out the bottle of 409 and starts scouring the stove, but thankfully Jim doesn't ask.

Jamie shows up with takeout for Jim after she gets off work, and the smell is good enough to make Stephan's stomach rumble with the realization that he hasn't eaten anything since the scone he grabbed with his espresso from the coffee cart that morning. He starts to ask what they're having and guilt trip them into offering him some, but then he thinks about actually eating the food, putting it in his mouth and chewing it up, and his stomach positively *lurches* and he feels like he's going to hurl.

And wouldn't that be ironic, since the last time he saw Eric in person, Stephan was puking his guts out in the street? So maybe not.

Eric finally calls and says he's at the Student Center grabbing some food. He asks if Stephan has already eaten or if he wants Eric to bring something back. Eric sounds so casual, so *normal*, that it makes Stephan's head spin. Maybe nothing is wrong? Maybe he's gotten himself all worked up over stuff that's not a big deal? Maybe things are *fine* with Eric, and if he hadn't spent the last two weeks twisting himself up in knots, he'd be able to see that everything is all right. That they're good. Maybe?

Trying to get a grip on the possibility of *nothing being wrong*, Stephan puts in an order for a sandwich and salad, and he can actually hear Eric's smile as Eric ribs him for getting healthy food and then says he'll be there soon. Stephan's head starts to throb. He can't tell if it's from relief or what.

Eric arrives, handing him his food with a kiss on the cheek. They settle down in front of the TV, Jim and Jamie still at the table, and everything is so goddamned normal, so ordinary. Eric seems fine, everything is good. There's still this weird feeling in the air, that feeling like when you're dreaming but you're positive that you're awake, except that even in the dream you know everything seems a little off. It's probably just Stephan's own anxieties and stuff. He's such a spaz, right? He tries to relax, tentatively, laughing a little too loud at the TV show they're watching, but making an effort to just be cool.

It's during a commercial break when Jamie says, "So how are things, Eric? I don't think I've seen you since you guys were getting ready for that costume party a few weeks ago. How was that, by the way?"

Eric mumbles something, so Stephan answers. "It was great. Good music, dancing, you know. Eric's friends know how to party. He even won a prize as Mercury-the-bike-messenger," he says, reaching over to ruffle Eric's hair.

"Yeah, thanks again for your help with the wings. It was fun. Although someone who will remain nameless lost his costume fairly quickly," Eric says, with a smile and a wink.

Eric's teasing him. *Thank God.* "Well, it was hot, dancing. And the E helped too. If I recall correctly, you weren't exactly complaining about my lack of clothes when we were alone together outside," he says, wiggling his eyebrows suggestively.

Jamie and Jim laugh, and so does Stephan. At least he laughs until he notices that Eric's got a humorless smile pasted on his face, making him look more constipated than anything else. Stephan feels that knot of tension back in his stomach.

When the show starts again, the other two start cleaning up their mess from dinner. When they finish with the dishes and leftovers, they go into Jim's room, and Eric grabs the remote and turns off the TV.

"Uh, I think we're going to have to talk about that party and some stuff," Eric says in a quiet voice.

Stephan blinks, his nerves coming back full force. Everything seemed like it was going well just a few minutes ago. What the hell happened? Shit, he should have known. "Uh, that doesn't sound good."

"No. It's really not." Eric gets up and waits for Steph to join him.

"Ohhhkay… so I guess we should go to my room?"

Eric nods and precedes him, holding the door, and once Stephan is in, closes it behind them.

"I've been thinking a lot, ever since that party. And after driving you home that night you went to the Red Room and got wasted."

Stephan can feel the hairs on his neck prickle and starts to get defensive. He didn't do anything *wrong*, either of those nights. He's not an alcoholic, and it's not like he was screwing around on Eric or anything. But Eric seems to have some kind of speech rehearsed, so Stephan takes a breath and tries to just listen.

"I had a lot of time over the summer to think about what I wanted out of life, the kind of person I want to be. I see how my mom drinks all the time, and I don't want to be like that. I know I'm friends with Chad and he's a fucking mess, and you're nothing like that. I know it's just recreational for you and your friends—well, except for Mike, maybe—and you don't see it as a problem, but... it kind of is for me." He bites his lip and meets Stephan's eyes for the first time since he shut the bedroom door. "I know you're just blowing off steam and having fun. And—" He swallows a little, forcing the next few words out. "I love you, but I don't... I don't think we want the same things."

Stephan's knees threaten to buckle, so he sits down on his bed. *Holy shit.* After a moment, Eric sits down beside him, but they're still far enough apart that they're not touching at all.

After a while, Stephan says, "I didn't realize it was something relating to your family. Guess I should have, when you seemed to sort of change how you felt about drinking and stuff after you came back this fall." Eric shrugs and nods at the same time, picking at a thread at the cuff of his jeans. "It's not like it's something I have to do, though," Stephan says. "I mean, I'm twenty-four. I could settle down some. Stop acting like a kid."

Eric sighs, shaking his head a little. "It's not like you're *forty*. You shouldn't have to settle. Settle down or settle for me. And I don't want to feel like I'm what you're settling for."

Stephan opens his mouth to deny that, but then finds that he can't. Eric's watching him, and Stephan knows those are the words he should say, but they seem stuck somehow, and won't come out.

Biting his lip, Eric nods. "I think everything else has been really good with us, hanging out and being friends and stuff, but maybe we shouldn't have sex."

No sex? Stephan clears his throat. "So... does that mean we're breaking up?"

"I guess so."

The two deep breaths Stephan takes don't help with the pressure in his chest at all. It's not like this was a huge surprise or anything, but somehow dreading it doesn't seem to have actually prepared him or made this easier to deal with in any way. He can hear his voice getting all scratchy as he talks around the tightness in his throat. "So... what then? That's it? I mean, I could stop. It's not like drinking or drugs are that important to me. I want to try to make this work. With you." God, he sounds so fucking pathetic. What's wrong with him?

Eric's mouth twists into a half-smile for a second, there and then gone. He reaches out a hand and holds Stephan's. They're both clammy. "I don't know. Maybe I'm just really self-involved. I mean, it's been almost two weeks and I didn't even call you. I think there are other problems too." He squeezes Stephan's hand, closing his eyes as he continues, hesitant. "I like being with you, and all, and the sex was really great, at least for me. But I think maybe we're not that compatible. It doesn't seem like you get what you want from me very often. And I don't want to feel like you're not satisfied. I want to be enough for someone."

"Maybe I just want too much."

Eric shakes his head. "I don't think so. I think we just want different things."

They both sit for a while, thinking about that. It's sad and it hurts, but it feels like the truth. And there's not much Stephan can do to argue with the truth.

"So what do we do?" he asks.

"I guess I leave." Eric's voice is rough, nearly a whisper. He touches Stephan's hand a little hesitantly, twining their fingers for what they both know is the last time. Neither of them knows what to say. They nod and dredge up weak half-smiles for each other.

"So yeah. I guess I'll see you later," Eric says, getting up.

Stephan nods again. "Yeah. I mean, I hope so."

"Me too."

And Eric leaves, closing the bedroom door behind him.

Chapter 16
Rain

AFTER Eric leaves, Stephan sits on his bed for a long time, staring into space. He has no idea what to do with himself. He tries to study after a while, but feels like that's too normal. Like he should be more upset or something. Not get drunk or all dramatic, but *something*. Like, if he smoked, he could go outside and sit and smoke and be all pensive or stoic or some shit. Or he could totally fag out and eat a pint of Ben and Jerry's ice cream, make Danielle come over to watch chick flicks, and cry or something. Neither of those sounds like good enough ideas to actually do, though, so instead he reads for a while, answers an e-mail from his mom, and then goes out to the living room to see what Jim and Jamie are doing.

Jamie's gone and Jim is watching hockey on TV. Stephan has no idea if it's a live game, or a best-of, or if it's even hockey season. He had no idea that Jim *watched* hockey, but whatever. He grabs a beer and joins him on the sofa.

They watch and drink, and men on skates hit a little puck around on the ice. It's kind of boring, but better than a chick flick.

"Jamie gave Eric a ride home. Did you guys break up?" Jim asks during a commercial break.

"Yeah."

Jim nods. "Sorry."

"Yeah. Me too." Stephan finishes his beer and starts picking at the label. "I knew it was coming, but…. Yeah."

"Yeah."

There's a silence, not too awkward, just *there*. Jim gets up, goes to the fridge, and brings back another beer for each of them, and they sit and watch the rest of the game.

Thank God for straight men.

SOMETIME in the night the first rain of autumn starts. It's not particularly cold, but without the sunshine everyone suddenly realizes that it's not actually summer anymore and maybe it's time to stop wearing shorts and flip-flops. Midterms are next week, and aside from the required first-rain-of-the-school-year-naked-Frisbee game it's a fairly mellow day in the apartments. And sure, Stephan went to check out the ridiculous undergrads, but he only ogled the guys a little, and he would have done that even if he was still with Eric.

Also, girl boobs? Very weird. They're round and jiggly and he kind of gets how that could be appealing, only not really. Not in bed, certainly. He is so very, very gay.

The library is empty that afternoon, and his table is free, so he settles in for some serious work and manages to be pretty productive. He has three Americanos and one latte, pretending that the milk counts as food because he's not hungry. Anyway, that evening is the "grading party" at Jeff's, with Lauren and Will and pizza, so he'll eat then.

It dawns on him that he's in kind of a funk sometime around sunset. He's not depressed, exactly, and he's a little embarrassed to consider it, but he kind of wonders if he's faking being upset simply because he thinks he *should* be upset. His longest relationship to date is over, and he still has no real clue what he did wrong, if anything. Or what went wrong, what he could maybe have done to make things better. And deep down, even though he wishes he had some answers to that and he feels some sadness when he thinks about not seeing or touching Eric ever again, mostly he feels kind of relieved.

That makes him a totally horrible person, he knows. Then again, things have sucked for about a month now, and well, at least it's over, right? He can move on with his life and do whatever he wants. Now, if only he knew what that was....

Sighing, Stephan packs up his messenger bag, debates going home first and decides to just go to Jeff's a little early. At least that way he can get in his vote for pizza toppings before anyone else. The rain has faded into a drizzle, so he walks, enjoying the brisk air and the feeling of being washed clean by nature. The campus is beautiful like this, with patches of fog hanging around the tops of the trees, making everything feel ethereal and otherworldly.

Okay, yeah—he might be a little lightheaded from lack of protein.

Jeff answers the door, hair wet and obviously fresh out of the shower. He offers Stephan a coffee or beer, but Stephan decides to go with a soda since his stomach is so empty. It growls, and when Jeff raises an eyebrow at him, he admits he hasn't eaten all day.

"I made a green salad, and I've got some olives and cheese and stuff to snack on. Help me set it all up, and you can start on that while we wait for the other two to get here," Jeff offers.

Sounds like a deal, so Stephan is opening boxes of breadsticks and slicing cheese and stuff while Jeff manages to turn out a fairly nice-looking appetizer platter.

"Look at you, all Martha Stewarty," he teases.

Jeff snorts and shoves him a little. "Shut up. This is the first time I've had anything resembling 'company' in my new house."

"Well then, let's party," Stephan grins, carrying the platter into the living room and starting to demolish it immediately. Jeff follows with plates and napkins, making a show of tsking at Stephan's lack of table manners. Stephan retaliates with an impressive belch, and they're both still laughing when Will knocks on the door.

Lauren arrives shortly after, and they get settled in after minimal chatting and placing an order to the Student Center for a couple of pizzas. Jeff distributes the papers the students turned in yesterday, and they start by each reading one. When they're finished, Jeff goes over the assignment instructions, and then they start talking about how well the papers they just read met the criteria.

"What about these atrocious grammar mistakes?" Will asks. "This guy doesn't seem to know that sentences need an active verb in them."

"Oh please. Mine started her paper with 'Since the dawn of history…'," Lauren scoffs.

"Come on now, guys, most of these kids are freshmen. Be nice," Stephan says. "We were all idiots when we were that age."

"I thought you said you were going to be the hard-ass, way back when?" Jeff reminds him. "But he's right; you have to go easy. You can correct the mistakes, sure, but be careful not to be too condescending. If you get a paper that's really awful, don't cover it with red ink; just make a note at the end suggesting that the kid get some help from the writing tutors. Try to follow the guideline of one compliment for each couple criticisms. Be liberal with comments like 'good point' and 'insightful'."

With that in mind, Jeff has them each actually grade the papers they read, and then they pass them over to Jeff, who looks at them and gives some feedback. They discuss each one, what the student did right and what they got wrong. That's pretty much the model they follow for the next few papers, working at their own pace and handing them to Jeff as they finish until the pizza arrives.

It's not the most exciting Saturday evening Stephan's ever had, but it's actually kind of nice having some company while he works. At some point Jeff tells them each that they've got the hang of it, and he doesn't need to see their comments anymore. He opens his laptop and starts on his own work, keeping them company and fielding questions as they come up.

Then Will gets a paper that makes him stop. "Wait. Stephan, that first paper that you read, can I see it for a minute?" Stephan passes it over, and after a minute Will groans. "We have a problem."

"What?" Lauren asks.

"I don't know who wrote the original, but these two are almost completely identical. Whoever the cheater is, she paraphrased the other girl, but the content is exactly the same and in the same order."

They both turn to Jeff, who sighs. "Just give them to me. I'll deal with it."

"But… she's my student," Will starts to insist. "I should say something, shouldn't I?"

Jeff shakes his head. "No, I'm the official instructor, and I'll have to file the paperwork with the Academic Provost. I think I'm supposed to meet with the students first, though… I'll have to call the department and see. But don't worry about it; it's one of the annoying things you don't have to deal with until you're faculty."

"Big Daddy gonna have to open a can of whup-ass, huh?" Lauren says with a laugh.

For some reason that makes Stephan have a very disturbing flashback to being in the library with Jeff and talking about kinky sex. He shoves almost a whole slice of pizza in his mouth, trying to cover up his sudden flustered feeling, and almost chokes.

Lauren pounds him on the back. "You have to relax your throat," she winks.

Being swallowed up by a hole in the ground would be nice right about now, but no such luck. He can die of embarrassment or laugh it off. "Never had any complaints so far," he manages, after a drink of soda. Jeff winks at him when he glances that direction, and something hot flashes through Stephan's body. His heart beats faster, and he can't quite believe he made a joke about sucking cock in front of his *professor*. But then, Jeff's not just his professor or his boss; he's a friend. Right?

After a few hours, they decide to call it quits. It's still early, and they're only about halfway done with the papers, but they've got the hang of it, and Jeff says he feels confident in them. That gives Stephan another warm fuzzy, but in a different way. They're instructed to e-mail Jeff with any questions they have, no matter how small; he'd rather answer them than have them worry about making a mistake. It's a good feeling to know that he's got their backs on this whole TA business, and Will and Lauren take off with smiles and hugs, respectively.

Stephan lingers a few minutes longer, helping clean up. He kind of wants to hang out, but feels awkward and weird, and after hesitating for a few seconds, he grabs his backpack and gets ready to take off. "All right, I'm going to get out of your hair," he calls into the kitchen.

Jeff ambles out, drying his hands on a dishtowel. He nods. "You did good tonight, Steph. I'm proud of you guys."

His ears are hot and Stephan knows he's blushing like an idiot, not to mention grinning like one. He feels hot and his blood is circulating too fast and his hands are sweating, and he really needs to get out *now*, before he does something stupid like hug Jeff or something. He lifts a hand in a dork-assed little wave and practically runs for the door, a strangled, "See ya," catching in his throat.

The mist from earlier has turned into a drizzle with the evening temperature drop, and by the time Stephan's walked to the shuttle stop, it's full-on raining. He waits, trying to fit under the kiosk and mostly getting himself wet in favor of keeping his bag with his laptop dry. After a while, once the water is running down his face and he's starting to get chilled, he looks at the timetable posted on the kiosk wall. No shuttles on the weekend after eight o'clock. It's nine-thirty. Fucking great.

He starts walking up the hill back to his apartment. He's tired but it's not that late and he feels… well, weird. A little wired, not as relaxed and happy with life as he usually does after hanging out with Jeff. Usually it's easy, being with Jeff. Tonight wasn't hard or strained or anything, but it was strange having Will and Lauren there, like it threw off the balance somehow. He's so used to working with Jeff when it's just the two of them in the library….

And Jesus, he should be all emo about Eric breaking up with him last night. He is, sort of, but… not like he thinks he should be. He'd much rather think about Jeff. He doesn't know what happened with Eric, and it's sad, but it's over. It just didn't work out, and really, it feels like it's been over for a long time anyway. It was a long summer, and they never reconnected after that, and now that it's done…. Well, it's *done*.

He mostly feels relieved to be able to stop stressing out about it.

Which is due in no small part to Jeff. Sure, his crush is epic and ridiculous and trite, but Jesus fucking Christ, Jeff is hot. He's got a body that seems solid and strongly muscular, yet he's actually pretty lean from what Stephan has been able to see. The gray in his beard makes him look a lot older than he is, but it's sexy, and not because Stephan has twinky Daddy issues.

Besides all of that, though, Jeff is... he's great. He's smart—obviously—but he's smart in the things Stephan wants to know about. And he listens to Stephan like he's not an idiot, and he's had some insightful things to say when he's listened to Stephan bitch and moan about school. And his love life. Hell, they even like the same kinds of music and food.

Jeff would probably make a way better boyfriend than Eric ever had. If he wasn't straight.

But maybe he's *not*. He hadn't freaked out or seemed weird at all when he'd found out Stephan was gay. Not that not being a homophobe meant that Jeff secretly liked dick himself, but still. He hadn't been uncomfortable listening to Stephan talk about being queer. Sure, the guy had been married to a woman, but maybe he was bi?

In fact, now that he's thinking about it, Stephan wonders if Jeff's been flirting with him. Sometimes he gets this look in his eyes that makes Stephan's whole body react, and he knows he's got it bad for Jeff, and no, he *hasn't* been getting laid enough, but still. He's not making it all up, is he?

Is he?

Stephan looks up and sees that somehow, he's walked in a complete circle and is standing on Jeff's porch. He's drenched, soaked through, water running down his face like he's in the shower. He has no idea what he's doing here, or even when he turned around and started walking back.

The lightbulb cover on Jeff's porch is cracked and appears to be largely held together by spider webs. This seems somehow more significant than it probably is, and Stephan wonders briefly if he got high or drunk somehow without noticing it. Or maybe he's gone insane. Maybe the stress of school and life and crushes and ending a relationship has caused him to have a mental breakdown. Maybe he's finally lost it.

That seems likely.

He's still standing there, looking at the spider webs, when the door opens.

"Stephan? I thought I heard something out here. Did you forget something?"

Stephan blinks and his eyelashes are wet and they stick together. *Did* he forget something? He isn't sure. Jeff has changed into a T-shirt that's tight around his shoulders, and Stephan is utterly distracted by the tattoos he can finally see, that he hasn't even known had been driving him crazy with curiosity until just now. He starts to reach out to touch his fingertip to a Celtic-style cross but gets distracted and pauses to watch as water drips down his hand.

"You're fucking soaked," Jeff says with a chuckle, sounding a little confused, but he's got nothing on Stephan, who seems to be struck dumb. He feels like he's stuck in slow motion when Jeff grabs his wrist and tugs him forward, then lets go and turns around. "Let me go get you a towel."

"No, wait." Time speeds up again for a moment, and Stephan is moving, reaching for Jeff, grabbing him by the arms and sliding his hands up Jeff's shoulders. It's like he's watching his body from somewhere outside, seeing every detail of the wet handprints he's leaving on Jeff's shirt, the way Jeff's forehead crinkles in confusion for a moment, the way his mouth opens in surprise a second before Stephan's lips touch his.

Jeff's stubble is longer than he's used to and it prickles, making Jeff's lips seem so, so soft. Jeff's surprised—hell, *Stephan* is surprised—but after a moment of just standing there, Jeff's hands lightly touch Stephan's waist, and the kiss turns from something tentative and uncertain into something soft and sweet. It feels like longing and perfection and everything Stephan's ever wanted, and it's nearly too much, too *gentle,* or something.

Jeff makes a small noise in the back of his throat, but then his body goes tense under Stephan's hands. He pulls his head back, breaking the kiss, even as he wraps his arms around Stephan and pulls him close. It's only for a moment—Stephan's cold, wet clothing soaking up the warmth of Jeff's body—and then Jeff is holding him at arm's length.

"Stephan. We really can't do this."

Stephan looks at the dark spots his wet clothes have left on Jeff's. He blinks a moment and a slight breeze from the still-open door behind him raises goose bumps on the back of his neck. He bites his lip so hard it almost bleeds as he nods. One step backward and he's back out in the rain, his pace picking up into a jog as he hears the distant sound of Jeff's voice behind him, calling his name.

Chapter 17
Midterms

STEPHAN *really* does not want to go to class on Monday afternoon. He slides in the door at the last possible minute with the final stragglers, and takes a seat in the front row next to Will and Lauren, cringing at almost being late. He'd spent all of Sunday at home rather than at his table in the library, in case Jeff showed up. He hadn't left his apartment except to do laundry in the next-door building, even though he'd meant to go to the grocery store too. But there's only one store close to the campus, and well. He's hiding from Jeff, basically.

He can't fucking believe he kissed Jeff. It was like he was in a trance or something, all logical thought and reasoning totally suspended. It was unplanned, impulsive, and frankly a little weird. Not like he's always planning things out, but… well. It was a mistake. One he'd wanted to make for about two months, but a mistake all the same.

Jeff knows that. Probably knew all about Stephan's gay little crush; he certainly knows now. God, he can't believe he's so fucking stupid sometimes….

At the end of the lecture, when Stephan is hoping for a quick getaway, Jeff asks the TAs to hang back for a few minutes. The kids clear out and he can't run; this is his *job*. He joins the other three at the table at the front of the classroom.

"I just wanted to check in and see that you guys were doing okay, if you'd run into any problems?" They all respond in the negative, and Jeff nods, pleased by their answer. "Will the papers be ready to return by Wednesday?" They will, and Jeff makes a note in his planner, saying that he's going to go over some of the common problems of writing about history in the next session, now that the students have all had a little taste of the process. A mini-historiography lecture, he says, winking at Stephan. He drags up a pretty feeble smile in return, and Jeff's expression changes into something concerned. "All right then, see you guys on Wednesday," he says. "Don't forget to call or e-mail if you have any questions at all, okay?"

Will and Lauren take off, and Stephan tries to slink away with them, but is stopped when Jeff grabs him by the arm. "Hang on, Stephan, I want to talk to you for a minute."

He turns around, trying not to cringe, unable to meet Jeff's eyes. Is he going to get fired? Told to find another TA job? Reported for violating the student conduct rules? *Shit.* He starts to hyperventilate.

"Stephan." A quick glance shows that Jeff looks concerned, not angry. "Hey, look," he says, squeezing Stephan's shoulder. "It's fine. Really. You don't have to feel weird about this, okay?"

He doesn't? Why not? Huh.

He nods.

"Feel like getting a beer?"

Stephan shrugs. This is not what he expected, Jeff being all... *normal.* Not that he'd expected anything, but he thought it would be bad, whatever it was. He takes a deep breath, hesitating.

"Come on. Have a beer with me," Jeff wheedles. He shoves his papers and miscellaneous stuff into his messenger bag and slings it over his shoulder. "Just at the Student Center. I'll even buy."

"Well, if you're buying, that changes everything," Stephan manages to joke, and they turn to go. Their walk is filled with Jeff talking about his discovery that the Student Center makes falafel and gyro wraps, and that he'd spent a lazy Sunday afternoon there watching some kids play pool, working on his class notes, and talking to Demetrios, the café owner.

Jeff insists on buying him lunch, too, and Jeff was right—Stephan had forgotten how good the Greek food is here. The sandwiches suck, the pizza and salads are all right, and everything else is kind of "eh," but the falafel really is damn good. The lunch special comes with a huge plate of fries, which they share. If Stephan jerks back like his fingers have been burned the one time their hands meet reaching for fries at the same time, well, Jeff has the good grace to ignore it.

Maybe things will be sort of all right after all.

Not that Stephan isn't a *huge* fucking idiot or anything, but still. Maybe the consequences of his brain taking a vacation and letting his body lead the show for one horribly mistaken minute aren't that big of a deal. If Jeff's willing to not only ignore it, but still try to be friends with Stephan, he's not going to argue. It's way more than he hoped for.

THE rest of the week drags by in fits of anxiousness and stress, interspersed with huge lulls of boredom. Midterms are this week, but Stephan's only test is in French. Instead, he has paper proposals due for Method and Theory and American Lit. He's been working on those for the last couple of weeks, so he's feeling fairly set. At least, when he's being rational. These are the only big assignments he will turn in for both classes, and he's a little freaked out. He's not sure what exactly he's freaked out about, aside from some nebulous feeling that the professors are going to tell him his proposals suck, he sucks, and he should just drop out of school now and save them all the trouble of failing him.

Yeah. Because that's even slightly realistic. He's a hard worker, a good student, always prepared, and he usually has something to contribute to the discussions. He's even totally caught up in his reading, after a weekend of being a loser and hiding out in the library and his apartment. His professors seem to like him. So why does he still have a knot in his stomach?

Maybe it's vicarious—tension on campus ratchets up to a huge degree during midterms week, to say nothing of finals. Everyone's got that sleepless, terrified look in their eyes, and the freshmen look like they could cry at any moment. The girls are all in sweats with their hair twisted into sloppy buns held in place with pencils, and the guys look like they've been wearing the same clothes since they arrived in August. Kids are sleeping on the sofas scattered around the library, and the people working at the coffee carts can barely keep up with the demand.

It's actually kind of funny, in a *schadenfreude* sort of way.

Of course when Madame Georges starts prepping them for the French midterm, Stephan totally freaks out. Memorization is *not* his strongest skill, and while he's been doing fine on the weekly quizzes, he's worried about being able to recall stuff from two months ago.

Plus, the teacher is some kind of sadist or something because it's not "just" a test; she's giving them a project instead. They have to pretend that they're travel agents and pitch a trip to a French-speaking country to the teacher, one on one. The brochure is something they can make at home and use their textbooks for, but they're not allowed to bring any notes with them to the presentation aside from the brochure itself. She'll ask questions and they'll have to answer. It's the cruelest thing Stephan's ever heard of, and he kind of admires Mme. Georges as much as he fears her evil sense of humor.

"I want to see an obituary for any grandmothers who happen to pass away on Friday," she says, and he can tell that she's only mostly joking. He went to her office once, and her white board had a number of silhouettes of bent-over stick figures with walking canes sketched next to the last three years and the note "Deceased Grandparents— Don't Let this Happen to Yours!" Funny woman. Crazy, but funny.

Anyway, he turns in his paper proposals and focuses on the stupid French presentation, deciding to go to Montreal, since he's actually been there and doesn't have to do a ton of new research. She's only given them a few days to prepare, which is a little unfair, he thinks. On the other hand, making up a brochure at home and then answering no more than ten minutes' worth of questions can't be *that* hard.

Probably.

Jamie's knowledge of Microsoft Office's programs is truly impressive, and Stephan manages to talk her into helping him design the brochure in exchange for washing and vacuuming out her car before she drives Jim home to meet her extended family for Thanksgiving. She's got this weird look in her eyes when she talks about it, and Stephan wonders if she's going to come back from the holiday with a sparkly ring on her finger, and makes a note to ask Jim later. Not that

Jim could *afford* a diamond, although if he can, Stephan is totally going to start drinking more of his excellent beer and not feel at all bad about it.

They get the thing done in record time, and then Stephan's spending every waking minute of Thursday trying to memorize all of the phrases he used and anticipate what Mme. Georges might ask him and how he'll answer. He's twisting a coffee-stirrer straw into knots, glad that his students are mostly too busy studying to show up to his office hours in the Student Center, as he rehearses his script.

"If any more kids ask me to quiz them on German nouns, I'm going to strangle them," Kristine says, sitting down at Stephan's table. "Seriously, how hard is it to study on your own or force your housemates to help you? I've got better things to do with my time."

"So do I," Stephan says, giving her a significant look as he taps the straw against his papers.

"Like I care," she says, rolling her eyes at him. "You're so over-prepared for your classes, you can probably teach them all next year. Tina said you were making everybody else look bad in M&T."

He shrugs. "Not my fault your girlfriend's a slacker." She punches him in the shoulder, of course, and *damn*, she hits hard. "All right, all right. Sorry."

They bitch and moan at each other for a while, until another frazzled-looking student comes up to Kristine to ask for help. At least this one isn't just asking her to do drills with him, but it seems like he's been floundering and behind on his memorization for about the last five weeks—out of eight. He silently wishes her luck as he goes to get more coffee for himself and a cookie for her. At least his Intro Am Hist students are all relaxed because they've already turned in their papers, and aren't bugging *him*.

The barista is cute, about Stephan's height or a little shorter, slim build, loose blond curls, and big blue eyes. He's got the lithe build that probably means he surfs, and the tan to go with it. Stephan bets he looks hot in a wetsuit.

The guy is friendly, maybe overly friendly. Stephan could totally hit on him. He smiles a little bigger than is necessary and gets a blinding grin in return. When the barista drops the lid to the coffee cup, the apron strings outline a nice, perky ass, and Stephan feels lust swirl around his body and center in his groin.

He could probably have that, if he wanted to. But instead, he lets the tension linger there between them while they trade dollar bills for coffee and food. When the barista offers his name—Dylan—Stephan gives his in return. Then he just turns away and says, "Catch you later, Dylan," wondering what the fuck is wrong with him that he could totally *have* this hot guy—with a nice body, who makes *coffee*—but he doesn't want him.

At all.

FRIDAY is a fucking relief. Stephan is one of the first in line to see Mme. Georges, bright and early at nine-thirty. He's got his coffee, he's got a muffin, his brochure is awesome, and he's nervous but trying to relax. It's only a midterm. It counts as one-fourth of his grade, and he knows he won't totally bomb it.

The ten minutes fly by, and although she smirks that he's chosen *Canada*, he actually remembers all the right words and only has to ask her to repeat herself twice when her accent and talking speed confuse him. He's sure he's speaking as slowly as someone who just woke up from a coma, but she doesn't make any horrible faces or correct him, so he assumes it's going all right. When he's done, she says in English that he did well. He needs to work on his confidence—ha!—and accent, and could stand a review of verb tenses, but she's pretty lenient and he gets an A.

The rest of the day floats by on a cloud of relief, and he goes back to Danielle's place after American Lit to celebrate midterms being over. Her housemate and her respective boyfriend talk them into going out for Chinese together, and then watching a movie on TV at home. It's cozy, curling up with Danni on the sofa; when he wraps his arms around her, she feels like she's managed to put a little meat back on her bones. Life is good.

Mostly.

Chapter 18
Mud Bathing

HEY guys. Just wanted to give you a heads-up that I posted a message on the class webpage and will be making an announcement in class on Monday—all TA sections are cancelled for the week (as are my office hours). I think everyone needs a break, and this is a good point in the semester to take one. Enjoy your time off! - Jeff

The e-mail is addressed to all three TAs, but Stephan's is followed by another short message, only to him: *Will my canceling the TA sessions free you up enough to take me hiking on Tuesday or Thursday afternoon this week? The library is nice, but I miss the trees. I remember you said you liked hiking.*

He's got to give the guy credit for making an effort to not act weird, that's for sure. Maybe things like that are simply easier when you're older. Sure, it's embarrassing to kiss a friend and not have them kiss you back, but not any more of a big deal than getting caught tripping over a shoelace or farting on the toilet. Everyone does it at some point, and it's best if you both try to forget about it as fast as possible.

And a day of hiking *does* sound pretty fabulous. The weather has been crisp and cool, but sunny. In another few weeks, it'll be cold and perpetually overcast; winter on the Pacific Coast equals rain and lots of it, so this is an ideal time to sneak in some outdoor activity before it gets overly cold and wet. He'd love to blow off M&T and take the whole day, but there's no way he can do that, so he e-mails Jeff and suggests they meet at Grad Student Housing around noon.

The next few days are uneventful for Stephan. He's been trying not to brood too much, but he finds that he misses Eric. Or, well, maybe not Eric himself, but having a boyfriend, or at least the *idea* of having a boyfriend. And he can't believe he was such a fucking idiot with Jeff. He's such a loser. Stephan knows he's handsome, yeah; he's smart; he's also *alone*. His iPod is on "emo whiner music" and he's not changing it, no matter who makes fun of him (Kristine). If he's not allowed to mope over being single and fucking up yet *another* relationship—and he still isn't even sure what happened there, really— then when is he allowed to mope? He can't ever make things work, and maybe he should stop trying and just be satisfied with casual sex. That should be fine, right? Right. Simple, uncomplicated sex. Now, if only he'd stop lusting after inappropriate people....

Stephan is making a sincere effort to be relaxed, calm, and poised on Tuesday afternoon as he waits for Jeff, but of course all his intentions go to shit when Jeff turns up wearing a T-shirt that is simply not *fair*. How is he supposed to get over his stupid crush and focus on only being friends when Jeff insists on wearing something that soft and clingy? Stephan can barely resist reaching out and touching it, tracing his fingers across the muscles of Jeff's shoulders, licking the tattoo on his forearm, running his hands across that flat stomach, and dipping his fingertips into Jeff's bellybutton. Seriously, how is that fair?

It's not. Jeff clearly hates him. God too.

This is nothing different from how Stephan usually feels, so he just takes a deep breath and looks away when Jeff bends over to fix the laces on his hiking boots. He's not going to look at his ass. Uh-uh.

"So I thought we'd stay on campus, actually, if that's okay with you?" Stephan asks. He gets a quirked brow, and adds, "'Campus' technically includes this huge parcel of land, almost double the size that all the buildings and stuff are on. It was a ranch, way back when, and lime quarry. They also did some logging up there, and there are a ton of trails through the forest that makes up the north part of the property."

"Yeah? Sounds great. How far back does it go?"

"I'm not sure. Jim says something like three hundred acres and then it switches into state park land, but there's not exactly a line drawn to show you when you cross over. It's really gorgeous, though. If you like redwoods."

"Love them," Jeff says with a wink. "It'll feel just like back home, only less wet."

That remark turns out to be a massive jinx. They're about an hour and a half from the trailhead, up in the woods, enjoying each other's company but not talking a whole lot. It's quiet and serene, and Jeff has secret wilderness skills and can identify most of the plants and animals, so Stephan obligingly asks him to show off when they run across something he doesn't recognize. It's still, very quiet, and when Stephan comments on how the only birds he hears are the occasional screeches of the ever-present scrub jays, Jeff stops walking.

"You're right. It's quiet. Too quiet. And is it always this humid?"

Stephan shrugs. "I don't know. Been a while since I've come up here. It's a little late in the season, but it's not cold yet." He's trying to figure out why Jeff's looking uneasy and hesitating when a fat drop of rain hits him on the head. "Aw, fuck."

The fat drops turn into a heavy downpour before Stephan can get his wits about him. The trees are so dense that they can't see the sky very well at all, and Jeff says he can't tell if this is a storm or a brief cloudburst, without seeing. Stephan points out that it doesn't matter anyway because they're both soaked to the bone already, and since they're uphill, their trail is now a tiny stream, and it's just going to get bigger and more slippery as the water washes downhill and turns the red dust into clay, even if the rain itself stops.

"Well then, I guess it's a bust. Head back?"

"Yeah." Stephan leads the way, since he's the one who knows the trail better, although Jeff could probably find his way back without help. He's even got a walking stick that he picked up early on in their walk. As the mud gets slippery, Stephan begins to wish he had one of his own, but oh no, he was too cocky for that. He'd teased Jeff about it, ribbing him for being an overly careful old man. Jeff had laughed and said it was for fighting off mountain lions, but maybe he'd let the lions eat Stephan's young, tasty flesh while he ran for it, instead.

"Fuck!" A piece of rocky shale breaks off under his foot unexpectedly, and Stephan's down. His ankle hurts when he flexes it, and his ego may be fatally wounded. "Ow."

Jeff plants his stick in the mud carefully, then leans down to give Stephan a hand up. "You all right? You went down pretty hard."

"Fine. Just bruises, I think." He takes Jeff's hand and lets him assist. The rain is *still* coming down in buckets, and now Stephan is drenched and cold and muddy. He tries to put his weight on his good ankle, and manages to slip again, pulling Jeff down on top of him.

"Ow," he says again, once he catches his breath. Jeff is *heavy*. Well, okay, anyone would be heavy if they just *fell* on you, even Danielle. But still. This was definitely *not* how he'd imagined it. "Goddamnit."

"Oof. That went well," Jeff says, struggling back off of Stephan.

The shared body heat is kind of nice—too nice, and not just because Jeff's body is shielding Stephan from the relentless rain—but there's a rock digging into Stephan's shoulder and his ankle hurts and fucking *fuck*. "Fuck," he says with meaning.

"Yeah. Okay, we're gonna try this real slow, all right?" Jeff asks. Stephan nods. Jeff carefully gets on all fours, then pushes up to his feet. He plants his body weight in cautiously, using the stick as a balance point, then leans over and helps Stephan shift around. "On three," he says, and they manage to heave Stephan's huge ass out of the squelching, sucking mud, and he's up, one hand in Jeff's, one sharing Jeff's walking stick, and standing on one foot like some kind of bird—a flamingo or something.

He carefully puts his foot down, testing it, while the rain sluices the mud off his backside. "I think I'll be all right, just have to go slow."

"Not sprained, then?" Jeff asks. "Just a bad twist?"

"Yeah, I think so." He's kind of mortified when Jeff reaches out and wraps an arm around his waist, insisting on taking some of Stephan's weight for the first few steps, just in case. Again, Jeff's body heat is disconcerting, but it's more than that. Stephan's ankle hurts and his shoulder is killing him, and he's cold and wet and pretty sure he's got mud in his hair and down the back of his pants, and he must look ridiculous. And the guy he's got a fucking *humongous* crush on is being so nice and helpful, even after Stephan threw himself at him, despite the fact that Jeff's obviously *straight*, or at the very least, not into Stephan....

"Life sucks."

"Aw, poor baby. Come on, we'll get you down the hill, and you can take a bubble bath and I'll make you some cocoa."

"Fuck off," Stephan says, but he smiles despite himself. "You'd better put a shot of Bailey's in that cocoa, at least."

Jeff grins. "Absolutely, princess. Anything for you."

They hobble for a few steps, and Stephan tentatively gets confident enough to shrug out of Jeff's embrace. He misses the arm around him, but he's not going to milk the situation for false physical comfort. He might be pathetic, but he's got his limits.

The way back down to the trailhead is steep, but they arrive without further incident. Stephan's mostly walked off the pain in his ankle, so there's obviously no serious damage. They're both cold and wet, so he's not surprised that Jeff follows him into his apartment without discussion.

"Jesus Christ," Jim says. "What the hell did you do, go play in the mud?"

"Yes, that's it exactly," Stephan says in his driest voice as he bends over to unlace his clay-coated boots. "This genius is my housemate, Jim," he tells Jeff. "How about some towels, asshole?"

Jim scowls at him. "Not if you're going to be a dick."

Jamie appears from the hallway, arms full of towels. "Play nicely, boys, or I'll send you to your rooms."

"Sounds good to me," Jim says, wiggling his eyebrows. A moment later he's swooping her up his arms and carrying her into his room to the sound of giggles and smooching. Stephan ignores them, tossing a towel to Jeff with a belated, "The domestic goddess is Jamie. I still don't know what she's doing with Jim."

Jeff quirks his eyebrow. "Sounds like she's fucking him," he says, then, "oh, that's better," as he dries off his face.

Stephan does the same, running it over the back of his head, and isn't surprised when it comes away covered in mud. He strips off his T-shirt and begins the frustrating process of peeling off his wet and filthy jeans. He's carefully not looking at Jeff, beyond a few glances out of the corner of his eye that confirm that Jeff is stripping too. Thank God he's shivering with cold and unlikely to pop a boner. Then again, he's not going to tempt fate by looking, because God hasn't been on Stephan's side lately.

"Damn, kid. How is it fair that you get a body like that as well as such a gorgeous face?" Jeff asks, shaking his head.

Stephan's startled into a quick look. *Shit!* "Not like you have anything to be jealous of," he responds automatically. Fucking *Christ*, Jeff's body is… It's… *it's in his living room. Almost naked!*

He feels his cock stir in his soaking wet boxers and casually bends forward to dry off, ignoring the compliment. "You're the guest, do you want the first shower?"

"I didn't realize we were still standing on formalities," Jeff snorts. "But hell yeah, I can tell you're going to be in there for a long time, getting all the crap off of you. I'll be fast, I promise."

Stephan sighs, but Jeff's got a point. He goes to get some sweats or something for Jeff to put on after, and has a sudden bad moment when he turns into a teenager again, thinking of Jeff wearing his clothes. His *underwear*. Then he remembers that he's in his mid-twenties and should try to act like it, and throws a pair of relatively unworn boxers in the pile, along with some socks. Are Jeff's feet the same size as his? Would he want to borrow shoes or just wear his own wet boots home?

Stephan is banging the loose mud off Jeff's boots and putting them in front of the heater to dry a little when Jeff opens the bathroom door and a wave of steam comes rushing out. He's got a towel wrapped around his waist, his cheeks are flushed, the hair on his chest is matted down with moisture, and Stephan needs his own goddamned towel again because he's suddenly so fucking *hard* he feels lightheaded from how fast all the blood in his brain just rushed into his cock.

He only realizes he's staring—and possibly made some kind of embarrassing noise—when Jeff smirks at him.

"Your turn," Jeff says, and, "thanks," when Stephan wordlessly thrusts the pile of clothes he's gathered at him. "I'm gonna start some coffee while you're in the shower, okay?"

Stephan nods, trying not to die of humiliation and lust, and closes the bathroom door behind him, trying and failing not to think about Jeff being naked in here just a few seconds ago. In *here*, in Stephan's shower, using Stephan's soap all over his naked, gorgeous body that Stephan really wants to lick every inch of. He feels like he's being turned inside-out by *want*.

Jesus, he shouldn't want the guy this strongly. He and Eric just broke up; it's disrespectful or something. He doesn't mean it to be; this thing with Jeff was just supposed to be a stupid crush, not this full-out, every-cell-in-his-body-*yearning* lust thing. He's let this get way out of hand....

The hot water feels amazingly good; he hadn't realized how cold he was, and it's almost sinful feeling the soap slide around on his body as he washes himself clean. By the time he's done shampooing his hair, his dick is aching, and there's no arguing for even a moment before he gets a handful of conditioner and starts stroking. His legs are shaking, and he considers getting down on his knees so he can slide some fingers up his ass, but there's no time for that, so he wedges himself back against the tiles in the corner and lets the pleasure build while he thinks about Jeff's body, the way it felt on top of his in the mud, the way the damp white towel barely concealed Jeff's dick, the way his arms held Stephan that night in the rain and how his stubble felt against Stephan's mouth. He's pretty sure there's no way the sound of the shower or the bathroom fan totally covers his groan, but he can't stop because he's coming so hard he's going to fall over and die or something, it's so fucking *good*.

Thank God for the stupid little stickies Jim insisted they put in the bathtub—they're pretty much the only thing that just saved Stephan from a truly humiliating death from breaking his neck while jerking off in the shower. Ah well. And at least he didn't die with his fingers up his ass.

It's important to look on the bright side.

By the time Stephan gets out of the shower because he can't hide in there anymore without developing jungle rot, Jeff is watching a game with Jim and Jamie. Jamie's face has that post-coital flush, and Jim looks immensely satisfied with himself, and no one gives Stephan a second look, so maybe if any sounds leaked out of the bathroom, they were attributed to his horny housemates instead. Awesome.

Jeff gives him a raised eyebrow as he grabs a cup of coffee, though, and he's not sure if that's about anything other than the fact that he's only wearing a towel. "What?"

Jeff shakes his head, and Jim grins. "Hey, at least he's wearing a towel. Very little gets between Stephan and his coffee."

Pouting, Stephan flounces dramatically into the hallway and his bedroom for some clothes, tossing back, "You only wish you had my hot body," at Jim. He hears a snort in reply, but isn't sure if it was Jim or Jeff, as the door closes. He's still smiling in satisfaction when he emerges, dressed, and joins the others. They sit around watching a game on ESPN until Jamie's stomach rumbles, and they decide to order out for Chinese. Jeff decides to join them, admitting he doesn't have any food at his house anyway. It's relaxed and easy, comfortable, and if anything, it's a surprise how well Jeff fits in with Jim and Jamie, with Stephan's life, and it sort of feels good but at the same time kind of makes something ache in his chest.

"Hey, I forgot to tell you; Billy has a gig this Saturday," Stephan remembers, halfway through his chow mien.

"Yeah? Where at, the Catalyst?" Jim asks.

"Yeah. Hey, you want to come?" he asks, turning to Jeff.

"Sure. What kind of music? And who's Billy?" Jeff asks.

Jamie snorts. "Billy is Stephan's self-appointed big brother. He vets all of Stephan's boyfriends and tries to warn them off before they break Stephan's pretty little heart. They've known each other forever. And mostly country, with some rock."

Stephan makes a face, but can't really argue. "I don't think Billy remembers that I'm not eighteen anymore."

"Can you blame him, when you consistently date people who are so wrong for you?" Jim says.

"Fuck off." He knows Jim was just mouthing off and thinking more about guys who aren't Eric, but still. That sort of hurt.

"So, country," Jeff says, coming to the rescue. "Like, serious twang and steel guitars? Or what?"

"Like folksy-country," Jamie answers. "Good lyrics, nothing about women leaving and taking the dog and having to drown his sorrows in a bottle of JD. But maybe that's because it would be a man instead," she adds, smiling.

"Yup, he's a genuine gay cowboy," Jim says, laughing. "Just don't make any Village People jokes around him or insult his boots and you'll be fine. So, you in?"

Jeff agrees to join them on Saturday, and they finish eating with the game in the background, conversation between the four of them flowing easily. It's still kind of early when Jeff gets up and starts gathering his dirty clothes to go back home, but then again, it is a school night. Jeff's boots aren't even close to dry, but they don't squelch when he walks, and he says that's good enough for him to get back to his place. It's still raining, but not nearly as hard, and it's early enough that the campus shuttles are running.

Stephan walks with him down the stairs of the building and then suddenly gets all flappy-handed when it's time to say goodbye. Should he hug Jeff? Is that too weird? He hugs most of his friends, but... he hasn't tried to kiss most of his friends, either. But Jeff's being all normal, and he doesn't know Stephan jerked off in the shower thinking about him only a couple of hours ago, so. Normal, then.

He leans in for a quick hug, awkward as hell as his hands flit around Jeff's shoulders. He can't help remembering that night, the way Jeff had pulled him in to an embrace, strong and comfortable, *comforting*, and oh, this was a bad idea. He pulls back, feeling his face flush.

Jeff is laughing at him. "Night, Steph. See you in class tomorrow. And hey, e-mail me the details of the concert, okay?"

"Yeah, I will." He raises his hand in a wave, which Jeff doesn't see because he's already turned around, tucking his head down and hurrying to the bus stop kiosk. Stephan's stomach feels tight and strange, and Jesus, he's so sick of feeling confused and embarrassed or whatever the hell it is inside his brain. Mixed up and tentative and so horny he can't think straight.

Maybe it's the Chinese food.

Chapter 19
Rebound

"COME help my big studly boyfriend move the sofa, Steph. He has an *enormous penis*," Jamie yells over her shoulder to the living room before turning back to Stephan, "but I think he's going to hurt his back if he tries to do this on his own. You know how heavy the furniture is here."

Sounds like a great excuse for a study break, *and* he gets to rib Jim about being a pussy and having his girlfriend be overprotective. Win-win. Evidently the sofa was directly over the heating vent, which explains why the central areas are so fucking cold in the mornings, now that the temperature is dropping at night. The guys manage to move the sofa without any fuss, aside from Jim's grumbles that he *totally* could have done it himself and didn't need any help and Stephan's scoffing that Jim isn't *actually* Superman.

"What's this?" Jamie asks, picking up a dusty blue rag or something that had fallen behind the sofa. She shakes it out, and it turns out to be a T-shirt.

Jim shakes his head, and Stephan takes a second to recognize it, since it's familiar but not his. "Oh. I think it must be Eric's." He takes it and tosses it into his bedroom, and he and Jim finish moving the chairs and coffee table and TV into more optimal positions, with Jamie supervising.

He doesn't remember the shirt again until a few hours later—they had to test the set-up of everything by watching a movie and eating lunch. It's really dusty; maybe he should wash it before he gives it back to Eric. If he gives it back to Eric. He hasn't seen his ex since they broke up, but they did say they were going to try to stay on friendly terms…. He should probably wash it first. He'll call Eric once it's clean.

Stephan opens his books again but finds that he can't concentrate very well. He feels… he doesn't know how he feels. He feels kind of tight in the chest and headachey. Sad maybe? He decides to just take two aspirin and maybe a short nap.

The rest of the week is a whirlwind of studying. His paper proposals were all approved—of course—and now the serious research and writing begins. The Lit one looks fun and easy; the M&T paper has him sort of in knots, although he feels pretty confident that he's got a good project in the works. He found several biographies of Robert E. Lee, one apparently by someone who was a big fan, and one by someone who was clearly not a fan at all, both semi-contemporaries. There's also one written in the 1960s, attempting to be objective but clearly reflecting the Civil Rights Movement at that time, and finally a biography less than a decade old. He plans to compare the works, seeing what is different, where the biases come out, and how each is a product of the authors themselves and of their own eras. He wants to explore how perspectives can never be totally neutral, and that it's only through comparing different accounts that a historian can begin to piece together a slightly more objective picture, and recognize that he himself will have inserted his own point of view into his own work, no matter how much he tries to avoid it. The only subjects a historian can be truly neutral on are ones that he doesn't care about at all, and why study those?

That's his plan, anyway. Jeff said it was a good topic, and the M&T prof got all excited about it, but their enthusiasm frankly makes Stephan suspect that he's bitten off more than he can chew—this sounds almost more like a thesis topic than a twenty-thousand-word research paper. Ah well. If he gets that into it, maybe it can become the basis for his thesis next year.

Scott e-mails Stephan with all the details about the show, including that Billy is totally freaked out about his first solo gig in a long while and that *"Stephan had better come over or he's going to*

lose his place as honorary little brother and get his ass kicked."
Apparently Billy is having a bitch attack, and Scott figures that if he
has to suffer, so does someone else. Stephan goes over Friday night
with a few six-packs and the DVD of *Tombstone*. Between him and
Scott, they manage to get Billy calmed down enough to decide on
which jeans and plain black T-shirt he's going to wear tomorrow and
whether he ought to clean off his cowboy boots or just leave them.
Stephan is so fucking proud of himself for not laughing in Billy's face
that he thinks he should get an award, until he realizes that Scott has to
deal with this *all the time*, and if anyone deserves a medal for putting
up with Billy, it's Scott.

The movie (plus a joint or two) gets Billy settled enough to stop
twitching, and Scott drags him into the bedroom without so much as a
"thank you and good night" for Stephan. Fuckers. He knows they love
him, though.

The show on Saturday is *packed*. Country music's not a big draw
in a college/surfer town, usually, but Billy has a reputation for putting
on a good show, and he knows damn near everybody, so it's not really
a surprise.

A few songs into the show, someone taps Stephan on the
shoulder, and when he turns around, it's Jeff. He's had a few beers and
is feeling them, so he gives Jeff a huge grin and equally huge hug. The
concert's not that long: two half-hour sets and a short break between.
There are some girls dancing to the more rockin' songs, but it's mostly
just folks milling around, having a good time, listening to the music.
Jeff seems like he's having fun, and Stephan's glad he's there, sharing
this with Stephan and his friends. Most of Stephan's "gang" has turned
out for support, and brought all their friends, too, so it's almost like a
party. Only with a way better sound system.

Billy calls Scott up to join him during the second set, and you'd
have to know Scott pretty well to see how surprised he is, but Stephan
does. He's deeply amused when Billy plays the song he wrote for
Scott's birthday, Scott playing backup and doing the harmony. It's
clearly not something they've rehearsed, but it's perfect—beautiful, to
be honest. Stephan is unashamed of the knot in his throat and the grin

on his face as he whoops and applauds loud enough to be heard over the rest of the audience once the song is over.

Of course, no good deed goes unpunished, and Billy is hellbent on calling *him* up on stage next, it seems. He tries to argue that he doesn't have his instrument or anything, but Scott just smirks and passes his guitar to Stephan, and he's well and truly stuck. Luckily, all he has to do is play harmony for a familiar song, although when he hesitates on the backup vocals, Billy kicks him. And honestly? It's fun. It's been ages since Stephan played with Billy, and while he's not big on audiences of more than a handful of close friends, it's still a rush.

Thankfully, Billy lets him flee once the song is done and he's been subjected to a smattering of applause "For my friend Stephan, who's way too pretty to be a 'real' cowboy." Jeff gives him a congratulatory smack on the ass when he returns to where they were standing, and hands him a beer. Stephan would like to take a moment to savor the fucking *ease* with which Jeff just spanked him, but he's kind of high on adrenaline and he'll have to try to replay it later.

Alone-later. A lot, probably. God, he needs to get laid.

After the show ends, pretty much everyone decides to invade their local bar, 99 Bottles. Billy and some of the guys grab some tables and start ordering pub food, but most of them head to the bar and dance floor. Stephan manages to sweep Jeff along with him, arguing that it's still early and he probably owed Jeff at least one drink by now.

"What do you want? Beer? Shot of Jameson's? A drink with an umbrella? Rum and coke?" Stephan teases.

"Jameson's, if you're buying. Go ahead and get yourself something pretty, sweetheart," Jeff drawls.

Stephan sticks his tongue out in response, and emerges from the crush of bodies at the bar in a few minutes with the whisky in one hand and his drink in the other.

"No umbrella?"

Stephan takes a drink, kicking Jeff lightly in the shin at the same time. "Greyhound."

"Ah. Grapefruit and vodka, right?" Jeff asks.

"You can even pretend it's breakfast, like a mimosa," Stephan says with a grin. He's so wired he doesn't even need the booze, but it tastes good and the juice is refreshing. He can barely stand still, and is edging toward the dance floor, not so subtly luring Jeff onto it with him.

"I'm not much of a dancer," Jeff argues, as his feet hit the parquet floor. "You go ahead, I'm gonna just lean here and savor this while I ogle you young'uns."

Shaking his head, Stephan shrugs his shoulders and hands Jeff his mostly drained glass, admonishing him to keep it safe. Then he's on the dance floor, letting some people he sort of knows pull him into their circle and writhing around to the heady beat. It's hot and crowded and the blood in his body is thrumming in time with the music, and Stephan loves, loves, *loves* this. He can feel Jeff watching him, and he's totally doing his best to dance seductively; why not? Jeff's been cool about the kiss, and Stephan's always been a bit of a flirt, and he's a little drunk and life is good, so why not?

Every time he turns around facing Jeff, the guy is staring right at him, sometimes not even noticing that Stephan's looking back at him for a few moments, and then he looks away. Jeff's not the blushing type, but Stephan can tell he's a little flustered, and fuck—maybe Jeff *is* bi after all.

When the music finally changes to a song he doesn't like, he realizes he's breathless and drenched in sweat, totally soaked through his T-shirt. He grins at Jeff, who gives him a kind of strange look back, and shouts over the music that he's going outside for some air. He snags a cup of water off the end of the bar as he walks past it, Jeff following behind, and then they're outside in the fucking *fabulous*, refreshing, wonderful air.

"You were watching a lot, wanna come join me when we go back inside?" Stephan asks, wiping the sweat off his face with the hem of his shirt. He catches Jeff's eyes fixed on his stomach. He licks his lips. Oh yeah. Jeff wants him.

Jeff clears his throat. "Actually, I think I'm gonna take off. Will someone else give you a ride home?"

Wait, what? *What?* "Um?"

"Hey, I had a great time," Jeff says, and he's got his usual easy smile, but Stephan thinks it looks a little forced.

Whatever. He's confused and wired and maybe a lot more drunk than he thought. It seemed like Jeff was checking him out—he was *positive* of it—but... maybe he was wrong? In which case, he's been hitting on his friend—his *boss*—again. And pretty fucking obviously, writhing around on the dance floor like a tramp.

God-fucking-dammit.

"I.... Yeah. No worries; I can get a ride."

"Good. The concert was great; maybe sometime I can meet Billy for real, talk to him and stuff. Clubs aren't really my scene, though. But you should stay and have fun."

Seriously? Stephan's going to lose *another* guy who thinks all he wants to do is party and drink and fuck around?

God fucking *damm*it.

He mumbles some reply and gives Jeff a fleeting hug—he's drenched with sweat and if Jeff's not going to fuck him, he probably thinks it's gross, not sexy. He wanders back inside, and it's loud and crowded, and his head hurts and his heart hurts too. He's completely surrounded by people, the place is packed, but he feels alone. He's so stupid; it's just a crush. He needs to get the fuck over it. Everyone thinks he's just some stupid, pretty party-boy, so why not act like one?

He gets another drink, downs it, and goes to dance again.

The floor is even more crowded now, mixed groups and couples of all pairings. It's not a gay bar per se, but the owner is a loud member of Dykes on Bikes so it's definitely a queer-friendly place. There's a group of college-age boys, who look like they're barely old enough to be in a bar, dancing together, if "humping and grinding to the music" can pass for "dancing." Which Stephan supposes it can, especially when one of the guys starts looking at Stephan and smiling a lot.

Soon they're "dancing" together, him and this kid, and damn—guys have been telling Stephan he's "pretty" since he was barely a teenager, but this kid? *Definitely* prettier. He's got huge eyes, a head of floppy, tousled, damp curls, and a mouth that's just a little too large to keep it from being impossibly perfect. Instead, it makes Stephan think of blowjobs. Topless, the kid's got the finest down on his lean chest, and a dangerously sparse trail leading past his navel into his pants. He has a huge smile, too-big boyish hands, and a fucking *filthy* mouth he's been using to tell Stephan how much he wants Stephan to fuck his tight, young ass.

He's allowed to rebound right? It's expected. It's what you're supposed to do when you get dumped. So, yeah. And Stephan has to do something to get Jeff out of his head.

They have a quick exchange where Stephan confirms that this gorgeous kid is actually twenty-two (he says) and that he lives three blocks down, in an apartment above some of the shops downtown. Thank God, because Stephan is so ready to go, his dick is straining to get out of his pants, and he *wants*, and he's going to *have*.

The apartment is more of an open-plan loft with three beds, but no one else is there and Stephan doesn't care. Condoms and lube are in a fishbowl next to the kid's futon, and their kisses are sloppy and wet, full of tongue and urgency. Stephan's hands are pinning pale wrists down against the bed, his cock sliding inside a tight ass, deep, to the sound of groans.

It's a fast, crazy ride, the sound of the music still pounding in Stephan's blood and brain and his dick, which is *so* happy to be having sex and to be *topping* that he knows he's not going to be able to hold back for very long. It doesn't matter at all, though, because the kid's working his cock in time to Stephan's thrusts, moaning, "Yeah, yeah, yeah," like it's his new mantra. He comes so fast it's almost a surprise, and then just keeps fucking right on going. He never softens while Stephan fucks him through it, and shit, he's going to come a second time, isn't he? That is so hot that Stephan can't help speeding up, slamming in deeper and harder than he means to, but it seems to be what works, because the kid is shooting again, adding more cream to the puddle on his chest and squeezing so tight around Stephan's dick that Stephan thinks he's going to pass out when he comes.

He does sort of gray out for a minute. It takes him a second to catch his breath and his throat hurts; he must have been making some noise himself.

"Fuck, that was good," his partner slurs, eyes mostly closed, hand lazily fumbling for the roll of toilet paper next to the bed. "You're brilliant."

Stephan chuckles tiredly. "Thanks. Not bad yourself."

The kid snickers. "So, who's Jeff?"

"What?"

"That's the name you said when you came."

"Oh my God. I'm so sorry. Wow, I *suck*, seriously. I'm really sorry," he apologizes, frantically trying to remember the kid's name, going over everything they actually said with words, and concluding that he never asked. God, Stephan is such a *slut*. And has abysmal manners on top of everything else. Shit. He *sucks*.

The little tart is laughing at him; thank God. "No biggie. I'm Óskar. Pretty sure I didn't tell you. And you are?"

"Stephan," he says, and they shake hands, pretending to be all serious and stop laughing.

"Nice to meet you," Óskar says very formally, and for the first time Stephan notices he's got a slight Northern-European accent. "Now, I'm gonna go clean up and then have a Red Bull and vodka back at 99, I think. You want to come?"

Stephan's got to give him credit; that's a pretty polite way to chuck someone out after a random hookup. "Nah, I think I'm going to head on home. See if I can get someone to give me a ride."

"I thought someone just did," Óskar says with a wink.

Stephan laughs and leans over to kiss his generous mouth one last time. "Thanks. See you around."

"Yeah. Bye, Stephan."

The walk back to the bar takes longer than the walk to Óskar's apartment had seemed to, but that can almost certainly be chalked up to

Stephan's satiated lethargy. His brain feels a little less satisfied than his body, though. Aside from the *massive* social blunder of calling someone by the wrong name while fucking them and the resulting embarrassment, he's pretty unsettled that his mouth had betrayed him so. It's irritating to be given away by your own brain when you're working so hard to be in denial. The kid was gorgeous, his body had felt great, *Stephan's* body had felt great fucking him... but he wasn't Jeff.

God-fucking-dammit.

Chapter 20
With Friends Like These...

ON TUESDAY Stephan is hanging out at the Student Center for his office hours when someone comes up behind him and a familiar voice says, "Help me, Mr. Burke, you're my only hope!"

Stephan rolls his eyes as Billy sprawls into the chair opposite. "What the fuck are you doing here? You graduated how many years ago? I can't believe they let you on campus."

"I'm kidnapping you. Bringing some excitement to your dreary life," Billy says with an easy grin.

"Oh please."

"I'm taking you home for dinner. Scott thinks you're too skinny."

"I've got work to do!"

"Wasn't a request, darlin'. You're coming to dinner."

Stephan rolls his eyes again, knowing how futile it is to try and argue with Billy once he's made his mind up about something. Plus, Scott is a good cook. "Fine, I give. I've got twenty more minutes, though, in case any actual students show up and need my help."

"As if; what could you help them with?" Billy scoffs.

"Fuck you; I'm a good teacher."

There's a snort from the next table over. "Come on, Burke, just go," Kristine says. "I'll tell your students to e-mail you or something if anyone comes looking."

Grumbling, Stephan packs up his stuff and lets Billy drag him outside. There're no TA sections this week, either, because there's a required movie night instead, so he's technically free for the rest of the evening, but he'd planned to get some work done. Billy has a way of derailing Stephan's plans, and always has.

There's got to be something up for Billy to show up out of the blue, but he's not talking, and Stephan knows from many years of experience that he'll just have to wait until Billy is ready. Instead, they sit around and shoot the breeze, drinking beer and talking about the gig on Saturday until Scott gets home from work. Billy predictably preens over the compliments, so Stephan switches to criticism of what could have been better, trying to take his friend down a few pegs.

"You really need someone else to play harmony and sing backup or something. The sound is a lot more effective with another voice smoothing out your twang."

"Hm. You might be right, but it's hard to find someone who doesn't mind me hogging the limelight, you know?"

"Yeah. And on that subject, I know you and Scott can't perform together without fighting a lot, but that song you guys cowrote was the best one, by far. Maybe you could find a way to work creatively without pissing each other off too much."

"Maybe," Billy agrees, lifting his bottle to take another drink. "Maybe we've been together long enough now not to end up fighting about every note."

Stephan snorts. "When pigs fly, man," he says and gets a kick in the shin in return.

Dinner is fantastic, as always. Scott makes some kind of Thai-style salad rolls, with marinated strips of Asian-spiced beef and lots of veggies, and they each make their own, burrito-bar style. It's good and it's fun, too, the three of them sitting around the table that's usually way too cluttered to eat at. Scott's working for a computer company, doing their audio stuff and apparently enjoying the electronic side of music a lot more than he expected to. Billy is, again, "taking a break from work."

"Man, are you ever going to get a real job, one that you *like*, or what?" Stephan asks.

"Got one," Billy says. "Not my fault that fucking Scott and playing music doesn't pay the bills."

Scott snorts. "I don't earn enough money to pay you for sex, hon, sorry. Plus, I kind of think you might have ruined that plan by giving it away for so long."

"Yeah. Why buy the cow?" Stephan agrees, smirking at Billy.

"Play with the bull, boy, you'll get the horns," Billy warns him.

Cracking up at that, Stephan manages to choke on his beer, and everybody's laughing by the time he can breathe again. Fuckers.

"So, who was the guy you brought with you on Saturday?" Scott asks. "Your new flame?"

"Jeff. He's just a friend."

"Just a friend, huh? Never heard that line before," Billy snorts.

"Fuck off. He's my boss, kind of, the professor I'm TAing for. He's new in town, and we're sort of friends now. He's cool. But *just a friend*," Stephan repeats.

"Aw, Stephanie, you protest like a little girl."

"Not to mention that you don't look at him like a 'friend'," Scott adds, teasing but also defusing the banter before Billy sincerely pisses Stephan off. Calling him "Stephanie" always gets his hackles up, and Billy knows it. Dick.

"And he's totally your type," Billy manages to add before Scott smacks him on the arm. "What? He is. He's hot. And older, and smart."

Scott makes a face at Billy, but agrees. "He is pretty attractive."

"Yeah. He's also straight. I think. He just got divorced from a woman this past summer, anyway."

"Hmmm...." Scott gives him a look, but doesn't actually say anything.

"Bummer. I noticed you getting all hot-n-heavy with some twink on the dance floor later though," Billy says, leering. "Not wasting any time pining over Eric, I see."

Stephan shrugs. "It was just a random hookup. Not gonna sit at home moping about someone I can't have, you know?"

"Good for you," Billy says, saluting him with his bottle, while Scott gives Stephan another inscrutable look.

"What?"

"Nothing," Scott says. "Nothing wrong with getting laid, and no need to sit around sobbing over Eric for any specified length of time. I gather that was kind of fucked up for a while; good for you for moving on."

There's totally something Scott's not saying. Stephan might not know Scott as well as he knows Billy, but he's still been friends with the guy for over four years. "But?"

Scott shrugs. "But you talk about Jeff a lot. Have been for months."

Billy nods, oh so helpfully. "He's right; you do."

Stephan picks at the label on his bottle for a few moments, feeling both of them looking at him and unsure what to say. "He's *straight*. At least, I think so… I don't know; sometimes he looks at me like… But whatever. He's awesome and he's smart, and we're totally into the same stuff, and I have this hugely epic fucking crush on him and I'm a total idiot, okay? Is that what you wanted to hear? I have a crush on my new friend, who is a really amazing guy, the most amazing guy I've probably ever met, but he's my *boss* and he's straight. Probably. My life sucks."

"Aw, poor Stephanie."

"Fuck off, Billy. That sucks, Stephan. I'm sorry," Scott says.

"I'll live," Stephan shrugs.

"Yeah, you will. Hey, why don't we grab the guitars and go work on your following and blending for a while? You sounded a little rusty on Saturday night," Billy suggests, in a surprising show of sensitivity.

Scott must really be rubbing off on him. Which is *not* an image Stephan needed, thank you very much.

The three of them relocate to the living room, Stephan borrowing one of Billy's guitars. They goof around for a while first, working on a few songs together, playing old favorites as well as some of Billy's and Scott's original pieces. Scott's working on something instrumental, more folksy and kind of ethereal—"New-Agey bullshit," Billy mutters, getting smacked in retaliation. It's nice, though, really peaceful, and Stephan picks it up after not too long. The song conveys a lot of emotion even without any lyrics, and Stephan decides he likes it a lot.

Then they start to improv, and it's sort of hard for Stephan, actually, using a part of his brain that hasn't had much exercise lately. He can't remember when he last held a guitar before the gig Saturday, and that's kind of sad. It's been months, and he's missed it without realizing it. Stephan doesn't think of himself as a musician—especially not compared to his friends who actually earn money at it and hope to make music for a living someday—but still. It's part of him. He should make time for it more often.

Right. In all his free time when he's not doing massive amounts of research and analysis, memorizing irregular French verbs, and helping clueless undergrads learn how to be decent students.

Or having stupid, pointless crushes.

Or picking up cute undergrads, he adds, smiling a little to himself. He's surprised he hasn't been harassed too much about that—Billy tends to tease the crap out of him whenever he's getting laid. Billy has some scary kind of sixth sense about the details of Stephan's sex life, like how long it took—or didn't—and who moaned like a needy slut. Seriously, it's disturbing.

What's *also* disturbing is the front-row seat Stephan seems to have on Billy and Scott flirting with each other tonight like a couple of newlyweds, rather than two guys in their late twenties who have been together forever. Billy's "suggestive" comments about fingering have turned from double entendres about sex and music to bald recitations of how it feels to have his fingers inside Scott's ass. Stephan did *not* need to know this stuff.

Scott, of course, is no pushover, although he's a little more flustered or inhibited or something than usual, tonight. He can generally keep up with Billy's obnoxious mouth pretty well, but tonight he's responding with a lot more shoving and smacking than arguing—he's handsy, basically. When he pulls Billy's guitar away, pausing for a second to lay it on the floor before tackling Billy backward into the sofa, Stephan decides he's had enough.

"Hey, get a room! I sleep on that couch sometimes."

"My couch, my rules," Billy says, mouth muffled against Scott's neck, one hand grabbing Scott's ass while the other slides under his T-shirt and up his back.

"No spooge on the couch *is* your rule," Stephan points out as the two of them start grinding together. Oh great, now they're kissing, and he so did not need to see Scott's tongue doing things like that to Billy's. Gross. It's like watching his *brother* make out or something.

Billy gasps, then manages, "My spooge doesn't count. Neither does Scott's."

"Gross, dude."

"Go away, Stephan. We want to fuck," Scott says, pausing long enough to look up at Stephan and grin.

"Jesus, all right, I'm going." Stephan gets up as fast as he can, but apparently that's still not fast enough since he gets hit in the face with a flying T-shirt, because Billy is an asshole. "Damn, keep it in your pants for just a few more seconds, can't you? I'm trying to leave!"

"My house," Billy gasps, and Stephan is so damn glad he can't see what's going on now that he's on the other side of the couch. "His rules," Scott adds, breathless, and they both giggle.

"Horny bastards," Stephan grumbles. "I should film this and put it on the Internet. See how much money I can make on you two fucking exhibitionists."

"Exhibitionists, fucking," Scott corrects him, and then lets out a long, guttural moan that has Stephan grabbing his messenger bag and running out the door.

That was almost worse than hearing Danielle and her boyfriends that one year, and ew—Stephan does not need to see *or* hear any more of his friends fucking ever again. He thought he'd left that stage behind when he finished living in the dorms; even when he was crashing on Billy's sofa this fall before school started, Billy and Scott had pretty much always kept it in their bedroom. Jesus Christ.

Seriously, next time he has a steady SO, he's totally going to make sure to screw where Billy and Scott have to see it. That was just disturbing, man. It's one thing when you live together (or next door), but that was just uncalled for.

Plus, now Stephan's horny again. His life is so fucking unfair.

Chapter 21
Lederhosen Hell

"ARE you still single?"

"Hi, Danni, how are you doing? I'm super, thanks for asking," Stephan says into his phone, not at all trying to hide his irritation. She interrupted his study time—and he was totally on a roll with his writing today—just to rub salt into his wounds? Bitch. "What the hell?"

"Oh, suck it up, Burke. Halloween is this weekend, and you're going to the party at the House of Ill Repute with me. Unless you're too busy moping around or having a rebound or something to be my date."

He sighs. She has that determined voice that he knows from long experience there is simply no point in arguing with. "Not really. I had a random hookup after Billy's show last weekend, but it was just sex. I'm assuming you have costumes in mind? I won't do drag again," he says firmly.

"Oh baby, if you're already getting laid when it's been *months* since I've seen any action, you're going to do whatever the hell I tell you to do. But no, you get to be a boy. I'm thinking Hansel and Gretel."

Stephan groaned. "Oh God. You're going to make me wear those little shorts, aren't you?"

"Lederhosen. And yes. With the suspenders and knee socks too."

"What did I ever do to you to deserve this? What did I ever do in life to deserve *you* as my best friend?" he whines.

"Must have been something pretty bad," Danielle agrees. "Maybe all that hot underage gay sex, I'm thinking. Plus, you're a tease. You deserve punishment for that alone."

"Me? I'm a tease? I can totally picture your costume; it's going to be one of those slutty short poofy skirts and lots of cleavage, am I right? You're going out to tease the hell out of every straight guy there, and then maybe if you deem one good enough, you'll take him home and fuck him stupid, and then throw him out so you can go to sleep and won't have to deal with him in the morning and risk getting hurt again."

"Watch it, Stephan. I know your sore spots too," she says, and he realizes he's almost crossed a line. She must be feeling a little sensitive about being single, and he guesses he *hasn't* heard her talk about anyone since her breakup. Or even the breakup much, now that he thinks about it. Sometimes he's an insensitive asshole.

"I'm sorry, baby. I suck. I didn't mean to be a jerk. Sometimes you're just kind of a barracuda, you know? Not in a bad way, but you go through men like… krill," he finishes lamely. Yeah, his foot? So far down his throat he's going to asphyxiate if he doesn't shut the fuck up.

There's a long pause. "Krill?"

"Uh. I was trying to stay with the fish metaphor."

He's very, very lucky, because she laughs instead of swearing at him and hanging up the phone and changing her number. Or swearing a vendetta, and seriously, the last person Danielle decided she hated? Did not go on to happy and prosperous things in life. She can kind of be a total bitch when she wants to.

Anyway, if she's forgiving him, he's not going to complain about some stupid-ass costume. "So, what's the deal? Are we buying these things ready-made from the Halloween store or do you have something else in mind?"

"Nah, I hate getting caught in the crowd there. I ordered stuff online a few weeks ago."

He snorts. "Pretty sure of yourself, aren't you?"

"Aw, Steph, you're wrapped around my little finger. You always have been. I'm the hag to your fag; where would you be without me?"

"Not in lederhosen, for a start."

"Keep whining and I'll get you a wig with platinum-blond ringlets to wear, and a little hat too."

Stephan knows when it's time to surrender. "All right, I give. I'm sure the lederhosen will be very... alluring. To pedophiles," he can't help adding.

She laughs. "Given your penchant for older men, I can't see how that's anything but a plus for you."

They banter a bit more, planning to get together when the package arrives—she confirms that it's already shipped and she'll bring it up to campus on Thursday and they can play dress-up. He tries to argue for doing it at her place instead, but Danielle insists that it's only logical, since she has her TA sections in the evening and he has the movie he has to go to for Intro Am Hist, and they can do it between classes.

"Fabulous. I'm sure Jim would love to give his input," Stephan sighs. Maybe he can bribe Jim to not be home. Or harass him about drinking so much beer and developing a belly until he goes out for another superhuman run. Hmmm... that idea has merit....

ON THURSDAY Danielle is waiting outside his door when he gets home, bags in hand, and a shit-eating grin on her face. As far as a sign of things to come, this is *so* not good.

She insists on showing hers off first, and frankly, Stephan would give anything to delay seeing his for as long as possible, so he's fine with that. She starts stripping, right there in front of him like he's her faithful dog or something, and he flees before he can see anything icky.

"Goddamnit, Danni, I'm gay not *blind*! Warn a guy, next time."

"Oh please. We've been naked hot tubbing. When did you turn into such a prude?"

Huh. Stephan actually thinks about it. Maybe she's right. First Billy and Scott, now Danielle—what the fuck is wrong with him? He never used to care about his friends being naked or making out in front of him. Maybe it's a leftover thing from Eric? He doesn't know.

Anyway, she comes out in her tiny little dress, with predicted poofy underskirt thing and most of her boobs showing. She has him tighten the laces on the fake corset while she braids her hair into two short plaits. She adds white socks that go over her knees and some Mary Janes, and Stephan has to admit, she looks pretty damn good.

"If I were straight, I'd probably want to do you," he says, making her laugh.

"Damn right you would; I'm a total babe. Now, it's your turn!"

"You really are," he says, pulling her into his arms and kissing her neck. "And you're smart and funny and you like sports and you're a good cook, and any guy who can't see that must be a fucking idiot." It's all true, and he means every word; she's a good friend and she's apparently been a little more depressed than he realized, as self-centered as he's been for the last few months.

And he's trying to delay seeing his costume for as long as possible.

"I love you too," she says, turning to kiss his cheek. "Now stop stalling and go put on your shorts."

Naturally, she follows him in, and since he's not taking off his boxers, he decides not to protest. If she wants to look at his body, well, fine by him. He knows he's hot, and he keeps telling himself that as she starts removing things from the second bag and laying them out on his bed.

"Melissa and her boyfriend—John, you remember—they do Renaissance Faire, so I borrowed the shirt from him. The hat and lederhosen are from the store. Oh, and I borrowed socks from John too. Do you have brown shoes?"

He nods speechlessly as he looks at the clothes. The socks have little tassels on them. They are green and perfectly match the embroidery on the front chest-thingy on the... lederhosen. Which are beige. And have a flap on the front crotch, with buttons. The hat is small and pointy, like a cone, with a feather in the brim.

"You're really mad at me about something, aren't you?"

"Wuss. Put it on, or I'll put it on you myself," she threatens, and he knows that's not an empty threat, so he starts pulling on the shirt.

The… *lederhosen* go on next and, wow, are they tight. "They don't fit; they're too small," he protests, but Danielle tugs and smoothes (gropes him, basically), and says that they're fine, or they will be if he goes commando.

Great.

STEPHAN spends Friday evening and Saturday morning in the library, anticipating that Sunday will most likely be consumed by a hangover. Given his costume, he's going to need to get totally shitfaced in order to make it through the night with his sense of humor intact, so really, it's just good planning to try and get as much as possible done beforehand.

Jeff joins him on Saturday, but resists Stephan's attempts to talk him into coming to the party. "Sounds like fun, but college parties aren't really my scene anymore"—Jeff shrugs—"especially if I'm going to run into my students there," and that's that. Much as Stephan would like to keep pushing Jeff into socializing and whatnot, all it does is frustrate Stephan and make him want things he can't have, so why bother?

Maybe he can just have some more meaningless sex and try to keep his mouth shut this time and *actually* forget about Jeff for a while…. The real question, though, is why isn't Stephan trying to find someone else to crush on or fall for, if he can't have Jeff? He's still mooning, he supposes. Or maybe it's too soon after Eric, he tells himself, even though he knows it's a lie. No, all he wants is no-strings sex, if he can't have Jeff.

Damn it.

Then again, there's nothing wrong with a few random fucks, right? That's what everyone else does when they're single. It's what he used to do....

Stephan is still brooding a little when Danielle picks him up and takes him back to her apartment to get ready. Most of their friends will be at the party, so she doesn't want Jim or Jamie or anyone who might be wandering around campus to see them before they get there. She wants to make a grand entrance, basically, which has Stephan cringing inside.

The party is, of course, awesome. The House of Ill Repute is a huge Victorian that's been stripped down inside and is rentable for events, and the owners do theme parties once a month. There's a cover charge, but it's well worth it for the open bar and all-out decorations. A bunch of Art-type graduates got together a few years ago and decided that the parties they had in college were fabulous, but wouldn't it be great if they could do it up right, for a small entrance fee? It's still sort of invite-only, so it's got that cozy, private-party feel, but no one has to clean up the puke the next day and the DJs are really good.

And Halloween is, as always, the best fucking party of the year. Instead of going for cheesy haunted-house stuff, they've decorated the four-story house so that every section is a different version of Hell— Dante's *Inferno*, Hieronymus Bosch's *Garden of Earthly Delights*, and something of William Blake's that Stephan can't quite identify aside from the art style. It's freaking *amazing*.

Stephan gets a drink for himself and Danielle as they wander around, looking at the artistic décor and all the cool costumes people have come up with. People laugh at him a lot, but he gets a few gratifying leers from guys, so maybe Danni was right about the tight stupid lederhosen, after all. There's a costume contest planned in a few hours, and she enters them in the "couples" division, against his protests. Great, now he's going to have to get on stage and prance around and pose and shit.

This is totally going to end up on the Internet. Fucking *wonderful*.

Downstairs is a dungeon—kinky, not fake-torture, despite the Parisian catacomb theme of human-bone art. Okay, it's a little creepy. But still, the "torture" implements are crosses and spanking benches, not Iron Maidens and stretching racks. There are several sexy dominatrixes—dominatrices? He's too tipsy for good grammar: Dommes, in leather and latex, and a couple of Doms. One guy is tall, broad, and seriously smokin' hot. He catches Stephan checking him out, and before Stephan can protest—not that he was going to—he's cuffed to chains hanging from the ceiling and getting spanked with a crop.

And he's getting hard from it too.

Which isn't a terribly big surprise, but it's been a while, a *long* while. The Dom's not hitting him hard at all, and he's still fully dressed, so it doesn't sting. But it feels exhilarating to be all tied up and mock-helpless, people watching as a sexy topless guy in black leather swats him and tells him how gorgeous he is, how well he's doing. He'd forgotten what a turn-on it can be, being watched....

The crop runs down the length of his leg, ticking the back of his bare knee, and then giving him a smack on the thigh that hurts, but not nearly as much as it would without the layer of clothing. Grinning, the guy walks around to Stephan's front, trailing the crop over to Stephan's cock, stroking him through the stupid lederhosen.

The buttons on the shorts are straining, and he must look ridiculous, but there's absolutely nothing Stephan can do about it. The thought makes him even more excited, arousal thrumming through his entire body.

"Wanna take this some place a little more private, beautiful?" the Dom asks, brushing the corner of Stephan's mouth with his lips.

"Uh...."

"Or are you only kinky when there's an audience, huh? Are you a submissive little tease?" he adds, challenging, but with humor in his eyes.

"A little kinky," Stephan admits. "But I think tonight I'm just a tease."

The Dom laughs and rubs the end of the crop against Stephan's cock again. "Well, that's honest." His voice is low and throaty, and makes Stephan shiver. He pulls what looks like a business card out of his back pocket and pushes it into Stephan's shirt. "Call me if you ever want to fool around. I would *love* to hear you call me 'Daddy'."

Stephan can't help moaning as his cock twitches in response, but the guy merely laughs and goes back behind him. A few minutes later he's uncuffed and standing off to the side while the next victim—a cute college-boy who's already calling the Dom "Master" and begging to be spanked—is strung up. Stephan sort of envies the kid, but not really. He's not into Daddies and boys, and while he likes rough sex—a lot— he's not into the head games.

And there's really only one guy in his head these days, one Stephan's intent on drinking away into oblivion as much as possible. He heads back upstairs to the bar and to dance, ready to put his plan into action.

Chapter 22
Den of Iniquity

THE phone wakes him up at what feels like the ass-crack of dawn, but can't possibly be, since Stephan recalls seeing the sky lighten as he fell into bed. It, sadly, is just after noon, and the caller is Jeff, and Stephan is smitten, so he answers. Jeff's voice is his usual growly low-pitch tone, Stephan knows, but it still feels like Jeff is yelling at him through a megaphone.

"Rise and shine, beautiful. You up for a study date?"

"A what?" Stephan tries to say, and after a few garbled tries and a cough, manages to get out.

"I'll bring you a vat of coffee. I need your help, kiddo, if you don't feel too horrible?"

"Guh. Uh. Um…." There's a long pause while Stephan waits for all of those words to make sense. "'Kay?"

"Library? Or I could come over to your place and make you a nice fried breakfast to help with the hangover. You won't even have to get dressed."

"Um. 'M naked?" It's not really a question—he sleeps in the nude—but there's some part of what Jeff said that didn't make sense, and it had something to do with clothes. Unless Jeff wants to come over while Stephan is naked, which sounds great, although there may be some reason why it's not, but he can't remember right at the moment.

Jeff's laughter is *not* helping. And it's loud.

"Shhhhh."

"Stephan. I'm going to say this really slowly, all right?" Jeff's voice thankfully hushes a little. "Are you sick or just hung over?"

"Um. Queasy. Okay, though."

"Good. I'm going to come over in twenty minutes. Get up, take a leak, brush your teeth, get in the shower, put on some sweats." He waits for Stephan to respond with an affirmative noise. "I'll bring food—and coffee."

Stephan makes a happy noise.

"All right. Now, don't go back to sleep. Are you sitting up?"

A very, very sad noise answers Jeff's query, and Stephan kicks off the covers and slowly eases into an upright position, grumbling all the way. It's cold. He whimpers.

"It'll be warm in the shower," Jeff points out.

The shower is a million miles away. But it *is* cold, sitting up naked in his room. And now he really has to piss in the worst way. It's all Jeff's fault. Life is hard.

"Get out of bed, you lazy fuck!"

Stephan shouts, drops the phone, and bangs his head on the desk chair picking it up. "You suck."

Jeff laughs. "Yeah, but you're awake now. Go shower. I am coming over, and if your ass isn't clean and dressed by the time I get there, you don't get any coffee."

"So cruel." Stephan is helpless against such merciless manipulation. He would sell his right kidney for coffee on a regular day—right now, he'd happily trade organs he only has one of in exchange for the precious elixir. "I will never forgive you for this."

"I have an unopened bag of Peruvian beans, just ground yesterday at The Coffee Cat downtown."

"That… will do nicely. I'm unlocking the door for you," Stephan says, padding naked into the living room. "God, I have to piss." Jeff laughs and hangs up, and it's a minor miracle that Stephan remembers not to take the phone into the shower with him.

THE smell of coffee clears up Stephan's nausea, and he sucks down about half the pot before he realizes Jeff is simply sitting at the table with him, watching and smirking.

"What?"

"You human yet?" Jeff asks. "Because I didn't come over and bring you coffee out of the goodness of my heart."

"Bastard. What do you want?"

"Well, first, here are your clothes back," he says, passing over a bag. "They're clean. Do you want food?"

"I want to know what your motives are," Stephan points out suspiciously.

"Gossip, basically. I'm being assigned to the committee reviewing divisional graduation requirements, and I want the dirt on my colleagues. I need your brain. Braiinnnsss…," he moans, reaching out his hands like a hungry zombie.

"Halloween was yesterday," Stephan says. "I have the hangover to prove it."

"So I see. Good party?"

"Not bad. Danielle dressed us up like Hansel and Gretel," he sighs. "I looked like a dweeb. But we did win the 'best couple' part of the costume contest."

"Oh yeah? Is there photographic evidence?" Jeff grins, reaching for his laptop.

Stephan groans. "Probably."

Jeff types some, asks the name of the venue again, and in a few seconds has found pictures from the party. People are *fast* at getting shit onto the Internet it seems, to Stephan's dismay, if not surprise.

"Wow. Nice legs," Jeff snickers.

"Fuck you."

"Seriously, those are the most bowed legs I've seen outside of a dude ranch."

"*Fuck you*," Stephan repeats, then thinks for a second. "You've been to a dude ranch?"

Jeff nods. "Worked at one in Montana one summer when I was an undergrad."

Man, the guy just has so many *layers*. It feels like there are a billion things about him that Stephan would never even guess at, and they're all pretty cool. Of course he realizes it's always this way with new friends, discovering all the awesome things about them, but still. Jeff is just so damn interesting.

"So," Jeff drawls, with an obvious leer, "did you get those bowlegs from riding horses or wrapped around someone's back?"

"Dick," Stephan says and hits him on the shoulder. "They're not *that* curved. And my grandparents had a ranch with a few horses. I rode a lot when I was a kid, until I moved here for college."

"Hm. I guess the knee socks do kind of make them seem more curved than they are. Not to mention how tight your little shorts are…. Did you even have anything on underneath?"

"Uh. No. They got all bunched up, and Danielle made me take them off," he admits.

"Who is this Danielle?"

"My hag," Stephan says, pointing at her in another picture on the web page.

"That is not a hag," Jeff says, brows raising as he checks out her boobs. "Although maybe compared to you…," he adds.

Stephan laughs, shaking his head. It's nice, the banter and flirting, but he's nowhere near ready for it with Jeff. Not yet. It still kind of hurts that he's off-limits, and while Stephan embraces a "flirt with the universe" mentality, flirting with someone you really, really like who doesn't like you back as anything more than a friend… sucks.

Luckily, Jeff follows when Stephan changes the topic, surfing to the Humanities division's web pages and getting a faculty list. They go over who does what, and who is horrible to work with, and who is pretty decent. Jeff takes some notes and promises Stephan not to blackmail him with his honest opinions. Stephan promises the same.

They shake on it, laughing, and Stephan pretends not to notice how strong and nice Jeff's hand feels.

THE whole week kind of feels like a hangover. There are five weeks left in the semester, but really only four, since Thanksgiving is coming up. Another paper is due in his TA class next week, and the students are nervous again, hoping to do better on these papers than they did on their first ones. Stephan is researching and reading every snippet of information he can find for his two big papers, and it's an all-work-and-no-play week for the most part.

Which means that when the weekend comes and Mike insists Stephan come over and try the new cannabis strain he's cross-bred, Stephan accepts. Pot—or hashish—won't give him the hangover booze would, and even if Mike has several friends over, it will still be super mellow, unlike a night out clubbing would be.

After all, there's no one who's going to tell him that he can't or shouldn't, or look at him with disapproval and wrinkle their nose at the smell of the smoke on his clothes. Or anyone who will turn him down because they think he's a brainless little twink who likes to party every night and isn't ready for anything serious. Nope, Stephan can do whatever he wants.

So there, he thinks, sticking his tongue out at invisible, judgmental someones as he knocks on Mike's door.

So of course that's when Mike opens it. "Don't stick that out unless you're going to use it," he winks.

"Guess I'll just have to use it, then," Stephan says, leaning in as if to kiss Mike on the cheek and licking him instead.

"Dirty boy!"

Stephan smiles, although it feels a little forced. "You know it; I'm a free agent."

"Well, come on in, then." Mike shows him inside and introduces him to the handful of friends hanging around the living room. His huge hookah from Morocco is all ready to go, the coals smoldering and casting a shadow around the room. Apparently Mike's decided on an Arabic theme for snacks and music, which means hummus, pita chips, and something mellow with a lot of drums. Maybe an oud, too.

There's a guy there whose name Stephan can never remember but has been a stoner friend of Mike's for as long as Stephan's known him. The guy is nice, friendly, but has always kind of given Stephan the creeps. He's not flirty, per se, but he's touchy-feely in a way that could be harmless or could be sexual. It's so indirect that Stephan always feels like an asshole if he tries to get out of the hugs and, well, *cuddling*, but it's a serious personal-space invasion. The best way to deal with it, he's found, is to simply get really, really high and stop worrying about it.

Of course, that means that since he didn't even put up a token protest tonight, the guy—Ian—is not even being subtle. Tonight's touching is sexual, for sure, and hands are massaging, stroking, *groping* all over him. Stephan isn't sure if he could resist and shove Ian away even if he wanted to, and he can't tell whether he wants to. That should probably be upsetting, but he's too messed up to care.

Besides, it feels good to be held, tonight. Ian is sort of spooning him, and they're all on the floor, sprawled across a bunch of futons and papasan-chair cushions, like an opium den or something. The air is blue with smoke, and the gurgle of the water in the hookah is a nice counterpoint to the drum-heavy music. He's relaxed and kind of vaguely aroused, Ian's fingers running over and under his T-shirt, down his spine, across his chest, lips kissing the back of his neck.

"Good smoke," he tells Mike, who is curled up at his feet and alternately giving them a massage and playing This Little Piggy with his toes. His piggies are very pervy, it seems, at least according to Mike. Stephan had no idea.

"Yeah, smooth, isn't it? Pollinated with strains from all over the world…," Mike says in a dreamy voice. He's got a girl's head in his lap, and she could be doing anything from resting to nuzzling to giving Mike a blowjob, but Stephan would put his money on the nuzzling if he had to.

"Is it just me or is this kind of… making everyone horny?" he asks.

There's a giggle from the couple in the opposite corner. "Not just you, dude."

He considers staggering on home, if this is going to turn into an orgy or something, but honestly, no one seems to have the energy to go all the way and fuck. They're just touching and cuddling. Well, and kissing; there's definitely *some* making out. Mike brought out pillows and a few blankets a while ago, and he wouldn't be surprised to see that the boy-girl couple is partially or totally naked and having sex underneath theirs. But they were a couple when they got here, and the others are only friends.

Friends who cuddle. And kiss each other's necks, apparently. Stephan wiggles a little, rolling onto his back, and is not surprised when Ian's lips immediately meet his. It's not a sexy kiss, but it's... all right. He feels mellow; it's nice. Ian is starting to move on top of him, though, and that's not really as all right as the kissing. Stephan makes a negative noise, and Ian pulls back, laughing a little as he's replaced by Mike, and the girl from Mike's lap pulls Ian down to cuddle with her.

"You invited me to an orgy, you jerk," Stephan chuckles, breaking away from Mike's kiss.

"Hey, I didn't know it was going to be an orgy when we started. I had no idea I accidentally invented an aphrodisiac."

Stephan snorts. "It's like mellow, smokeable Ecstasy."

"Maybe it's your fault," Mike suggests. "You're just too hot to resist. Everyone wants a piece of you."

Everyone but Jeff, anyway. But that thought is depressing, and Stephan would far rather close his eyes and let himself be kissed and touched. Female lips occasionally press against his, too, but mostly they're male lips, and he refuses to figure out whether they belong to Ian or Mike. Hands are all over his body, and he is blindly caressing the other three too. It's half like a group massage and half like four people very, very slowing making out with no intention of having sex. Eventually he falls asleep, all four of them still in a pile, drifting off into a cloud of blue haze.

Chapter 23
It's Just Sex

STEPHAN wakes up with a crick in his neck, a hard-on pressed against his hip, and a face full of long, curly hair that smells like some kind of flowers. By the time he disentangles himself from the other three people, staggers home, showers, and sucks down a few cups of coffee, he mostly feels all right. His head is a little cottony and slow, but it's nothing like a booze hangover, thank God.

He's puttering around later that afternoon, tidying up the clothes that cover far too many surfaces in his room and taking a break from working on his M&T paper, when his phone rings.

"Stephan. Come dancing with me tonight."

"I'm *working*. You're a bad influence, you know."

Danielle laughs. "No point trying to resist temptation."

"Noted. Where do you want to go?"

"Just the Blue Lagoon."

The Blue is the local gay bar, although of course there're always a lot of straight people there too. They go because the music is good—it's the only real "dance club" in town—and the straight girls go because it's a safe-feeling place where they won't get hit on by asshole guys. The guys, of course, go because that's where the girls are. Still, it's definitely queer space, and Stephan's kind of been a regular since the night he turned twenty-one. In fact, he and Eric used to go there all the time when they first got together.

"Huh. You sure you want to go there instead of the Red Room or something? Do you just want to dance or, you know, go trawling?"

There's a pause while she thinks. "Good point. I'd kind of like to get laid, at the very least. I know I'm probably not going to meet anyone decent at a bar, but whatever. I need to get back in the game."

"Well, we can start going out more often. You'll meet someone worthy of your pancakes eventually. And by that I mean breakfast the morning after, not some weird vagina euphemism," he clarifies before she can even ask.

"Thank God. I might need to find someone else to go out with, though. No offense, but I'm never going to find anyone good if you're with me all the time. Guys aren't going to come up to me if you're there. You can't be my wingman, Steph, you're too pretty."

He makes a face even though she can't see it. "I'll try to be as ugly as I can."

"Good," she says, impatience creeping into her voice. "Okay, so. You need a date for tonight; who can we call?"

"I don't need a date," Stephan disagrees.

"Fine, you just need to *look* like you're dating someone. Someone not me. Mike?"

Stephan snorts. "You'll have to fend him off, too, if he smells that you're on the prowl."

"Oh please, he's totally afraid of me. And it's perfect because no one would ever seriously think I'm there with *Mike*."

"But they'll think I am? Thanks."

They trade a few more friendly barbs, and the banter ends with Stephan agreeing to call Mike to see if he's available, and the two guys will meet up at Danielle's house that night. If all goes well, she and Stephan will both find a hot stranger to go home with and fuck silly. Mike, sadly, is on his own.

WHEN Stephan calls, Mike is not only available, he's enthusiastic about going out to shake his groove thing with Stephan and Danielle. He tells Mike over and over that they are only *pretending* to be together so that Danielle's potential suitors won't think she's with Stephan. So she can potentially get laid, which Mike agrees is not exactly a matter of her finding someone, but of her *choosing* a guy she thinks is worthy. The girl is definitely hot enough to pick up anyone she wants to, after all.

It is a definite plus that Mike and Danielle have no interest in each other at all. Sure, Mike would try to put the moves on her if he thought he could get anywhere, but just for show. Which is good because Danielle would probably kill and dismember Mike, and then Stephan would have to help her hide the body. And Stephan likes Mike, so that would suck. He'd hate to have to choose between them when they inevitably broke up, if only because there's no way he'd cross Danielle by not choosing her. She's scary. And while Mike *likes* scary, he's not that stupid. He's generally pretty drama-free in his dating, actually.

Stephan kind of envies him a little, now that he thinks about it. Mike's never had a serious relationship that he knows about, or at least none in the last six years or so. Mike likes boys as well as girls, kink and vanilla, but he's pretty consistent about a lack of conflict in his life. This seems to result in him dating people for about a month or two at the most, although he's had a few fuck buddies who were strictly just friends who hung around for a while.

It sounds kind of nice, to be honest. Straightforward, easy, and if Stephan can't have the guy he's kind of pining for... well, maybe fuck buddies are the way to go. No drama, no complicated emotions, just a booty call every now and then with someone he trusts. The more he thinks about it, the better the plan sounds. Sex with no strings attached and no messy emotions.

With that in mind, Stephan turns on the charm and flirts his way into at least a dozen free drinks and some anonymous grinding on the dance floor. No one really catches his eye, although there are a few guys who are pretty hot. He's starting to think maybe he's just too damn picky, but he doesn't *want* another college boy younger than he is. Sure, Eric was totally hot—as was Òskar—but they're not what Stephan wants. He wants someone with some experience in life, who isn't going to be looking to him to take the lead. Someone assertive. Older.

Jeff.

But Jeff's not here. He doesn't go out clubbing, doesn't like to have fun, doesn't approve of drugs and parties and casual sex outdoors. Even if he is bi, he wouldn't want Stephan until Stephan grows up and settles down and gets boring. Maybe *Jeff* is the one who is boring, and Stephan should stop wanting him.

Even in his own head, Stephan knows he's being unreasonable, and also possibly confusing Eric's disapproval with Jeff's rejection. It just feels like every guy he has feelings for thinks he's some asshole party-boy, and so fuck it, he's going to act like one. Maybe if he tries hard enough, he won't even care that they think so little of him; he just thought they knew him better than that.

"No more booze for you," Mike declares, wrapping his arms around Stephan from behind. "It's a depressant, you know, and you're looking all mopey. Come outside with me, and let's see if I have something in my pants that will turn that frown upside down."

That starts a chuckle out of him. "I imagine you have *several* things in your pants that would make me laugh, dude."

"I'm wounded! Well, now I need a toke, too, to get over your casual ego-crushing of such a good friend. A good friend who not only drove you here, and is letting you pretend to be my boyfriend, but also is offering to share some of his finest weed with you. You're just ungrateful, Stephan, you know that? No gratitude at all," Mike says, shaking his head sadly over Stephan's rudeness.

Rolling his eyes, Stephan drags Mike outside and into the alley. It smells like pot out there already, and soon enough they're adding their own share to it. It's not the same as last night's hashish, of course, but it's still pretty smooth and very strong.

"You going to be okay to drive home?" Stephan asks in a moment of practicality.

"Hm, good point. Well, I only had one hit; the rest is all yours," Mike grins, holding the joint and lighter out to Stephan.

It's more than he wants, and when they're joined by a few other smokers, it's not hard to find someone willing to share. Stephan wants to get high, yeah, but not seriously fucked up. Not two nights in a row, anyway.

When he goes back inside, Danielle is looking for him, but for a good reason; she's found a guy from one of her classes last year and is going back to his place. This is a coded message, because Stephan knows she doesn't ever fuck a guy for the first time anywhere but her own bed, but he's glad she's found someone to at least fool around with for a while. The guy seems like a decent-enough person; Stephan gives him the older-brother once-over, and the guy just grins and says he's glad Danni's got someone burly looking out for her. She, of course, is less happy about that and glares at them both and reminds them that she has a brown belt in jujitsu and can take care of herself.

That done, she leaves, promising Stephan that she'll call him tomorrow. It's getting a little late, and Stephan is thinking about taking off too. He finds Mike sitting at a table against the wall with Jim and Jamie, who stopped in for a drink after a movie. It's nice to run into them somewhere outside of the apartment. Jamie looks happy and a little drunk, and Jim is all relaxed. He's goofing around with Mike while Stephan and Jamie watch indulgently as they roughhouse like little boys and laugh far too loud and generally are disruptive jerks. The bartender glares at them eventually, and while they've been coming here long enough that they probably won't get thrown out, it's best to just call it quits, so the four of them leave without incident.

Mike drives them home, and Stephan is way too out of it to walk back up the hill to his own apartment. His jerk friend should have driven him home first, he points out, but Mike just shrugs.

"How else am I going to get you into my bed? You took off this morning before I had a chance to lure you in any further."

Stephan laughs. "I thought last night was one of those things we don't discuss. What happens with the hookah stays with the hookah."

"You can 'not discuss' it all you like; I'm planning to tell everyone I know that I finally got to mess around with the Great Stephan Burke."

"Yeah, you and Ian and… what was that chick's name, anyway? I can't believe I kissed a *girl*," he says, making an *"ew ick"* face.

"Stacy. That was some damn amazing shit…. Seriously, I can't believe I got you into an orgy, or a languorous massage, or whatever. And you're a surprisingly good kisser. So many hot guys are awful in bed," Mike laments.

"Fuck off; I'm great in bed," Stephan pouts.

"Oh yeah? Wanna prove it?"

Stephan rolls his eyes, but wraps his hands around Mike's head and pulls him in for a kiss. Like last night, it feels good to be touched. He's a little drunk, a little high, and feeling pretty damn good. Mike is comfortable and familiar and maybe he's not so sexy that he gives Stephan a boner every time they see each other, but still. And maybe some of that is from overfamiliarity; Stephan's known Mike for what feels like forever. He just never knew Mike could feel so good to touch and kiss and hold.

They end up in Mike's room, on the bed, making out without much conversation. Stephan feels… good. Just good. Not the lusty urgency he felt with Òskar, not the bone-melting one-sided desire he felt for Eric the last few months… and not the frustrated longing he feels for Jeff. But good. He's a little horny, and they're kissing, rubbing against each other, and he's enjoying it.

He's just not sure he's enjoying it *enough*. He's on the bottom, Mike sprawled on top, both of them shirtless and with bare feet. Mike's starting to make happy little sounds as he reaches for Stephan's jeans, and Stephan's trying to keep up, to get into it, honestly. He's hard and everything, and he's trying not to lie there like a dead fish, but he's not exactly pulling off Mike's pants or thinking about where condoms and lube might be stashed.

"Hey," Mike says, poking him in the belly to get his attention. "We're friends, right?" Stephan nods. "It's just sex. But it's fine if you're not into it. Me and my unrequited lust will survive," he grins.

Stephan laughs. "It's not… it's not you. I just don't feel…."

"Oh my *God*, shut up before you embarrass us both, dumbshit."

Rolling his eyes, Stephan wraps his arms around Mike and pulls him into a loose embrace. Mike makes a protesting noise, but hugs him back.

"So, no sex. This okay?"

"Yeah, s'good…," Stephan mumbles, letting his eyes close as his body relaxes. No sex. No pressure. Just holding. Nice.

"Great." They cuddle for a while, Mike's hands roaming over Stephan's body in a soothing kind of way. Stephan's kind of drifting on the edge of sleep when he notices that Mike's dick is still poking him in the thigh and rubbing against him. He reaches a hand down to Mike's hip and holds him still.

Mike stops moving, and there's a moment of silence before he speaks. "Okay, I'm going to go jerk off in the bathroom before I die of blue balls, all right? Don't go anywhere."

"You don't have to. I mean, you can stay here, if you want. I don't wanna drive you out of your own bed," Stephan offers, intending to move to the sofa in the living room.

"Nah. We've already pushed the boundaries of friendship far enough without my jerking off on you. Besides, this way you won't get all pissy when I moan Matt Damon's name when I shoot," Mike says, winking as he gets up.

They both laugh again. "Okay. You sure it's cool for me to stay here? I could go home."

"Nah. I'll let you share my bed even if you don't put out. I'm a gentleman like that."

Stephan snorts, and Mike closes the door behind him. He hears the bathroom door close a moment later, and then wriggles out of his jeans, making himself comfortable in Mike's bed with the pillows fluffed just right. He's pretty much asleep when a warm body slides into bed next to him and a kiss is pressed to his cheek.

Mike's awesome.

Chapter 24
Women

"GOOD weekend?" Stephan asks Danielle after their class together on Monday afternoon.

She hits him with her book, smirking. "Not bad. We went back to my place Sunday afternoon and he stayed the night."

"Yeah? What's his name? And I thought I was supposed to be picking out your boyfriends, you know. Do I need to interrogate this guy?"

"Hm, maybe. His name is Rob." She thinks for a moment. "He's good in bed. Smart. Funny. And we cooked well together…. What else is on your list?"

"Money. Life goals. Musical taste. Movies. You should have known something was wrong with Bryan when he said he'd never heard of Mel Brooks."

She laughs. "Yeah, I should have. Sure, if all goes well and I keep him around, you can grill him with my blessing the next time we're all together. I won't hide him from you, I promise."

"Good." He totally means it; he's going to do his best to make sure this guy isn't as much of a dick as Danni's last boyfriend. She deserves someone who will respect her, take care of her, and treat her like a queen when she's not doing naughty things to him in the bedroom.

Heck, *everyone* deserves that. Even him.

"That was a world-weary sigh," Danielle says. "What's up with you? Did you go home with anyone on Saturday or just Mike?"

Stephan tries really hard not to let his facial expression change or blush or anything stupid, but she knows him too well.

"Uh-oh. Tell me."

"Uh. Well… Mike and I messed around," he says, going for the blunt approach to get it over with.

"What? Oh my God," she says and starts to laugh hysterically.

"Shut up! It was actually kind of okay. We didn't do anything, really. Made out a little, fell asleep."

She's still laughing. He rolls his eyes and waits for her to get a hold of herself.

"Bitch."

"I'm sorry, baby. It's just funny, you've got to admit." He smacks her lightly on the arm, and she smacks him back. "Seriously, Mike? Are you okay?" she asks, sobering. "I mean, I thought you were just messing around, but…?"

Stephan shrugs. "I'm fine. Just, you know, kind of playing the field. Mike's a good kisser, surprisingly enough. But it was weird, so we stopped and just fell asleep. It was nice to share a bed with someone again," he adds thoughtfully.

"Getting lonely?" she asks, in her far-too-insightful way.

He rolls his eyes, denying it. "Nah. I'm having fun, just screwing around, like you're supposed to after a breakup, right?"

She gives him a probing look but doesn't push the issue. "Fine. So, tell me about school—how is your TA stuff going? I bet your kids all have massive crushes on you."

He's not sure why she's fluffing his ego, but he'll take it. "Some. Just girls, though. I can't tell if any of the guys are queer; you know how closeted most guys are their first year or two."

"Not you—you were pretty much always out and proud."

Stephan shrugs. "Well, out, anyway. I never got the point of hiding. I like guys. Girl parts are weird and—" he manages to catch himself before he says gross and she kicks his ass. "Squishy?"

Danielle rolls her eyes. "I'll let you get away with that, but only if you buy me lunch."

It's not a bad offer, and he knows he got off lightly for insulting her womanly bits. They head to the Student Center and settle in for some food while they commiserate over how their Lit papers are going. Stephan's almost done with his first draft, although he needs to spend some more time in the library doing research to fill in the holes and support his ideas a little better. They make a date to meet there on Tuesday afternoon.

"Thanks for lunch," she says, kissing his cheeks as she gets ready to take off for her last class of the day. "Say hi to Mike from me, when you see him"—she grins—"and try to keep your pants on this time."

He throws a balled-up napkin at her as she walks out the door. "Brat!"

STEPHAN thinks about his conversation with Danielle for a while that night while he's trying to study French stuff. He's not lonely. He's just… drifting. Maybe the thing with Mike was a mistake, but at least it wasn't a big huge catastrophe or anything. They fooled around, it didn't work, and while he hasn't exactly *talked* to Mike about it, he doesn't think it will probably be a big deal. They just didn't have any chemistry together, he thinks, and then rolls his eyes at the idea of a biochem PhD lacking chemistry.

It just wasn't there though, that *feeling*, that urge to touch and taste and *fuck*. Not like it was with Eric or that guy at the club, or even with Jeff. He's been doing a pretty good job of not thinking about Jeff, despite seeing the guy in class three times a week. He kind of misses their budding friendship, but…. It's hard to be around him. They haven't really talked since the morning after Halloween, and he wonders what Jeff's been up to. Maybe he should call him or something….

Speak of the Devil; Stephan's phone rings and nearly scares him to death.

"Stephan? It's Lauren. Are you free by any chance? I'm fucking dying, here."

He closes his book, concerned. "Yeah, what's up? Are you okay?"

"I'm fine," she says, in a voice that is totally *not*. "It's my TA sections. This guy and girl got in a huge screaming fight tonight, and I couldn't shut them up, and I had no fucking idea what to do. I've totally lost control of them, Stephan. At first, I couldn't get anyone to talk about anything at all, and now I can't get these two idiots to shut the fuck up!"

"Breathe," he says, since she sounds like she's going to start crying, and he totally does not know her well enough to deal with her crying at him over the phone. "Okay, so what were they fighting about? Is it an ideological disagreement or is it personal with them? Has it happened before? Do they just hate each other for some reason? Did they used to date?"

He hears her taking deep breaths before she answers, clearly trying to calm down. "Huh, I hadn't thought of that. I mean, they're *freshmen*—I totally should have remembered what that's like. I bet it's personal, whether they dated or not; they argue all the time, and I know they live in the same dorm. Now that I think about it, they used to sit next to each other at the beginning of the semester, but they don't anymore. God, I'm so stupid; I can't believe I missed that."

"Nah, don't beat yourself up about it. It's not like it was unreasonable to expect them to act like adults and not get into a brawl in the middle of your class. So now you have a guess as to why they're behaving like dumbasses, what can you do about it?"

There's a long pause. "Well, much as I'd like to rip them both new ones and yell at them for disrupting my class, I suppose *that* might also be disruptive. So I guess talk to them one-on-one, before or after section. I probably can't just e-mail them and tell them to sit down and shut up, can I?"

"Probably not," he laughs. "How bad was it? Do you think you need to say something in section, to the rest of the students, or can you just move forward?"

"I think it'll be okay to move forward. I'll get all dressed up and put on my bitch-boots and stop taking their shit."

"You go, girl," he says, doing the snaps even though she can't see him, and they both laugh.

"Wow, Steph, thank you. Seriously, I guess I just needed someone to be rational and help me see what the hell was going on. I appreciate you letting me interrupt whatever you were doing tonight. Getting lucky, maybe?" she teases.

"Nah, just studying."

"Your boyfriend sure must love you, to put up with being ignored so much."

She's totally teasing, but wow—that still kind of hurts. "Uh. We broke up," he finally says.

"Damn, I *suck*. I'm so sorry."

"Nah, it's okay. It was a few weeks ago. And, you know, I've been going out and doing the swinging-single thing," he says, to forestall any weird sympathy she might have. It's not like he's sitting at home alone every night moping or anything, after all. "Hanging out with friends, random hookups. Wild and carefree."

She laughs. "Well then, we should go out. Hey, how about tomorrow night? I'll buy you a drink to thank you for your help. And you should know—I *never* buy guys drinks, so you're special."

They arrange to meet at her place, which is just on the other end of the Graduate Student Housing complex, and she'll be the designated driver. It's a good plan, and he ends up looking forward to it all day because Tuesday is a *shitty* goddamned day. His M&T class is once again dragging, and listening to the guest speaker go on and on and fucking *on* about Karl Marx is killing him. Tina looks like she's going to fall asleep, and even the professor seems bored. Then, every time he gets into his own work during "office hours" at the Student Center he gets interrupted by stupid questions from his students.

In his TA section, the kids are whiny and upset at having to write an essay next week and then have their research paper due less than three weeks later. He has no sympathy; the essay is only about five pages, double-spaced, and is about the movie from a few weeks ago. Their panties are in a twist because they don't have written resources, and he tries not to roll his eyes when he points out that the Internet has all kinds of information they can use, including quotations from the movie and reviews from critics. Idiots.

He doesn't exactly *intend* to drink so much at the bar, but he doesn't stop when he notices that he's getting drunk, either. Lauren started him off with Jaeger shots, and he didn't feel like stopping or switching to something less lethal. He's dancing with her and a bunch of other girls, and he can tell she's totally laughing at him and the way the girls are throwing themselves at him, but he doesn't care. He's having a good time. He's allowed, right? So what if it's a Tuesday night?

They stay out entirely too late, and when she drives them back home, he can barely stagger upstairs to his own apartment. They pretty much closed down the bar at two a.m., and it's been a while since Stephan's seen the lights come on at the Red Room. Years.

When his alarm goes off at way-too-early o'clock, he briefly toys with ditching class. But it's French, and there's a quiz, so he really can't. Madame George doesn't do make-ups unless you've got a doctor's note or something, and he's stupid, not sick.

Really stupid. His double espresso is not enough to clear up the massive hangover from last night's overindulgence, and he's totally dragging. If that was Lauren's way of saying "thanks," he'd hate to see what she does to people she's angry with. And speaking of angry women, Mme. Georges takes one look at him staggering past her into the classroom, raises her eyebrow, and sniffs. He's pretty sure she smells licorice alcohol and sweat and the gross odors you pick up spending five hours in a bar. And no, he didn't shower this morning because it was that or grab some coffee on his way to class, and duh—caffeine.

"Today's quiz will be followed by oral exercises," she says, staring right at him. "We'll work on your pronunciation with a stimulating round of 'La Marseillaise', and then we'll see what other songs I have lyrics for. I'm sure you'll enjoy it."

She is pure evil. Women are scary creatures.

Chapter 25
The Right Ingredients

STEPHAN grabs a quick shower between French and Jeff's class. He still feels like shit, and he's got the nearly black circles under his eyes to prove it. At least he doesn't smell like Jaeger anymore, which is an improvement. He isn't going to be able to smell licorice without wanting to hurl for a *long* time.

He sits through the lecture without falling asleep by virtue of another double espresso and a handful of chocolate-covered espresso beans. Seriously, if he could just get an IV drip of caffeine, so many things in his life would be better. Jeff glances at him at one point, raising an eyebrow, probably as a reprimand for the crunching noises. Oops.

"Late night?" Jeff asks him when class is over and the students are filing out. "You look worse than you did after the Halloween party."

He shrugs. "Yeah. Lauren took me out for a drink last night that turned into closing down the bar doing shots. It was pretty stupid; I feel like utter shit."

"Well, no one died, right?" Jeff points out. "We all do stupid shit sometimes. What were you eating, anyway? Sounded like you were chewing gravel."

Stephan snorts as he fishes the bag out of his pocket. "Food of the gods: espresso beans covered with chocolate," he says, offering them to Jeff.

Jeff takes a handful and crunches on them while he packs up his stuff. "Have you eaten anything other than coffee today? Got time for lunch?"

"No and yes," he says, distracted for a moment watching Jeff's hands. There's nothing special about them, exactly, but....

Jeff clears his throat and raises an eyebrow when Stephan glances up.

"Yes, lunch. How about the taqueria on Science Hill?" he suggests.

They walk over, and it's extremely crowded, of course, but the food is worth it. They end up ordering the super nachos to share, and Stephan introduces Jeff to horchata when the older man confesses that he's always been a little scared to try it.

"So, are there any more concerts or shows coming up for your friend Billy? I was pretty impressed by him. And you too," Jeff adds. "I don't think I knew you played until he dragged you up on the stage with him."

Stephan shrugs. "I don't perform. Never been in a band or anything. I just play because I like it."

"Ah. Well, any shows?"

"Not that I know of, so nothing local for sure or he'd have told me about it." Jeff seems a little disappointed by that answer; maybe he's... lonely? Bored? Stephan clears his throat, then asks, "Do you want to do something this weekend?"

The grin Jeff gives him is amazing. "Yeah, I'd like that. Maybe not hiking, though, until the weather gets warm again," he says, winking.

Stephan snorts. "Okay, so indoors or out, then? We could drive up the coast, or go tidepooling, check out our fabulous local museums, shoot some pool, check out what bands are playing, or catch a movie...?"

"A movie might be good, actually. I think I saw a preview on TV for the new James Bond, if you're up for it."

That sounds good to him—admittedly because the new Bond is *hot*—and they plan on Saturday night. Jeff suggests dinner beforehand and he agrees.

"It's a date," Jeff says with another killer smile and a wink.

He's joking, of course, but that doesn't stop something inside Stephan from getting all twisted up and tight-feeling. He's still such an idiot.

STEPHAN still feels like crap the next day. He needs to get his shit together: stop drinking, get caught up on his French memorization, work out more, eat better. Do some laundry, even. He's made a mess of his body too many times over the last few weeks, and it's rebelling. He's not eighteen anymore, and he's sick of what he's been doing, going out too much, drinking too much, random almost-hookups, and generally doing the very things he was mad at Eric and Jeff for thinking he was doing, when he wasn't.

He's not that guy, the kind who smokes a bowl every day, or goes out clubbing on weeknights, getting off with random guys in dark alleys, flirting with girls he wouldn't touch if they were the last two humans on earth. Blowing off all the things that are important to him— school, his friends, self-respect—in favor of being kind of a jerk.

Not that he hasn't been seeing his friends, but still. He's acting stupid, and out of some sense of spiteful defiance at Eric's disapproval and hurt at Jeff's rejection, which is totally dumb because Jeff's either straight or just not into him, and neither of those are things he should take personally. Other guys think he's hot, after all; it's fine if Jeff doesn't.

But they have a *date*. Dinner and a movie, although of course they're just going out as friends. Man, how he wishes it was more.... Then again, that's not exactly helping with his stupid crush. His attempt at avoiding being social with Jeff until it faded doesn't seem to have worked at all, and on top of it, well, he kind of misses the guy.

There's not much he can do other than mope around and psychoanalyze himself, so he tries his best to focus on the things that he *can* do. He starts some laundry, drills his French flashcards, and on Friday night he calls Scott to get his recipe for minestrone soup. It's got ten vegetables in it, and Scott is always telling him how easy it is, so he's going to give it a try despite his general tentativeness to actually cook things with real ingredients.

Scott returns his call and offers to come over and help Stephan out. And also loans him a big soup pot, since he and Jim don't have one. Billy is gone for the weekend, playing a gig in Southern California, and Scott's work is too busy for him to take any time off right now, so he's home alone.

Scott brings over some bread, cheese, and beer, and supervises as Stephan chops the vegetables and throws them in the pot one at a time. He's nearly finished when Scott says, "You do know this is going to have to simmer for at least three or four hours, right?"

"What?"

"Yeah. Soups and stews take time."

Stephan blinks at him. "Well, what the fuck am I supposed to eat for dinner tonight, then?"

Scott smirks. "I knew you were clueless. Good thing I brought dinner, as well as snacks," he says, pulling some pasta and ready-made Alfredo sauce out of the grocery bag. "You're cooking, though. I came over here to give you a lesson and have a cute guy make me dinner."

Stephan wiggles his butt at Scott and gets a laugh in response. "You keep flirting with me like that and I won't let you go back home to Billy," he jokes.

"Right, like I'd ever get between you two; Billy would tear all three of us to shreds."

"Can't have that. I'm too young and pretty to be dismembered. Although my liver might disagree, after this month," he says ruefully. Scott gives him a look, and Stephan sighs then shrugs. "Been overindulging. Too much booze and pot and sex stuff."

"Your one-night-stand kid got weird?"

"Not him—he was fine. Just… too much flirting and messing around. Got really high at one of Mike's parties and fooled around with some people I probably shouldn't have. Like Mike."

Scott's laughter isn't quite as loud or long as Danielle's was, but it's still pretty goddamned annoying. Then again, if someone had told Stephan two months ago that he'd have made out with Mike not once but *twice*, he'd have laughed his ass off too.

It takes Scott a few minutes to get himself under control, and he apologizes once he has. "And not that there's anything wrong with Mike, either," he adds, "you two just would make a *terrible* couple. He's totally wrong for you."

Stephan raises an eyebrow, even though he doesn't disagree. "Oh yeah? And who do you think would be right for me?"

Scott takes a long drink of his beer and thinks about it. "Well, you and Eric were pretty good at first. So someone who's a friend, a guy you could hang out with, do stuff you enjoy together. Aside from sex," he clarifies, winking. "You've got to have common interests, and for you that's stuff like school, music, and being outside. Movies and food, too, but for you, I'd say having a guy who you can talk to about the things you're studying is really important."

"Huh. Yeah, I can see that, I guess. But someone who also likes to have fun is important," Stephan points out. "Eric was fine until he went home for the summer and had to deal with his alcoholic mom again. Not that I'm blaming him, I guess, but still—I don't want someone who's going to make me feel bad for having a little fun now and then. Or even a lot of fun, sometimes."

"Yeah, you don't need to deal with a lot of someone else's baggage, but everyone's got *some*. It's finding the baggage that goes with yours, that you can handle without it getting in the way."

Stephan snorts. "Matching baggage. I'd rather 'handle' the guy's package instead," he jokes.

Scott laughs. "Yeah, and that's important too—compatible sex stuff. Someone you wouldn't get bored with, who likes what you like, but can still surprise you sometimes."

His conversation with Jeff about the Marquis de Sade in the library that one time flashes through Stephan's mind. He flushes. So far, he and Scott have pretty much totally described Jeff, down to nearly the last detail.

"Great," he sighs. "So basically, my perfect match is the guy I have a huge unrequited crush on."

Scott shrugs. "Could be worse. At least he's a friend."

"True."

"So what's the problem? He likes you. He was staring at you like he wanted to lick every inch of your body at 99 Bottles that night after Billy's show," he teases. "Go get him."

Stephan shakes his head. "Can't. I tried already. I made a move the day after Eric broke up with me, like an asshole. I wasn't thinking, like, at all. I, uh, kissed him."

"Good for you. Did he kiss you back?" Scott asks.

"Not really."

"Did he shove you away?"

"No, not really."

Nodding, a satisfied look in his eyes, Scott says, "Exactly. Keep pushing. If at first you don't succeed, try, try again."

"I'm not going to keep throwing myself at him," Stephan argues. "I like him. I… I like him a lot. I want to at least be his friend, if I can't be anything else," he says pathetically.

Scott gives him a probing look, then shrugs and finishes his beer. "Huh. Well, hey… you're coming over for Thanksgiving, right? Bring him with you. Maybe he just needs to see how awesome you are outside of school and off the dance floor."

Stephan snorts. "You mean bring him over so you can play matchmaker and Billy can interrogate him and scare him away."

"You say 'tomato'…." Scott grins. "Come on, it'll be fun. And you said he's new here—he might not have anywhere else to go. It can't hurt to ask him."

"Okay, okay; I'll ask him. Damn, you don't take 'no' for an answer, do you?"

"If I did, Billy and I wouldn't be together," Scott points out. "Being stubborn is a good thing."

"Except in Billy," Stephan says snorting.

"Except in Billy. Bastard could write the book on being contrary."

"You hold your own pretty well," Stephan notes.

"Billy definitely taught me to go for what I want and not give up, keep working at it until I got it," Scott says, getting a sappy look in his eyes.

Stephan makes a puking noise and punches him on the shoulder. Scott manages to get him in a headlock, and they tumble to the ground, the remains of dinner going flying from the table. Which is when Jim comes in, hands on his hips and a scowl that would do any father of two rowdy, misbehaving boys proud.

"What the hell are you two—" is all he manages to get out before the combined team of Stephan and Scott leap up from the floor, united against a common enemy. Neither Jim nor the Alfredo sauce stood a chance.

STEPHAN can't stop thinking about his conversation with Scott all through his not-a-date with Jeff. Sure, he's had a crush on the guy since they met—or even before—but Jeff is honestly just *perfect* for him. There is nothing about Jeff that isn't right, and while it's true that he's only known the guy for three months and there's probably a lot of ex-wife baggage somewhere, everything Stephan *does* know is awesome.

The whole night is the most delicious torture—if only he got to go back to Jeff's place and fuck him stupid, it would be a perfect night. He's not delusional enough to think they're "meant to be" or some shit like that, but they *are* pretty compatible.

And damn Scott for making Stephan realize that Jeff maybe *hadn't* really rejected him that one night. Now that he's looking for it,

Jeff does seem to be flirting with him and checking him out whenever he's got his back turned. Maybe Jeff *is* bisexual. Maybe Jeff wants him. In which case, Stephan just needs to figure out why Jeff has been keeping him at arm's length, and convince Jeff to go for it. Show Jeff that he is ready and willing and practically begging for it....

He gets home that night, having given Jeff a longer hug than usual, and almost but not quite kissing him again. There had been that tension in the air between their faces, like the push-pull between two magnets, and Jeff hadn't moved away.

Stephan falls asleep with sticky hands after jerking off to fantasies of what could have happened, *would* have happened, maybe, if he'd kissed Jeff, pressed their bodies together until he could feel Jeff's hard dick next to his own, wanting.

Plans for seduction weave with satiation and a sense of determination. Stephan's going to make Jeff want him or die trying. Yes.

Chapter 26
The Early Bird Gets the Resentment

ON TUESDAY afternoon, Stephan's office hours are *swamped*. He feels like he should have one of those "take a number" machines next to the table that he's claimed, and a ten-minute limit per kid. He ends up more than doubling his one required hour. It's amazing to him how much these kids freak out about their assignments, yet they still attempt to do them at the last possible minute. This, Stephan thinks, is the quality that separates the truly good students from the rest— overcoming procrastination.

He tries to point this out to the kids who come to see him without being too heavy-handed, but knows he fails. It's just so stupid to stress out when you don't have to, and honestly, *no one* does a better job on a research paper by putting it off. Letting the ideas mull around in your head for as long as possible, gathering the facts and letting them simmer, and then writing based on all the connections that your subconscious has put together—that's how to write a good paper. Not unlike cooking, he supposes, based on his one soup experience. You can't just throw it all in the pot at the last minute and eat it right away and expect it to taste very good.

He's *totally* going to use that metaphor in his next TA section.

The last student leaves—or at least what Stephan *hopes* is the last student; there aren't any more obviously waiting, at any rate—and he goes to get a refill from the coffee cart. The same guy is working there as before, and Stephan struggles to remember his name, offering an apologetic grin when he can't come up with it.

"Dylan," he says, winking. "You're Stephan, right?" At Stephan's nod, he waves away the apology that's obviously coming. "I overheard one of your students a little while ago; I'm bad with names too. So what subject are you TAing? Are you going for an MA or PhD?"

Stephan answers his questions, flirting a little out of habit, and finds out the other guy is taking a break for a semester while he works on his BFA.

"Oh yeah? What kind of art do you do?"

"Theater, pretty much. I'm still wavering between acting and directing, which is why I'm taking some time off to think about it before I choose my concentration. Can't decide what I like better, bossing people around or getting applause from an audience," Dylan says with a wink.

"Bossing people around, for sure, for me," Stephan grins. "I get dragged on stage sometimes to play guitar with friends, but I'm far more comfortable out of the spotlight."

Dylan raises an eyebrow. "As hot as you are, that's a real shame. You should be a movie star or a model; you'd have millions of people wanting to jump your bones. Then again," he adds slyly, "that much competition might decrease my chances."

Stephan snorts. "Thanks." He never knows what to say when guys are so direct. It's flattering, yeah, but he also totally gets that it's objectifying as well. There's a fine line between sincere and smarmy, and frankly, guys his age and younger just come off as smarmy. Older guys, when they mention his looks, usually manage to do it so that there's some hint of irony, in a *I can't believe I'm telling you how sexy you are because that's so stupid, but I can't help myself because you're just that gorgeous.* Like Jeff, for a totally random example.

Anyway, he's not really interested in Dylan, so whatever. He's got his sights set on Jeff. Maybe if that doesn't work out, he'll chat up Dylan sometime and see if the guy can recover from his faux pas. Besides, actors, like musicians, are notorious flakes. Dylan's cute, but yeah—maybe later.

After the TA session that evening, Stephan's back at the Student Center for dinner and a study-date with Tina to go over their Method and Theory papers. Tina looks exhausted, which reminds Stephan that Kristine had looked pretty grouchy during their TA time earlier that day too. He meant to ask what was wrong but had never had a moment to talk to her. He doesn't mean to pry, but if they're both upset, then something's going on, and he wants to know what. Partially out of curiosity, and partially to see if he can help. He's *nosy*, but he's also trying to be a good friend.

"What's up, you look tired?" he tries. "Everything okay?"

Tina fiddles with her pen for a moment then sighs. "No. Kristine's mom is flipping out about the holidays. She wants Kristine to come home and see the family, but I'm definitely not invited. I don't want to go anyway and have it be awful, and her mom's kind of a bitch, so I'd just as soon stay here, you know? Only Kristine wants to go and have a big showdown and make her mom either totally accept or reject her for being a dyke, and I…. It's not my battle, you know?" she asks with a pleading, frustrated expression. "I'll go if she wants me there for moral support, but I'm fucking *tired* after this endless semester, and I just want to relax for my three-week vacation."

Stephan makes a sympathetic face. "That sucks. I'm sorry."

"Yeah, me too. Not much I can do, though. *My* family has known since I was in high school, and they were pretty much fine with it and any girlfriends I brought home, from the beginning. I wish we could just go see them," she sighs.

"Well, maybe you'll get lucky and Kristine will change her mind." When Tina gives him a highly skeptical look, he adds, "Or maybe her mom will change her mind, or they'll have it out over the phone, or maybe an asteroid will fall on their neighbor's house and suddenly a little muff-diving won't seem like such a big deal."

Tina snorts, smacking him on the shoulder, but he got a laugh and that's what matters. "Yeah, who knows? Maybe the world will end. I guess you're right and I shouldn't worry about it any more than I have to. So… M&T?"

Stephan nods and they get to work. He's mostly finished with his paper, has a first draft done and ready for someone to proofread and give him some feedback. Tina looks like she wants to murder him when he admits that he's so close, but hey, he likes to be done early. And he even kind of got into it a little; comparing the way the different biographers recounted the same events was pretty interesting. He just hopes the paper is interesting, too, and not a simple regurgitation of facts.

"It's not even Thanksgiving yet! How can you be done? I hate you forever," she moans.

"How about if I help you with yours, to make up for it?" He gives her his best puppy-dog eyes, and she rolls her eyes. "I'll even do some research for you, if you'll proof my paper," he offers.

"Hm. Throw in a mocha or two and you've got yourself a deal."

They shake on it, grinning, and spend the next hour or so talking about her topic and how to make it more interesting. It seems that some of Jeff's ideas about historiography managed to sink into his brain, and Stephan's actually kind of getting into it. While the topic in itself isn't that exciting, its application *is*. That's kind of cool, and in helping Tina, he realizes that he's learned something and sort of changed his mind about the subject too. Score!

The sound of billiard balls smacking into each other catches Stephan's attention as he's getting his stuff together to finally go home. He looks over at the pool tables and sees the cute twink from earlier in the semester, the one with the perky little ass who Stephan was *sure* was queer, right up until the kid started exploring the tonsils of some girl, in front of everyone.

Tonight, though, all is right with the world; the kid's got a permanent blush on his cheeks as he plays the game and flirts with a really built guy, touching him every time they move around each other, in ways straight guys definitely don't. It's cute, and Stephan is grinning as he leaves, glad both that the kid has come out of the closet and that his gaydar *totally* wasn't broken after all. Life is good.

A FEW days later, Stephan shows up for his Lit class with a brownie and soy latte for Danielle, who accepts them with a suspicious look.

"I'll take the food, but I want to know what you're bribing me for," she says. "I'm not letting you steal my new boyfriend."

"How's that going, anyway?" he asks.

"Great. What do you want?"

Stephan rolls his eyes. "I want you to proofread my paper for this class. I'll do yours, if you want. I'm just nervous."

Danielle shrugs. "Sure. We've talked about it enough that I'm kind of curious to see where you went with your research."

"Great; here," he says, handing her the printout.

She blinks. "Uh…?" She glances down at the papers in her hand and blinks again. "You're already finished? Oh my fucking God, you *suck*! I forgot what an overzealous little shit you are. This isn't even due for three more weeks!"

"It's only a draft! It probably needs revisions. I told you, I'm really nervous," he says defensively.

Grumbling, she shoves his paper in her bag and promises to review it before she leaves for the Thanksgiving break. He offers to take her out for dinner when she gives it back to him, to make up for his unspeakable crime of being almost done a little bit early.

"So what are you up to this weekend?" he asks.

"Not much. Hanging out with Rob," she answers, a little smile pulling at her lips.

"Are you blushing? Oh my God, you're blushing! Okay, dish with me," he laughs, nudging her with his shoulder.

She rolls her eyes, but launches into a description of how amazing Rob is, how they talk about school stuff, and go to movies together, and how the sex is amazing. "Mostly,," she says, looking a little embarrassed, "it's just how he treats me. No one has ever been so nice to me before, for no reason other than that they like me. Do you know what I mean? Like, he's not just doing stuff so I'll fuck him later; he actually *wants* to."

Stephan knows his smile is a little wistful, but he's genuinely happy for her. He wraps her in a big hug and squeezes. "Good. That's how it's supposed to be. I'm really glad you've found someone who treats you right. You deserve it."

She shoves him a little bit, face still a bit pink. "Shut up, jerk. I'll get all teary and my mascara will run."

"Well, we can't have that," he agrees, and he steals the last bite of her brownie.

"How about you; what are you up to this weekend? Want to come over and annoy me and check out Rob?"

Stephan grins. "I've got another TA grading 'party' at Jeff's tomorrow, but I'm pretty free otherwise. Dinner Sunday?"

They agree to meet at her place, and she'll cook if he brings some beer or wine and agrees to leave when she tells him to. As if he'd want to hang around and be a third wheel for their lovey-dovey crap or an unwilling voyeur when she gets horny. He's had enough of *that* to last a lifetime, thank you.

The grading session on Saturday goes smoothly. He and Lauren and Will have pretty much got the hang of it, but agreed that it was still good to do all together so they could talk about whatever issues arose, and make sure their standards are all more or less the same. Jeff's hosting mostly because he doesn't mind, and because his living room is more comfortable and quieter than any other place on campus, than to oversee their work or anything. It's casual and they plow through the papers, getting the relatively short essays graded in just a couple of hours.

Jeff is in a really good mood for some reason, and Stephan's pretty sure he's not drunk, although he's certainly putting away his share of the beer. He has the cutest giggle—not a laugh, but a genuine *giggle*—that Stephan's ever heard a grown man make. At one point they're joking about something, and Lauren makes a "your mama" retort, and Jeff just fucking *loses* it. He laughs, going all loose-limbed and helpless, and then actually snorts! It's fucking hilarious, and then they're all laughing, sort of at him and sort of for no good reason at all.

There's something about his laugh—his giggle!—that's just infectious. Stephan can't *not* smile in response to it. He's just so genuine, so honestly amused and willing to be a total dork, that it makes Stephan feel all mushy inside. Man, he's so doomed....

After Lauren and Will leave, Stephan seizes the moment to ask Jeff what he's doing for Thanksgiving.

"Not much. Maybe getting a Hungry Man and wallowing in my bachelorhood."

Stephan shakes his head. "Nope. You're coming with me. I'm going over to Billy and Scott's house. Scott's an awesome cook, and Billy probably won't be too annoying. And if he is, at least there's the game to watch."

"You trying to boss me around, boy?"

"I'm pretty sure I'm succeeding, so yeah," Stephan says with a shit-eating grin.

As intended, Jeff laughs again. "Fine. What time? And should I pick you up or are you going to drive, for once?"

"I'll pick you up," he answers, and they finish making arrangements. Jeff insists on bringing dessert and says he'll surprise them. "Cool, I'm looking forward to it," Stephan says and lets himself put every ounce of meaning into his words, even if he does look like a total sap. He *feels* like a sap, and Jeff probably already knows, so why bother trying to hide it? The guy already knows he's got a crush on him, after all. Stephan's not going try to put the moves on Jeff again, not without some serious confirmation that Jeff wants it, but he's not going to try to hide how he feels, either. It's exhausting, it doesn't work, and fuck it—he wants Jeff. He's only going to get him if the other man knows how he feels.

Determination feels good. Stephan walks back home with a spring in his step and a stupid grin that he's not even trying to hide.

Chapter 27
Giving Thanks

IT'S A short week, as Thanksgiving week always is. Monday and Tuesday fly by, and Madame Georges has a quiz on Wednesday morning to punish everyone who left early because she couldn't. He's not being a disgruntled student about that, either; she said those words exactly. Clearly, crossing this woman is a Bad Thing. Stephan wonders why she's not head of the languages department. Or the division. Or the whole university…. Obviously, it must be because she doesn't *want* to be.

Anyway, Scott calls on Wednesday afternoon to tell Stephan that he's e-mailing a totally simple recipe for a salad, and that Stephan had better bring it along with some beer when he shows up tomorrow around noon. The grocery store is *mobbed* with people who all have wild, frantic looks in their eyes, and the shelves are practically bare in some sections. Luckily, there's still plenty of fresh produce, so he gets everything Scott told him to, and then spends an absurd amount of time that evening assembling the salad and trying to make it look pretty. On the plus side, Jim and Jamie have already taken off to go see her family, so they're not around to make fun of him.

On the even more plus side, he gets to drink Jim's good (expensive) beer, because if that bastard is off getting engaged, Stephan is going to feel *old*. Happy for Jamie, yeah, but still. He's too young for his friends to be getting married already. Straight people—such nerve!

In the morning Stephan has a minor crisis while he debates whether to wear a button-down shirt or T-shirt, and whether to iron the button-down or not. He goes through five different shirts before he decides on a wrinkled one, left untucked. He looks decent but not like he put a lot of effort into it. Which is good because if he dresses up, Billy will make fun of him about it until Stephan has to kill him to get him to shut up. That would probably make Scott a little mad, and it's best not to piss Scott off when he's cooking if you want any of his food.

Right. So he grabs his keys and heads to the car to pick up Jeff, then doubles back to get his precious fucking salad, and phones Jeff to tell him that he's on his way. Jeff's locking the door when Stephan pulls up, a huge round plastic container at his feet and a bottle of wine.

"Shit, I forgot the beer," Stephan says by way of greeting, and Jeff laughs at him.

"Did you skip your coffee this morning or something?"

Stephan gives him a scornful look. "I wouldn't be dressed and able to form words if I had," he points out. Jeff teases him all the way back to Stephan's apartment, where he grabs the beer, and finally they're off campus and on their way to Billy's house.

Billy opens the door as they walk up the drive, offering to help carry stuff and obviously just relieved as hell to have some other people around. He's surprisingly polite and even sort of quiet when Stephan introduces him to Jeff, and doesn't say a word about Stephan's epic crush or that rash he had when he was nineteen or anything else obnoxious. He also doesn't launch into an interrogation of Jeff that would make the Spanish Inquisition proud. Yet the day is, of course, still young.

"Scott freaking out?" Stephan asks knowingly.

"Like you wouldn't believe. He's even wearing The Apron," Billy says with a shudder.

"The apron?" Jeff asks.

"No, *The Apron*," Stephan says. "Billy bought it for him as a joke, but Scott wears it when he's really stressed out about what he's cooking. The Apron usually only shows up at Thanksgiving and sometimes on Easter, for some reason," he says, turning to look at Billy questioningly.

"Easter is when he makes that whole leg-of-lamb thing."

"Oh right." Stephan turns back to Jeff. "Anyway, The Apron is never a good sign, although it does mean the food's going to be awesome. Basically, it means Scott is going to be a total bitch if you try to help and cuss you out if you don't offer."

The three men tentatively peek into the kitchen and catch Scott bent over the oven, basting the turkey. "They're here," Billy says to Scott's butt, in a low, *don't-startle-the-wildebeest* voice.

It doesn't work, and Scott whirls around, a squirt from the turkey baster spattering all over the floor. His hair is held back with a rainbow bandana, he's got a smudge of something orange and sticky-looking on his cheek, and he's wearing The Apron, which features a naked "bodybuilder" torso, dick strategically covered by a spatula, topped by the words "Manning the Grill."

So it's not really Stephan's *fault* that he laughs. And it's totally not Jeff's fault that he joins in too. It probably *is* Billy's, though; he should know better than to laugh at Scott when he's cooking.

Scott scowls at them. "Now look what you made me do! Fuck off, all of you," he says and turns to the oven as the three of them back away, trying to stifle their giggles. Billy gives Scott an apologetic look, and manages to put part of Jeff's dessert in the fridge without getting his head bitten off.

"Come on, Steph," Billy says when he's done, leading them into the living room, "I've been working on a new song, and I want your feedback. Jeff, feel free to help. Do you play?"

"Nope, just listen appreciatively," Jeff says, grinning.

Stephan gets roped into playing harmony, as always, which is fine. Jeff's looking at him with a slight smile on his face, mostly in his eyes, and Stephan's trying hard not to blush or something stupid like that. He closes his eyes, playing along while Billy makes some slight changes to the melody, getting a little lost in the repetition of the music as his self-consciousness fades away. When Billy starts with the lyrics, it's natural to add his own voice to the chorus. He does it without thinking; it's a really good jam session.

Jeff's applause startles him when they finish, or rather, when Billy finishes, since Stephan's just along for the ride. He blinks a few times, and Billy kicks him.

"Wow, that was great. You wrote that?" Jeff asks, and Stephan can practically see Billy glow from the praise. "And that was you working on a rough draft? I've never heard anything like it before; I'm impressed. You too, Stephan, wow. I don't know how you learned how to follow along like that, but it was so cool, the way your voice just blended with Billy's and everything. Just, wow. You guys are great."

Billy beams. "Thanks, man. You can come back any time."

Stephan laughs. "It was pretty good."

"Yeah, it was awesome, and you know it."

"Just because I'm a fantastic harmonizer," Stephan says, looking smug.

"You should sing more," Jeff suggests.

Billy laughs. "My boy's got a voice just *made* for backup."

"Fuck you." Stephan punches him, laughing. "I make you sound a million times better and don't you forget it."

"All right, all right." Billy throws his hands in the air defensively. "You've got a good voice. Not as gravelly rich as mine, but good enough," he says, winking. "Maybe one of these days I'll get you into the studio with me and we can record something."

"Right, because my lifelong dream is to be your backup singer," Stephan grouses. "The Richie Sambora to your Jon Bon Jovi."

"Shut up, Burke; that man is a god." Billy scowls at him.

"Whoa, sorry. I forgot about your secret Bon Jovi crush," he lies, winking at Jeff.

"Hey, I've been a Bon Jovi fan since way back, myself," Jeff says in an obvious attempt to defuse the conversation.

Billy snorts and kicks Stephan as he gets up, putting the guitars away. He stops at the stereo on his way back and puts on some music, with the volume low enough that it takes Stephan a moment to realize that it is, in fact, Bon Jovi's most recent release. He rolls his eyes and Jeff laughs.

Thankfully, they're saved from any more small talk by Scott announcing that dinner will be ready soon and if he doesn't get some help from "you ungrateful sons of bitches, you can just eat a turkey pot pie and fuck off." Billy is put to work doing God knows what in the kitchen, while Stephan and Jeff set the table.

"Here, open this," Scott adds, thrusting the bottle of wine Jeff brought at him, along with a corkscrew. "Also, hi. I'm usually not this much of a dick, and I promise I'll be nicer once the food is on the—not *that* bowl, asshole, the other one!" he shouts at Billy. "Uh. Table."

"Not a problem," Jeff says with a smile. "Just glad to be here; thanks for inviting me. I've cooked for a whole crowd, too, so I know how stressful it can be when it's all on your shoulders. I'm sure it will be fantastic; it smells great."

Scott flashes him an appreciative smile, and then turns back to the kitchen to keep supervising Billy as the food gets dished up and ready to go on the table. By the time it's all brought out, it's a damn good thing there are only four of them because the rest of the table space is taken up by food. Everyone sits in awed silence for a moment, taking it all in, while Scott sharpens the carving knife. He's outdone himself: turkey, stuffing, mashed potatoes, gravy, green beans, cranberry relish (and that horrible cranberry jelly from the jar, complete with ridges, because it's what Billy likes, the heathen), candied yams, and rolls. Plus Stephan's green salad and Jeff's dessert, which is still hidden in its carrying case. Everything is homemade except for the rolls, which Scott bought from a bakery because he says he can't do yeast bread.

"Holy shit."

Everyone nods, blown away by the sheer quantity of food before them.

"Well, eat up," Scott says, "Jeff, dark or light meat or some of both?"

The meal is fabulous, and while Stephan feels like his belly might explode from eating so many carbs, the satisfied look on Scott's face keeps him shoveling it in until there's honestly no more room left.

Everyone is making happy noises, which turn into dismayed noises as they start to clear their plates of their third or fourth helpings. Jeff asks Scott about the cranberry recipe, and they compare notes on the best ways to keep a turkey from getting too dry.

Billy gives him a kick in the shin and winks at him. "You should bring this guy around more often," Billy says, in what he probably thinks is a subtle way but totally isn't.

"I'd like to," he says, glancing at Jeff and feeling his mouth curve up into a little smile he couldn't stop even if he wanted to.

They adjourn to the living room to watch the game and succumb to a food coma—damn tryptophan. Or maybe it's the Beaujolais Nouveau that Jeff brought, because Stephan actually dozes off and misses part of the first quarter. Whichever, or both maybe. They are all more or less alert by halftime, though, and after cleaning up the table a little bit, Jeff finally unveils his dessert: pumpkin pecan pie with Bourbon-spiked whipped cream.

Stephan has about two bites, and it's like an orgasm in his mouth. In fact, his dick is kind of interested, just from the amount of pleasure his mouth is having. "Oh my God, I think I *love* you," he moans.

There is a moment of the most horrible silence ever before Billy laughs. "You're so easy, Stephan. I swear you'd try to steal Scott from me, just for his cooking, if you didn't know I'd kick your ass from here to Tuesday."

Billy is the best friend in the entire *universe*. Seriously, he can be a total asshole sometimes, but there's a reason Stephan loves him like a brother. He hopes Billy can read the massive *"Thank you!"* in his eyes as he flicks a dab of whipped cream at him.

"This is amazing," Scott says, and thank God Jeff turns to look at him because Stephan felt like he was going to explode into flame for a minute there from the heat of Jeff's gaze.

In fact, he keeps catching Jeff looking at him through the rest of dessert, and yeah, he's still flushed a little bit from embarrassment, but whatever. The next time he catches Jeff looking, he grins and licks his fork in the most obscene manner possible, and counts it a win when Jeff nearly chokes on his bite of pie.

The rest of the afternoon is mellow. It's a tight game between the Cowboys and the Redskins, and Stephan and Billy are acting like total jerks as they badmouth the Redskins. Scott and Jeff—who has formed some kind of alliance with Scott to oppose Stephan and Billy—are giving it right back, and it's all fun and games until the Cowboys win. It's their tenth victory in a row against the Redskins, and Billy and Stephan are doing a goofy dance of joy while the other two guys pout and pretend to be upset.

They're all laughing, having a good time hanging out together. Jeff is getting along with Scott like they've been friends forever, and Billy is actually being nice, too, which is weird but not something Stephan's going to question. The food was fucking *excellent*, working on Billy's new song was great, and the game was fun.

Jeff fits *perfectly*, like he was meant to be here all along. Life is good. Not even the looming specter of having to wash all the dishes with Billy can stop Stephan from smiling.

Chapter 28
Smooth Like Butter

STEPHAN spends the rest of Thanksgiving weekend lounging around his apartment, reveling in being alone and having nothing in particular to do. His papers are mostly finished, he can be naked in the kitchen, he can watch porn on the big screen TV and jerk off in the living room. Most of his friends are gone so he doesn't even feel like he *should* be being social. It's fucking great.

After two days of that, his place is a pig sty so he spends Sunday cleaning and doing laundry, and even hits the gym to work off some of Jeff's amazing pie. As he's folding the last of the clean clothes, he finds Eric's T-shirt again, the one that had been lost behind the sofa. He dithers for a few moments about what to do with it, and then sits down at his computer to send an e-mail.

He gets a reply back later that evening, with Eric suggesting that Stephan could bring it to him at the library any day next week after three p.m., saying, *"I'm pretty much going to be living there while I'm writing my final papers."*

Stephan agrees; he'll bring the shirt on Thursday evening, and he generously doesn't add anything about procrastination. Why yes, he does feel a little smug; shoot him. He's only human.

MEETING Eric at the library is weird. Stephan grabs an Americano to calm his nerves, and decides to be nice and get one for Eric too. He knows how stressed out Eric gets when he's writing his final papers from seeing it last year, when they were dating. He can be a nice guy. It's just *coffee*, after all, not like he's begging Eric to get back together with him or anything. He doesn't even want that; he just doesn't want his ex to think that, either.

He almost ditches the cup in the trash before he gets to Eric's usual study spot on the top floor, but his inherent thriftiness stops him; after all, he wouldn't throw away a five-dollar bill. Also, it's *coffee*— that would be, like, sacrilegious or something. Even if it is a double-mocha with extra whipped cream and barely has any actual "coffee" in it.

When he finds Eric, Stephan has to make a real effort to not smirk. Eric's hair is too long and sticking up in chaotic tufts, his shirt has a coffee stain on the front, his fingernails are ragged and his cuticles are a scabby mess, and his face looks so haggard that Stephan would bet the guy's not slept more than four hours a night for the last week. His skin looks like it's too tight for the size of his face; his features are more pointy than Stephan remembers from the last time they saw each other.

Eric's dimples are still really cute, though, when he smiles his gratitude and thanks Stephan for the drink. Stephan realizes he's kind of being a total bitch, even if it's just in his head; Eric looks mostly the same, it's just that there isn't that spark between them anymore. Absently, he wonders if it was ever *really* there or if he'd just wanted it to be....

They talk a little bit, mostly about school and how stressed Eric is about his papers. He bit off more than he could chew, as the cliché goes, and now he's choking on it, trying to figure out how to write a paper in the next week that is honestly more of a book-length idea than a ten-thousand word paper. Stephan sighs internally—he just finished his TA section and he's *tired*—but pulls out a chair and sits down. After about half an hour, he's helped Eric narrow his focus until he's got a much tighter outline and can use the research he's already done without needing to do very much more. To his surprise, it's not that difficult to be nice to Eric.

There honestly *aren't* any hard feelings between them. They're both moving on; Eric says he's dating someone, a girl named Kat, and laughs as he reassures Stephan that no, Stephan didn't turn him straight or anything. "It's just easier," he says, and while Stephan admits that that's almost certainly true, he does sort of want to punch Eric in the face for saying that. Must be nice, being bisexual, he thinks, but he's a big enough man to not say it out loud.

Eric decides he's definitely earned his dinner, and packs up his stuff and walks Stephan out of the library. They stand in the lobby for a few minutes, both a little awkward. Do they hug? Shake hands? Just leave?

Stephan laughs nervously. "I've never actually managed to be friends with someone I've slept with before."

There's something a little bittersweet in Eric's expression when he smiles back. "There aren't any rules. It was really good to see you, man. Thanks for the drink, and seriously, thank you *so much* for your help with my paper. I was about ready to cut my wrists or something."

"No problem," Stephan says, and they hug each other kind of clumsily, Stephan nearly elbowing Eric in the chest. Their bodies used to fit together, he's pretty sure, and can't imagine why they don't—at all—anymore. But they just *don't*. He's biting his lip, thinking about it, when he suddenly remembers the whole reason for this meeting wasn't to help his ex with his schoolwork. "Wait! Eric!"

They hand off the T-shirt, both laughing a little at how stupid they are to have forgotten, and Eric finally makes it out the door. Stephan stands, watching him go, and feels something strange happening inside that he can't really put into words. There's a kind of hurt feeling, and a kind of warmth, and a kind of letting-go, loosening sensation in his chest. It's weird to see someone you used to love, at least a little, and not hate them. This is better, yeah, but it's still weird....

Sometimes Stephan forgets how goddamned fucking *small* this campus is, and while he's avoided seeing Eric since the evening Eric walked out of his bedroom two months ago, he turns around to find Jeff standing at the coffee cart, watching him. When he notices, Jeff raises an arm, waving, and Stephan smiles and strolls over.

"Hey, how's it going?" he asks as he debates getting another coffee and whether he wants to actually sleep tonight or just lie in bed and wish he was sleeping.

"Good," Jeff says, raising an eyebrow. "You selling T-shirts now or something? Who was that? You look thoughtful."

"Him? That was my ex, Eric; I forgot you'd never met him. I was just returning a shirt he'd left at my house." Stephan shrugs. "It was good to see him. I guess. I mean, it was… weird. You know?"

Jeff nods. "Yeah. Yeah, I do know, trust me."

They stand there for a moment, and Stephan needs *something* in his hands, so he buys a muffin, even thought he doesn't really want to eat it. He wants dinner, he thinks; it's dinnertime, at any rate. His insides feel strange. His stomach growls, and so he asks Jeff if he wants to walk over to the Student Center and get some food.

The walk is quiet, Stephan still feeling a little unsettled, and Jeff evidently lost in thought as well. Finally Jeff comes out with, "So, Eric. He's an undergrad?"

Stephan nods.

"He's cute. Is he your usual type? Him and those kids you were dancing with at the bar that night of Billy's show?"

Jeff remembers that? Huh. "Not really, no," Stephan answers after a moment, deciding to be honest. "They're just easier to pick up than my usual type." He pauses for a moment, then adds, "And I did, you know, like Eric. A lot. We were really good friends, and for a while we had sex too…. That just wasn't really enough, I guess…."

Jeff makes a noncommittal sound. "Yeah…. So, I remember you were telling Billy that you were pretty much done with all of your papers?"

Not the best segue, but it's not like Stephan wants to talk about his failed relationships. Jeff probably doesn't either; the guy is pretty tight-lipped about his marriage and divorce, and has been the whole time Stephan's known him.

"Yeah, I am. Thank God; everyone in the library this week looks like they're about to go into cardiac arrest. That much ambient stress is practically infectious."

"No kidding. So, you have some free time, then? Want to catch another movie?"

"What, like a date?" Stephan says before his brain kicks in.

Luckily, Jeff just grins. "Like one, yeah...." He grabs one of the weekly free newspapers as they walk into the Student Center and get in line to order. They decide on a re-showing of a film from a few years ago, playing at the local art house theater, which Jeff has never been to. Stephan points out that the Nickelodeon is a crappy theater in nearly every way possible, but that going there is kind of required if you're an academic living in town. And on the plus side, the screen might be small, the seats hard and packed tight together, but the tickets are super cheap and the concessions stand has actual *food*, and good food at that—like, salads and sandwiches and fresh-baked cookies—and they note on their sign that the only thing they sell that goes "crunch" is the popcorn, which is made fresh and has real butter. And it costs a reasonable amount, not the usual highway-robbery prices most movie theaters charge.

Jeff laughs at him. "Wow, you really are a typical guy aren't you? Driven by food and sex."

"Nothing wrong with that," Stephan says with a wicked grin.

"Nothing at all," Jeff agrees.

THE theater is nearly empty, which is typical even for a weekend night. They buy their tickets and some food and take their place in an empty row. By the time the lights go down, there are maybe ten people in the theater, including them. It feels intimate, like having your own personal movie room or something, and people are spread far apart so that you forget they're there.

Once Stephan really *did* forget that other people were there, which was bad when his boyfriend-of-the-moment started moaning as

Stephan gave him a hand job. Still, he was only twenty and he's unlikely to ever repeat that again, certainly not with Jeff. Well, *probably* not with Jeff. At least not tonight.

He has been trying all evening, ever since Jeff picked him up, to not think of tonight as a date. The problem is that there is a very fine line between having dinner and catching a movie with a friend, and having a dinner-and-a-movie *date*. The usual way to tell is whether there is sexual tension and then sex or making out, or if there's just a friendly hug and then you go home.

With Jeff? The sexual tension is getting kind of impressive. The guy has *got* to be bisexual, at least. Right?

They joke about how small and close the seats are, and Stephan laughs and bounces on the butt-size spring, which is the cushion of his chair, to show Jeff how bad it is but also to burn off a tiny bit of nervous energy. Their shoulders are pressed together, their thighs are touching, and they really couldn't be much closer if they removed the dividing arm between their seats.

The movie is an artsy film noir kind of thing, which in this case means a lot of violence and a lot of sex. The sex isn't all skinny legs in black stockings and bouncing boobs, though; Stephan saw the movie when it came out a few years ago, but he'd forgotten that the fairly attractive male lead also visits a gay sex club. There are naked men fucking and sucking and grinding together and *shit*, is it hot in here? The pounding of the techno music is making Stephan's heartbeat speed up, and he's all pressed up alongside Jeff's body, and he's as hard as a rock.

He can't shift around much without Jeff noticing, plastered against each other as they are, and he certainly can't reach down and adjust his dick into a more comfortable position. Which means that he's embarrassed and uncomfortable, and yeah, those two feelings are not historically a deterrent for Stephan's libido when he's with a sexy guy. Quite the opposite, in fact....

He zones out for what's left of the film, unable to concentrate on anything other than how turned on he is. Jeff's thighs and shoulders are firm and warm, touching his, and it must actually *be* warm because he can smell Jeff now, his faint woodsy cologne as well as his body scent.

By the time the film fades to black and the credits start to scroll, Stephan's having to make a conscious effort to breathe at a regular pace and not do something stupid like cream his jeans *in a fucking movie theater*. He's almost shaking from how turned on he is, how much he needs to adjust his aching dick, how much he wants to just tackle Jeff and hump him right there in the goddamned Nickelodeon. His asshole is pulsing from where he's been unintentionally clenching and squeezing it, imagining Jeff fucking him, the feeling of a cock splitting him wide, and his tongue is rubbing against his teeth, imagining licking Jeff all over.

He is about to *burst*.

The lights come up, and Stephan is sitting there, silently vibrating and trying to somehow act normal and praying with every fiber of his being that Jeff doesn't notice. He stifles a moan as he twists around to get his coat on, the change in pressure against his cock almost a religious moment. Jeff makes a little sound, too, but when Stephan looks over, he's just struggling into his own jacket. They both stand up, and Stephan fakes a leg cramp from the too-small seats to cover the awkward way he's walking.

Jeff must have been more crowded than Stephan realized for the last two hours, since he's moving a little stiffly as well. The bright lights in the lobby cause Stephan to notice that there's also a lot of color in Jeff's cheeks, under the stubble, and without even meaning to, he glances at the other guy's crotch.

Oh. It seems as if Stephan wasn't the only one affected by the on-screen smut. Jeff's dick is bent at an awkward looking angle, but there is no mistaking the massive hard-on, and when he excuses himself to the restroom, it's all Stephan can do to resist following him inside and attacking him.

Instead he has a long, *long* drink of the ice-cold water from the drinking fountain and swipes a couple of napkins to get wet and press against his heated face. He tries to be subtle when he adjusts his dick and arranges his clothes to hide it better, then goes outside and hopes that the cold air will perform a miracle. The Coming Soon posters outside the theater have some pretty gruesome art for one of the indie horror films, and he forces himself to stare at it until fucking *finally* he starts to soften a little.

The drive home is kind of awkward, neither of them saying very much. Every time Stephan starts to make small talk about the movie, the conversation stalls out because the sex club scene was kind of crucial to the plot. And there's not much to say about that except that it was *hot*, although a big part of that was the company, not the film itself, at least for Stephan.

Jeff pulls up outside Grad Student Housing, and Stephan unbuckles his seatbelt. It still feels like this was a date, not a friend-date. There was food, a movie—a movie with hot gay sex—and undeniable sexual tension. Jeff's not his usual talkative self, not covering up the tension between them with all the things they usually talk about. No, tonight he's kind of quiet, and Stephan doesn't know what's wrong and has no damn clue how to fix it.

"No kiss goodnight?" he jokes, opening the door.

Jeff's knuckles tighten on the steering wheel. He licks his lips twice, and finally says, "No. See you Monday, Stephan" and drives off like a man running away from something.

Smooth, Stephan thinks, walking up the stairs to his apartment. He is so fucking smooth.

Chapter 29
Why Not?

THE days are flying by, as they always do at the end of the semester. Stephan is inundated with students needing help with their papers, he's cramming for his French exam, he's revising his papers with the feedback from Danielle and Tina, and why, *why* does he always forget that writing the bibliography takes at least one full afternoon, every single time?

It's finals week and he'd forgotten what it was like. Why did he decide to go back to school again?

Stephan is also spending far too much time staring off into space and wondering what the fuck happened with Jeff after the movie on the weekend. A few weeks ago Scott got him all pumped up to go out and "get his man" but Stephan doesn't know *how*. They're already friends, and he can't really make a move, since he did that and Jeff didn't respond. But it feels like there's something there between them, for sure; there's no way Stephan can be imagining that much sexual tension, is there?

Anyway, it's a pointless exercise to try and guess what's going on in Jeff's head, and Stephan's got plenty to do this week without driving himself nuts on purpose. Although sex *would* be a really great way to relieve some tension….

Last week he'd helped Tina and Danielle with their papers; this week he's doing a final proofread for both of them, to catch any last-minute mistakes. Their topics are both interesting, and it's frankly kind of a relief to be editing something other than the usual awful freshman papers. He knows when he tells Danielle to look up the rules about semicolons that she actually will, rather than just break down crying and tell everyone how mean he is.

He still owes her dinner for the atrocious crime of having had a draft finished before Thanksgiving, so he takes her out for Thai on Tuesday night. Her boyfriend Rob can't join them, since he's apparently in his own final-paper hell and told Danielle that he is hiding in his room until he's done. Stephan's still not entirely sure about the guy—no one is really *that* sweet without being a huge pushover—but only time will tell if they are good together or not.

"So, have you turned everything in yet? Do I have to eviscerate you with this knife?" she asks once they're seated.

"Papers are turned in, yes. But don't hurt me; I've still got my French final day after tomorrow."

She smiles. "Good. I'm glad you're suffering along with the rest of us. Hey, I thought I saw you at the library last week with someone who looked like Eric?"

He nods and takes a drink of his Thai iced tea. "Yeah, I was returning a shirt he left at my place and got suckered into helping him with a paper he was struggling with."

"Wow. That was generous," Danielle says, quirking an eyebrow.

"Yeah, I guess. It was weird seeing him again." She gives him another questioning look. "I don't know, he was just all nice about it, you know? Normal. Like it wasn't really a huge deal. And he's already hooked up with someone else, if you can believe. Some chick. That was fast."

Danielle rolls her eyes. "Excuse me, but didn't you go and do something really stupid the night after you and Eric broke up? Something about kissing Jeff? And wasn't there a rebound one-night stand not long after that?"

"Oh fine, be logical." He pouts as he drains the rest of his drink. "I haven't had any action since then, though," he points out. "It's been over a *month*."

"Hold on while I get some tissue so I can *weep* for you."

"Bitch."

"Dick."

Luckily, their food arrives and they get distracted with eating before the slightly bitchy humor can cross any lines. It feels like *forever* since he's gotten laid and that's no joke, even if it's not exactly a record at only, what, six weeks? Yeah. But what *is* a record for him is that the reason he hasn't had another hookup is because he's still pining for Jeff.

"What's that sad face for?" Danielle asks around a mouthful of red curry.

"Nothing."

"I'll seriously stab you with this fork."

"Jesus, you're such a bitch! Why am I even friends with you?"

"Because I know all of your secrets and you don't want me as an enemy," she says with a transparently sweet smile.

Stephan rolls his eyes and plays with the noodles on his plate, thinking. "This thing with Jeff is kind of messing with my head, I guess."

"Go on."

He talks slowly, putting things into words that he's only thought about before. "I just... I really like him. Like... more than I think I've ever liked anyone. I mean, things were good with Eric for a while, but it kind of felt like there was something missing, you know? I kept trying to convince myself that it was good enough, that I wanted too much, that I wasn't being realistic. But... I feel more of a connection with Jeff than I ever did with Eric. And we're not even together or anything." He bites his lip; he didn't mean to say that, but it's true. He did love Eric; he's pretty sure of that. But when he's with Jeff, he just feels so much *more*, excited and vibrant and alive.

"Hmmm," she says.

"'Hmmm'? That's it? I spill my guts and you just hum?"

"You're in a mood tonight, aren't you?" she says, smirking at him. "So what happened the last time you guys were together? I mean, did you touch him? Is there chemistry? Do you think he's just not attracted to you, or is he really straight or something?"

Stephan thinks for a moment. "I don't know. I mean, I don't think so. Logically, he's never done anything to give me a reason to think that he could be into guys—he was *married*, for Christ's sake—but there's all this tension between us. And he looks at me sometimes, you know, like really *looks*. I'd swear to God he wants me, but then every time there's an opportunity for it to go somewhere, he runs away or something. I don't know."

"So he's sending mixed signals, basically?" He nods and she sips her drink, thinking. "Do you know if he's got any reason for it?"

"None that I can think of, except, oh yeah—he's my boss, maybe he's not a fag, maybe he's not into *me*. Maybe I'm just an idiot, seeing what I want to see when there's nothing actually there."

"Okay, so you need to shut up." He scowls at her, and she rolls her eyes. "Your head is giving you all this information and getting you all wound up in knots. But you like being with him, he makes your insides go all goofy, and your eyes practically turn into little hearts when you talk about him. And obviously, you totally want to nail him. So you need to just make a move, Stephan. Find your balls and make a move."

"I *did*!" he almost shouts, then cringes when some of the other diners turn to look at him. "I already kissed him. I can't just throw myself at him again."

She tilts her head to the side and gives him a hard stare. "Why not?"

Stephan settles back into his chair, crossing his arms and scowling at her. "*I just can't*" is sitting on the tip of his tongue, but it won't come out his mouth. It's not a reason. So why not, then?

GOD damn Danielle to the furthest, coldest, most horrible reaches of hell. She's planted this question in Stephan's head that he can't let go of, and he *really* needs to be studying for his goddamned motherfucking French final tomorrow. He has four chapters left to review and a ton of prepositions he keeps getting mixed up, and all he can think of is *"Why not?"* Why not tackle Jeff down to the ground and hump him? Why not lick every inch of his chest and feel the way his chest hair tickles against his tongue? Why not take a hugely stupid risk and just *tell* the guy he's head over fucking heels in lust-and-maybe-love with him?

And because the universe still hates Stephan, Jeff sends him an e-mail sometime around two in the afternoon and asks if he can possibly come by Jeff's office to help sort out some of the final papers the students have turned in. It seems Jeff never got a conclusive list of which kids were in which sections after they'd all finished switching around, and it will probably only take a few minutes, and Jeff will buy him a beer to make up for it.

Great. Because what he totally needs right now is to be around Jeff, drunk, and try to keep his hands to himself when he can't come up with a single really convincing reason *why* he should do so.

"HEY," Stephan says through the open door. He's a little surprised, but this is the first time he's seen Jeff's office; there's never been any reason for him to come here until now. It's not very interesting, just a basic small office with the same too-old furniture from the 70s in the same rust-orange and avocado-green colors as everything else on campus. It's got a few windows, but they are thin and vertical and don't let in much light. Jeff hasn't brought very much to decorate aside from a few maps and a poster of the Constitution.

"Thank God," Jeff says, pushing back from his chair and getting up. He stretches, shoulders making a popping noise, and Stephan can't help drooling a little at the way Jeff's shirt pulls tight across his chest. He has a flash of memory of Jeff shirtless, wet from the shower, wearing only a towel, and has to clear his throat before he can reply.

"You needed me?"

Jeff smirks a little, but his expression is more sultry than amused. "Yeah. I've got the hard copies of all the final papers," he says, motioning to the stacks on his desk. "There are about a dozen kids that I think changed sections mid-semester, though, and I never got a list, so I don't know which of you guys to give the papers to for grading." His voice is extra-rough and gravelly, and Stephan really has to make an effort to ignore all the undercurrents in the tiny little office if he's going to make it out of there without embarrassing himself.

He walks around to join Jeff behind the desk and pulls the short stack toward him. In just a few moments he has it sorted between the piles that are his and Will's and Lauren's. He turns to ask Jeff if he wants to make a note of which students go where, just in case he needs to know again, but can't get the words out because Jeff is standing next to him, really close, and looking at Stephan like he wants to eat him alive. The guy has looked at him before, yeah, and even looked at him kind of lustfully, but either Stephan is forgetting how intense Jeff was or the situation was *nothing* like it is now because Stephan is suddenly getting hard, and shit, he is in so much trouble.

Or is he? Because he didn't do anything, did he? He's not dancing and being flirty, he's not teasing and kidding, and *fuck* he just wants Jeff like a man in a desert wants water, like he could *die*.

When he looks up, their eyes meet. Jeff takes a deep breath, and neither of them have moved a muscle, but Stephan would swear that they're somehow standing closer than they were a moment ago because he can feel the heat, the *desire* coming off of Jeff, and yeah—this is it. This is the moment he's been waiting for.

Stephan licks his lips, trying to think of what to say and coming up with nothing. It doesn't matter, apparently, because Jeff lets out a soft growl and steps forward, bringing their bodies into full contact, knees and thighs and chests and shoulders.

"Stephan."

He can't help it, he takes a step back, but it's an awfully cramped office and the wall is right behind him, Jeff moves closer, and he's only got maybe an inch on Stephan in height, but it feels like he's *looming* over Stephan, and Stephan can't help but shiver a little. Stephan licks his lips again, and Jeff shakes his head. "Jesus, Steph. You've been teasing me for four months... I can't fucking stand it anymore."

"Me?" Stephan says in a voice that sounds unnaturally high. "You're the one who's always pushing me away whenever things get like this." He can't hold eye contact with Jeff, not when the man's right there in his face. He focuses on Jeff's lips instead, but that's not much better. "I keep thinking you want... but then...."

"Shit, Stephan. Yeah, I want. I've *wanted* all fucking semester, and of course you *had* to be my TA, and it's damn near killed me trying to hold back and wait."

"Huh. The semester's pretty much over," Stephan says, only he doesn't quite manage to get the last word out because Jeff's mouth presses against his, and this is no soft, tentative little kiss, this is a breath-stealing, spine-melting, needy, hungry *taking*.

It's a good thing the wall behind Stephan is of industrial grade concrete because it's the only thing holding him up. That might not be strictly true; Stephan is gripping Jeff pretty tightly, one hand on his shoulder and the other on the back of Jeff's neck, making sure he doesn't move and run away, goddammit, not this fucking time. Jeff doesn't seem like he's going anywhere though, wedging a leg between Stephan's thighs to rub against him as they kiss, and Jeff is hard *for him*, definitely for him, all for him this time. And no fucking way is Stephan letting him go.

Not that he has to, because Jeff pulls back for a minute, does a weird sideways stretch reaching for the edge of the door, and then slams it hard enough that a few papers flutter off the desk and land on the floor. Jeff grabs him and pulls their bodies together again, wrapping strong arms around his back and sliding urgent hands under his shirt.

Jeff is mumbling between kisses, biting Stephan's jaw and neck and shoulder, rubbing his face raw with stubble. "Ever since the first fucking day I saw you, in the men's room before school even started, looking at me, and you *smiled*, and then you had to go and be my TA and be smart and funny and I've had to *wait*, and you, you just tease me, just by breathing. And I thought I could just be friends with you; I'm so damn stupid." He wrenches away and almost rips Stephan's T-shirt, pulling it up off him, throwing it to the floor, and grunts a little when Stephan reciprocates. Their bare chests rubbing together is *amazing* and fuck, it's not like Stephan's a virgin or anything, but this is mind-blowing.

Jeff is still talking, somehow. "Don't know how I managed to push you away when you kissed me that night, in the rain; all I wanted to do was bring you inside and dry you off and love you," he murmurs into Stephan's shoulders, hands sliding down his jeans and grabbing his ass. All Stephan can do is groan and jerk forward, pressing his cock against Jeff's thigh, already so hard and so ready to go that he'd be begging if he could form words, if he could get anything in between Jeff's.

Instead he uses his body to shift them around so he's almost sitting on the desk and lets Jeff keep talking while he busies himself with buttons and zipper. There's no fucking way they're not doing this, not now, and he's not going to give Jeff the chance to back out on him, not this time. Jeff takes the hint and starts on Stephan's pants, and Stephan remembers to grab his wallet out of the back pocket before he lifts up to let his jeans fall to the ground. They're grinding together, boxers damp, no more words, just breathless needy sounds now. The desk is pressing hard into Stephan's spine and the best fix for that seems obvious.

"Oh God," he gasps as Jeff presses forward, their hard lengths rubbing together, and that could be enough, it *could*, but…. "I want—I need—" he gasps.

"I know," Jeff says, pressing harder and shuddering a little. "I want it too."

Stephan pushes Jeff back just far enough that Stephan can turn around, fishing his emergency condom out of his wallet before he tosses it to the floor. There's a desperate moment before he sees a bottle of sunscreen on a shelf by Jeff's desk, and that will do nicely. He slaps them both down on top of the papers stacked beside his hip, and then leans forward like the eager slut that he is and spreads himself across the desk.

"*Fuck.*" Jeff's voice is wrecked, and his hands are tugging Stephan's boxer briefs down, and there's some shuffling, and then Jeff is leaning over him, covering Stephan with his body, and all Stephan can do is curl his fingers around the edge of the desk and hold on for dear life.

Lust is thrumming through Stephan's body with every beat of his heart, every thrust of Jeff's fingers inside his ass. He'd swear his heart actually pauses during the momentary break between Jeff pulling out his fingers and sliding in his cock, because when it resumes, it's with a thundering pounding that nearly deafens Stephan to the quiet noises Jeff is making, helpless and broken and the biggest turn-on Stephan's ever heard.

Stephan wants to reach back and wrap his arms around Jeff, hold him in an impossible embrace, so he does the best he can, opening his body and welcoming Jeff inside. Every thrust hits that spot that makes Stephan's dick leak, and he's flying as Jeff pants against his shoulder, grips his hips, pulling and pushing and *taking* him, taking everything he has to offer. He doesn't mean to be so loud, but the building is mostly empty, anyway, and it's probably not illegal to fuck in an office, and thoughts like that are the only thing keeping Stephan from losing control just yet, scattering papers all over the floor as he moans and gasps and shoves his body back on Jeff's cock, taking what he wants too.

Jeff slams in hard, finally, biting Stephan's shoulder and shuddering as he moans his name. He breathes for a moment, Stephan making desperate little noises as he tries to reach for his own cock, shaking with the need for release, pinned and immobile. "Here," Jeff says with a tired huff, shifting back just a little, his dick still a hard pressure in Stephan's ass, hand letting go of its grip on Stephan's hip to wrap around his cock.

It only takes a moment for it to register that Jeff's hand is touching his cock for the first time, and then Stephan is coming, fucking *bucketloads*, all the way from his toes, it feels like. He wails, loudly, and he doesn't even give a goddamn because Jeff just keeps going, jerking him through it until he's got nothing left, and Stephan crashes back down into his body, the unforgiving wood cutting into his thighs and Jeff's weight anchoring him down to the earth.

Jeff's hand gentles but doesn't let go of Stephan's dick. He's still breathing hard, little wafts of hot air against Stephan's neck, his beard tickling just a little as he says, "I don't think you can be my TA anymore."

Stephan laughs and nudges him some, until Jeff pulls out and they can stand up. There are papers all over the office, rumpled and a little mangled. "Yeah, not if we do this to the student's papers again," Stephan says with a snort. "We'd never be able to hand anything back."

Jeff grabs a wad of napkins from out of a drawer, and they clean up. It smells like sunscreen and sex and sweaty bodies and satisfaction, at least to Stephan. He's got a dorky-assed grin on his face, and not even the thought that he's definitely going to be walking funny tomorrow can get rid of it. The thought that he's got bruises from where Jeff was manhandling him, and possibly some beard burn, too, does nothing to remove it.

It turns out that most of the papers are only crumpled. There's a bit of spooge on one, but he wipes it off and hopes the girl won't be able to tell. After all, it's not like she's going to be doing DNA analysis over a little bit of something sticky on her paper. Heck, most students just look at the grade and ignore all of the comments in red anyway.

While Stephan re-sorts the papers, Jeff is bundling everything else up, pushing things into his messenger bag, and cleaning up. He finishes and catches Stephan looking at him. Running a hand through his hair, he sighs and looks away. "Damn, what you do to me."

Stephan grins. "Yeah? You too, to me." He wipes suddenly sweating hands against his jeans. "So… now what?"

There's a long silence, and Jeff is looking at his messenger bag, and a muscle in his jaw is flexing. The pause is too long, it's too quiet, and Stephan knows something is wrong; he feels it in a flash right before Jeff opens his mouth.

"I…. This wasn't right; I'm sorry. I'm in a position of authority over you; I'm always going to be," Jeff says in a voice that's almost a whisper. "We can't do this. I can't believe I fucked you in my *office*. Oh my God, what have I done?"

Someone has kicked Stephan in the stomach. That must be what happened because he can't breathe, and there's no way he's not hallucinating this, not when he can still feel Jeff's hands all over his body and his *dick* in Stephan's very-used ass.

"What?"

Jeff glances at him, then away, eyes full of guilt and shame and other things Stephan couldn't care less about. "I'm sorry. But we can't do this."

Chapter 30
Resolutions

STEPHAN wakes up on Friday morning, but not even the lure of coffee can pull him out of bed. He has only the vaguest impressions of yesterday. He knows he showered because he has a memory of warm steam, and that he went to his French final because he's not stupid. He has no clear memory of what was on the exam. He could have passed it with flying colors or left the entire thing totally blank. Madame Georges could have been naked. He has no idea. Vomiting might be a real possibility if he moves. It's simply safer to stay in bed and ignore the rest of the world.

Around noon his stomach begins to protest, hinting that nothing but coffee for forty-eight hours might be the cause of his nausea, at least in part. He can hear Jim in the kitchen, though, and Stephan doesn't feel like seeing anyone, so he goes to take a shower instead. His clothes from two days ago are still on the floor, and when he picks them up, his boxers smell like piña colada. That's all it takes to get him dry-heaving into the toilet: the smell of Jeff's sunscreen.

He decides to go back to bed and try again later.

JIM knocks on his door after a few more hours and opens it when Stephan grunts for him to come in; he's too lazy to drag his pathetic ass out of bed just to open the door.

"End of the semester flu?" Jim asks, sympathetic. "I picked up some chicken noodle soup for you, and 7UP, while I was at the store."

"Thanks," Stephan says, and is horrified to feel his eyes start to fill. Shit, is he going to cry because his housemate did something nice? *Fuck.*

"Um. You okay?" Jim's hovering in the doorway, looking hesitant but determined to be a good friend.

He shrugs. He's not going to unload all of his emo on Jim, he's really not, but his mouth doesn't get the message in time and says, "I fucked Jeff."

"Oh?" Jim picks at a flake of paint on the door frame. "I'm guessing that didn't go well."

Stephan closes his eyes and snorts. "Nope."

"I'm sorry."

"Me too."

Jim waits a moment longer, but when it's clear Stephan's not going to say anything else, he closes the door quietly and leaves Stephan alone to brood.

He's not going to cry or anything; that would be stupid. It's not like he and Jeff were even dating or anything. Yeah, he had this enormous crush for the whole semester, but it's not like he's in *love* with the guy or anything. So why does thinking those words hurt so much?

The more Stephan lays there and lets the scene in the office replay in his head, over and over, the angrier he gets. It's not like he led Jeff on or seduced him or anything; they've been having these "almost" moments for four fucking *months*, and it was inevitable that something would happen. Unfortunately, Stephan wonders if it was also inevitable that the "something" would involve both sex and Jeff running away afterward; a review of the past would seem to suggest that Stephan had more than one hint that such an outcome was likely.

What the hell is wrong with Jeff, anyway? Why doesn't Jeff want him?

Why doesn't anyone want him?

The shadows in the room get darker and deeper, the sound of the heater kicking on and the muffled noises of Jim moving around the apartment the only things that change as the hours pass by.

HE MUST have dozed off because when Jim knocks on the door, it wakes him up.

"Yeah?"

The door opens a little, letting a slash of too-bright light in from the hallway. "Uh, there's someone here for you." Stephan waits for him to continue. "It's Jeff. Should I tell him to fuck off?"

He thinks about it for a second, honestly considering, then sighs. He can't avoid the man forever; he's still Jeff's TA. "Thanks. Nah, send him back." He's not getting out of bed for Jeff; fuck him. He deserves to see what he's done to Stephan.

A few moments later Jeff is the one in the doorway; it's like Stephan can *feel* that it's him, without even looking. He sits up and turns on the bedside lamp.

"I sent you an e-mail and left a few messages on your phone, but you didn't answer. So I thought I'd hand-deliver these," Jeff says, holding out the stack of student papers that Stephan has the pleasure of grading before he can leave for winter break.

He rolls his eyes. "Thanks."

Jeff pauses before speaking again. "I'm here because I want to apologize. I want to explain what I said; I just want to say—"

"Yeah, I think you said enough on Wednesday, thanks," Stephan interrupts, "I get it."

"Stephan." Jeff sighs, and then sits down on his bed.

"What?" It's childish, yeah, but he refuses to look at Jeff, to make this easy for him in any way.

"I freaked out." He shifts around, and Stephan glances over, despite his best intentions, and their eyes meet briefly. "I'm sorry. I… I've wanted you all semester. I kept trying to resist, but you made it so hard…," Jeff says.

Stephan gives him an incredulous look.

"No, no, I'm not blaming you, I'm not saying it's your fault at all, I swear. I'm just saying… God, I don't know what I'm saying…. I'm saying I really like you." Jeff takes a deep breath. "I really like you and I really want you… I just have no idea how this can work out."

Stephan leans back against the wall, closing his eyes. "Yeah. Thanks, but you made that pretty clear in your office."

"Damn it; I'm trying to talk to you about this," Jeff says, an edge of irritation in his voice.

"Why? You've given me all your excuses; maybe you should go."

When he finally opens his eyes to see why Jeff hasn't left, Jeff is staring at him, a thoughtful look on his face. "No. Uh-uh. This sucks," Jeff says. He stares at the wall, at the calendar hanging there, in silence. The naked rugby hunks of "Dieux de Stade" are certainly worthy of such deep regard, but Stephan doubts that Jeff's even seeing them.

"I think… I think I've been getting things a little confused, in my head," Jeff says slowly. "As of next week, on Tuesday, or as soon as the grades are in, you won't be my student employee anymore. And if I refuse to be your thesis advisor, and you don't take any classes I teach, we might actually be okay…."

There's another silence while Stephan turns this over in his head, doing his best to ignore the way Jeff's looking at him, eyes all sincere and mouth curving up a touch, hopeful. It's kind of one of those moments where Stephan could go either way. It's up to him to choose whether to be hurt and defensive and cautious… or take what he wants.

He's still mulling it over when Jeff says, "I've been thinking about this since you left my office. I was an idiot." He smiles a little, contrite and amused, and hoping to be forgiven. And what Stephan wants? Is right there, being offered to him.

"I'm going to have to agree with that," he says, finally meeting Jeff's eyes, and he smiles a little.

Jeff's grin is almost blinding in the gloom of Stephan's bedroom. "Yeah? Okay. Well, do you have any ideas what I can do to win you back?"

Stephan shrugs, shaking his head and leaning back in the bed.

"Huh. You're going to make me work pretty hard, aren't you?"

He shrugs again. "Yeah, I would think so. I mean, you kind of fucked me over, you know."

Jeff snorts, but somehow manages to also look a little contrite. "It was only for two days," he protests.

"It's been a hell of a lot longer than two days."

Nodding his head as he concedes the point, Jeff says, "Yeah, okay. How about if I start making things up to you by taking you out for dinner tonight? Maybe celebrate the end of the term or something?"

"We could do that," Stephan agrees as his stomach growls. He still needs to take a shower though. God, his room is a mess; he doesn't know if he's got any clothes clean enough to wear out anywhere nice at all…. "Uh, I need to shower and find something to wear."

Jeff makes a kind of strangled noise, and Stephan looks at him, seeing already dark eyes gone even darker with lust. "You're gonna make me sit here, imagining you showering, hot and wet and naked—*again*?"

Smirking, Stephan admits, "Last time I had to jerk off in the shower after seeing you naked in that towel."

Jeff growls and the next thing Stephan knows, he's pinned to the bed, and Jeff's covering his body but not kissing him, at least not yet. "What's wrong?" he asks, his insides starting to feel like they've just turned into ice water, uncertain again.

"This isn't just about the sex," Jeff says. His eyes are saying a lot more than his mouth is, and Stephan reads him loud and clear.

"Okay." There's another pause; Jeff seems to be waiting for something more. "I mean, good," he says, nodding, and now he's starting to feel a little desperate. "There *will* be sex though, right?"

Jeff laughs, lips buzzing with humor as they finally touch his mouth. "Yeah."

This time their kisses start off gentle, exploring and tasting each other, learning the texture of lips and teeth and tongues, the fullness of lips, the scratch of stubble. His fingers are tangled in the hair covering the back of Jeff's neck, too long from the end of the semester and starting to curl. The other is gliding on a path up and down Jeff's body, exploring the shape of bone and muscle in his shoulder, spine, hip, and the curve of his ass. God, Jeff feels so good....

Jeff's hands are delving under the T-shirt and sweats Stephan put on that morning, and his fingertips against Stephan's skin feel electric, switching the mood from languorous and unhurried to urgent neediness. Ah well; there will be time to explore later, at least Stephan hopes there will be. He pulls Jeff's body all the way down on top of him, groaning as they come into full-body contact, and then they're kissing and licking and biting at each other's mouths, teeth clashing, grinding against each other through too many layers of clothes, and Stephan is seriously about to start losing any shred of control when his stomach growls again.

Really, *really* loudly.

Jeff rolls to the side, laughing, goddammit. "Sex or food first?"

As if Stephan has the ability to make important decisions like that with none of the blood in his body anywhere near his brain. "I, um...." If his hands were free, he'd be flapping them in the air with helpless indecision.

Jeff laughs again. "Never mind, we'll call it an appetizer." He winks as he backs away, moving down Stephan's body, pulling off the sweatpants and licking his lips like a man starving when Stephan's cock practically leaps out at him. Stephan can't help it when his hips jerk forward a little; *damn*, he needs this.

Jeff's mouth closes over his dick with no preliminaries, blatantly hungry and eager for it in a way that gets Stephan's blood pumping like nothing else. It's sloppy and wet; Jeff using one hand to more or less jerk Stephan off into his mouth, making these *ravenous* noises like he can't get enough, like he's greedy for Stephan's spunk and wants it as fast as he can get it.

While this might not be the most technically proficient blowjob Stephan's ever had in his life, it's definitely one of the sexiest, and the moments fly by as Jeff takes him higher and higher. He hovers for a long second, and it's the sound of Jeff groaning, and the vibration of it against his too-sensitive flesh, that finally breaks him. He comes in long drawn-out pulses, hands twisting in the sheets as he's overwhelmed with pleasure.

Stephan lies there, gasping like a fish, as Jeff licks and wipes him clean, every touch sending a tremor through his oversensitive body. When he opens his eyes, Jeff is grinning at him.

"I'm a little out of practice. I'll get better, I promise."

Stephan moans, "You'll kill me. But okay." It wouldn't be a bad way to go, really. He's willing to risk it....

He takes a few deep breaths, trying to remember how to make his arms move under his instruction, then nudges and pushes until he's got Jeff on his side. They're crowded in the twin bed, but it's not like they need much room right now anyway. His fingers make quick work of Jeff's jeans, shoving them down with his underwear just enough to free his erection, the fabric bunched up against his balls in a way Stephan knows feels pretty good when you're this turned on and about to get off.

He holds Jeff's gaze as he raises a hand and licks it, gratified when Jeff groans and presses his hips forward, the tip of his dick leaving a wet smear on Stephan's hip. Jeff's cock feels amazing in his hand, hard and ready. He sets a fast pace; after all, they have a dinner to get to, and Jeff doesn't seem like he wants to be teased. He pulls Jeff's head close and kisses him, tongues tangling as Jeff's breath speeds up to match Stephan's strokes.

"You wanna come all over my hand?" he asks, hoping he sounds more sultry than like a bad porno, but it seems to work because Jeff's groans get louder and his face twists up in a gorgeous grimace as he starts to peak. A few more strokes, and he's gasping and swearing, freezing totally still for a moment, and then shuddering as he splashes over Stephan's knuckles.

When he finally opens his eyes, Stephan grins and raises his hands to lick delicately at the bitter fluid. He gets the response he wanted; Jeff moans and wraps his arms around Stephan, pulling him in for long, slow kisses. Jeff's eyes are hazy when they finally separate, which is deeply gratifying.

"So, dinner?" Stephan asks, sitting up in bed with a pleased bounce.

They both need a shower, and Jim's either taken off in fear of a big dramatic scene or when the porn noises started, and the tub is definitely big enough, so they share. It *seems* like an efficient idea, both for time and hot water, but even though they're both too drained to go again, there's still a lot of making out, and finally the water runs cold.

"What do you want?" Jeff asks once he's dressed and Stephan is contemplating the limited choices in his closet. "For dinner, I mean."

"Something spicy," Stephan says with a wink, and decides to just go with the pastel-pink flowered shirt that he never wears; it's not like Jeff doesn't know he's gay.

The silence is mostly easy as they drive to a Cajun restaurant Jeff found a few weeks ago, although Stephan's fiddling with the radio. He's still a little wired, and everything inside him feels like a big tangled ball of twine or something. Jeff's looking thoughtful again, and that's not necessarily a good sign.

Finally, when they're stopped at a light, Jeff speaks. "My wife had an affair with one of her employees. He sued for sexual harassment when they broke up, although the suit was dropped before anything really happened." He drums his fingers on the steering wheel. "I had no idea it was going on at all. It was more of a symptom than the problem itself, I guess; we'd drifted pretty far apart over the years. She traveled a lot."

Stephan is quiet, digesting all of this sudden information about Jeff's marriage, when the guy never said anything at all about it or about his wife before. Makes sense now, he supposes.

Jeff continues, "It was kind of the final thing for us, though, and I threw a lot of those same words at her that I told myself—and you—on Tuesday. But it's not the same situation as with you, and I wanted to say again that I'm honestly sorry for throwing all my baggage at you." He turns to look at Stephan, a quick glance before the light changes.

Stephan nods, accepting the apology and explanation, and then snorts. When Jeff glances his way inquiringly, he shrugs and says, "Something Scott said about baggage a few weeks ago. Maybe ours will match."

Jeff smiles, eyes still on the road, and nods. "Yeah."

Chapter 31
The Ending

THE next few days, neither of them leave Jeff's house at all. They grade papers and fuck, watch TV and fuck, eat and fuck. Jim texts sometime on Saturday to make sure Stephan's still alive, which was thoughtful, although at the moment he's so post-coital that he could pretty much die happily.

He'd much rather stay alive and have more sex, though. Yeah, they're probably just getting a lot of it out of their systems after all the buildup and tension and stupid *longing*, but Stephan's not-so-secretly hoping that it lasts a while longer because this might be the best week he's *ever* had. Seriously—*ever*.

They do have to run out for food and beer and more lube at one point. Jeff has plenty of condoms—an unopened box that makes Stephan stupidly happy—but apparently the man's been going through the lubricant, which *also* makes Stephan pretty happy. In fact, there's really not a lot right now that could ruin his mood. Not even the looming specter of yet another uncomfortable Christmas at home with his family in a couple of weeks is making an impact.

He makes a mental note that he needs to go shopping for presents for his family, and idly wonders what he should get Jeff, if anything. Maybe it's too soon. Or maybe he'll just buy a super-size box of condoms and huge bottle of lube and put a bow on his dick....

They're in the kitchen, Jeff reaching up for some wine glasses in a top cupboard—he made pasta sauce and insists a merlot will be way better with it than beer—when Stephan is struck by the curves of Jeff's ass and can't help grabbing it. It's muscular and firm and wonderful, and Jeff might be giggling a little bit, in that adorable way, as Stephan squeezes and presses up against his back. He twists Jeff around to kiss his neck and jaw, and is so glad they're about the same height, although he wouldn't complain about being taller, for once. He's six foot one, for fuck's sake; he shouldn't *always* be the short guy....

Anyway, dinner's luckily at a point where they can walk away and let it simmer, so Stephan drags Jeff back into the bedroom, but not before stripping off Jeff's pants and kneeling on the linoleum to spend a few moments nibbling and licking the curves of his cheeks while Jeff is pressed up against the kitchen cabinets. Once in the bedroom, he pushes Jeff back on the bed, maybe a little too hard, but Jeff's not exactly complaining. Instead, he's got a smirk and somewhat speculative look on his face, and Stephan just has to jump on him and kiss that smugness away. He yanks Jeff's T-shirt off and then his own, wondering why they bothered to get dressed at all. Sure, it's December, but the heater in Jeff's place works just fine....

He finally gets them both naked—which takes longer than it should because he keeps getting distracted with Jeff's amazing brain-melting kisses—and they're rubbing together, grinding and groping. He's kind of manhandling Jeff a little, pushing him around, seeing how far Jeff will let him go. He grabs Jeff by the waist and pulls him onto his side so he can bite and nip at the curve of Jeff's hip and the top of his ass, and is gratified that it's clearly something Jeff is enjoying. That doesn't mean he's not a little surprised, when Jeff rolls the rest of the way onto his stomach and looks over his shoulder at Stephan and says, "Fuck me," as he spreads his legs.

Wait, what? Stephan blinks. Did he hear that right?

Jeff grins. "Please? I mean, if you don't top, that's fine," he says, but he's lifting his ass in the air a little bit, pushing against Stephan where he's being held down.

"No, no, I definitely top," Stephan says in a hurry. "I like both, I'm pretty versatile."

"Yeah? That's good," Jeff purrs, although it's unclear whether he's talking about Steph's preferences in bed or the way Steph's pushing his dick against the place where Jeff's ass and thigh meet.

It's not like Stephan doesn't know what he's doing, but he's still a little nervous, and it doesn't help that his fingers are clumsy with lust and tension. He fumbles with the lube, making a mess, and cringes when Jeff laughs at him.

"Come on, Steph, I won't break. Give me your fingers, loosen me up a little, and then let me feel that big dick of yours from the inside."

Stephan rolls his eyes and smacks Jeff on the ass with his clean hand. "Quit with the bad porno dialogue or I'm not gonna do anything."

"Oh, I think you will," Jeff challenges.

Furrowing his brow, Stephan grabs Jeff's wrists and pins them to the bed above his head. Where are the kinky sex toys when you need them? He contemplates grabbing some socks to tie his lover to the headboard, but decides it's too much trouble. "Hold on," he orders, wrapping Jeff's hands around the bars, "or do you need to be tied up?"

There's a pause while Jeff thinks about it, and Stephan wonders if he's gone too far, but the gods are smiling on Stephan today because Jeff seems to come to the same conclusion he did, and wraps his fingers around the bars compliantly.

That's about the extent of his compliance though, because Jeff is pretty much the *bossiest* goddamned bottom Stephan has ever been with. He demands more fingers, harder, deeper, and then Stephan's cock when he's had enough. The noises he's making are pretty fucking appreciative, and Stephan finds he doesn't mind all that much, especially when he finally sinks inside the unbelievable tight heat of Jeff's ass.

Sadly, he only gets in a few thrusts before Jeff starts to make complaining noises. "What?" he asks, trying not to get upset and wondering what the fuck he could be doing wrong. He let Jeff tell him what to do this whole time; it's totally not his fault if the guy's not getting what he wants.

"Off," Jeff says, bucking hard, and Stephan has no choice but to obey. Jeff rolls them over, pushes Stephan down onto his back, then straddles him, holding Stephan's cock and slowly easing down onto it.

The pleasure from that makes Stephan squeeze his eyes shut, trying not to come, and when he opens them again, Jeff is laughing again.

"Hold on to that headboard, boy," he teases, and Stephan childishly wants to stick his tongue out, but it's way easier to just do as he's told. Which turns out to be the smart thing, because Jeff is riding him like there's no tomorrow, and all he can do is hold on. He manages to keep his eyes open, awestruck by the sight of Jeff on top of him, strong and manly, one hand jerking his own cock as he bounces on Stephan's. His eyes are closed, and watching the waves of uninhibited pleasure chase across Jeff's face is so amazing that Stephan almost wishes he could focus on it without being distracted by the sensations wreaking havoc inside his own body. Almost.

Jeff's got him totally pinned down, using his body weight for leverage, pressing down on Stephan's knees with his ankles, and his thighs on Stephan's pelvis, and just *taking* what he wants. And what he wants? Is Stephan.

They both come at nearly the same time, Stephan losing it first, but not by much. Jeff catches most of his come in his hand, making cleanup easier as he slides off of Stephan in a semi-controlled fall to the side.

Stephan manages to uncurl his hands from where they were clenched on the headboard and wraps an arm around Jeff's sweaty back. He flexes and wiggles the sensation back into his fingers, breathing heavily. "God, that was amazing." Jeff grunts his agreement. "How did you know I'd like that?" Stephan asks after a few more moments.

He feels Jeff shrug beside him. "I figured it wouldn't hurt to ask."

"Hmm. You seem pretty sure of yourself. About all of this."

Jeff kisses the side of his head. "Pretty sure, yeah."

A small half-smile pulls at Stephan's sleepy lips. *Pretty sure.* That's good enough for him.

Epilogue
A New Year

THEY'RE late to the party because Jeff had needed help rolling up the sleeves of his shirt. He'd tried to defend his ineptitude by saying that he usually rolled up the sleeves before he put his shirts on, but he'd already been wearing this one when he asked Stephan for an opinion. The sleeves had definitely needed to be rolled up so he wouldn't look *too* nice; it was going to be a fairly casual New Year's Eve party, and Jeff didn't need to look *that* good, or if he did, Stephan would have to go back to his place and get different clothes too. And then they would be late.

Except that they're late anyway, because Stephan had rolled up Jeff's sleeves for him, revealing the tattoos on Jeff's forearms, and had traced them with his thumbs and then bent to touch the delicate skin with his tongue... And Jeff's shirt was still unbuttoned and untucked, and it was too easy to slide his hands inside and feel the warm texture of hair and skin on Jeff's chest and stomach and sides... And then it was just natural that he'd go down on his knees and undo Jeff's pants and suck him off. After all, waste not, want not, right? Jeff was hard and grinning and making those breathy-but-deep moans that Stephan fucking *loved*, and he wasn't going to pass up sex for a stupid holiday party, no way.

By the time Jeff climaxed, Stephan was pretty much ready to go himself, erection pushing at his jeans uncomfortably. Jeff, unimpeded by any clothing other than Stephan's boxer briefs, had him naked in moments, and his cock in Jeff's mouth was so fucking perfect that he's thinking of giving Jeff some kind of award for blowjobs or something. Later.

So that's why they're late. Of course it doesn't actually matter; it's a *party* not an appointment, and all the explanation anyone needs is there in the satiated smile on Stephan's face. Billy and Steve are hosting their usual Every Winter Holiday Party, which is on New Year's Eve but combines a white-elephant gift exchange and mistletoe-kissing games and some pretty lethal eggnog that Billy makes every year. Before the midnight countdown, they exchange the worst presents they've all received for Christmas; the rule is that it has to be a new gift you'd just been given *or*, if you absolutely have to buy something, you can only shop at the drugstore.

Stephan kind of hates the stupid game; last year he'd ended up with a douche kit, and the year before he'd been forced to go home with a holiday-themed Snoopy sweatshirt originally from Kristine's mother. This year he's hoping for the stack of twenty lottery tickets Scott always brings, as that holds at least a glimmer of a promise for something good. Jeff's number comes up first, and he gets a bottle of cheap wine, then a crystal vase, and then a monogrammed pen and mechanical pencil set with the initials "SC" on them, all of which are taken away. Stephan is getting ready to protest that everyone is picking on his new boyfriend, but the next thing Jeff opens is a box of his-and-hers lubricant, which he ends up with permanently.

Rob gets picked on a fair amount, too, much to Danielle's dismay. This is what their friends do to test out the new partners: bug the shit out of them and see if they run. It's kind of cruel yet effective.

School starts in three more days, so pretty much all of the student-types are back in town. Stephan introduces Jeff to Danielle and Rob, and Kristine and Tina. The girls all smirk a little too knowingly, so Stephan doesn't let them talk to Jeff much beyond the usual polite chitchat. Kristine manages to slip in something about seeing Jeff at the orientation at the beginning of the year, and then laughs when Stephan drags Jeff away before she can say anything else. Women are apparently still going to be evil this year too.

They talk with Jim and Jamie for a while instead; they're all pretty comfortable together from hanging out that evening after the hiking disaster. His housemate and his girlfriend are both acting a little weird, though, extra super cuddly, and finally Stephan notices the ring on Jamie's finger. It's apparently an engaged-to-be-engaged ring, whatever the fuck that means. It's gold with an amethyst, not a diamond. Straight people are weird.

He and Jeff are talking with Billy and some of his music friends about their upcoming gigs when a waft of herbal-scented breath hits Stephan's nose at the same time that arms wrap around his waist. Mike leans his head on Stephan's shoulder, looking at Jeff curiously.

"So, this is the guy you kicked me out of bed for?"

"Mike!" He shrugs out of the octopus-like embrace, trying not to blush as everyone watching laughs.

Sighing, Mike shakes his head. "That's all right, Stephan; one day you will be mine. I can wait."

"Get in line," Jeff says with a smile that shows a lot of teeth. "It's gonna be a while," he says, wrapping an arm around Stephan's waist in a protective move that makes Stephan's knees go a little wobbly. He runs a finger down Stephan's throat, tugging the collar of his shirt aside to reveal an enormous hickey, which had been carefully covered all evening. "See that bite mark? Those are *my* teeth."

"Oooh yum," Mike says, adding an admiring wolf-whistle. "Not sure which of you I'm most jealous of...." Mike wanders off, one arm around Jeff's shoulder, dragging the other man with him and babbling about how it's totally fine to end a sentence with a preposition since they're not speaking Latin.

Stephan meets Jeff's eyes and salutes him with the dregs of the glass of eggnog he's holding and just smiles. Life is good. It's going to be a great new year.

ALIX BEKINS lives in the coastal mountains of Northern California with her partner and their dog. She's been writing for as long as she can remember in a variety of genres, including fiction, erotica, poetry, and nonfiction and has even managed to get some of it published from time to time.

Sexuality is the cornerstone of her life and work and always has been, through two degrees and several life plans. Her work and writing focus on the themes of self-discovery and coming out, with a healthy dose of kink on the side.

Alix is pretty sure she's the only person in the world who wears a plastic Viking helmet as a thinking cap when she battles writer's block. She always wins.

Visit her blog at http://alix_bekins.livejournal.com.

Also by ALIX BEKINS

An
Academic
Dilemma

Alix Bekins

http://www.dreamspinnerpress.com

Also by ALIX BEKINS

http://www.dreamspinnerpress.com